I0729951

ELEMENTS V
FREEZING HEARTS

WILLIAM RICHARDS

STALKING P ART

Life can be scary.

But behind those fears,

opportunity awaits.

CHAPTER 1
OPERATION MAN HUNT

THE NIGHT SKIES OF TORONTO WERE PAINTED BLACK with thick, blotchy clouds. Not a glimmer of moonlight shone upon the bustling metropolis, but the streetlights and neon signage did their best to make up for it. The clock struck midnight, but the city's night owls remained active, enjoying their after-hour exploits.

The outskirts of the megacity were far less rambunctious than usual.

A black SUV sped along the desolate highway, which wrapped around the low-rising hills far off into the distance. The roads were barren and silent, except for the lone vehicle stealthily gliding through the night with impunity.

Cement barriers guided the roads, behind them a never-ending forest. Seeing through the trees at night would be impossible for anyone not readily equipped, although there was little reason to worry about such things; the forest would usually be silent at this time of night.

But those choosing to use the forest as cover always came prepared.

"License plate ACX 649…looks like that's our target."

Sitting high in the bushy branches was a tall, imposing woman. There was an authoritative air about her as she commanded the words into the comms strapped to the left side of her chest. The way she sat fearlessly in the trees with an ambiguous glare on her face suggested that she was in full control of the situation.

She reached for the binoculars around her neck, lifting them to her onyx eyes. Her focus remained fixated on the SUV continuing in her direction.

From her perch, it was difficult to tell if the driver was alone, but she couldn't see anyone in the passenger seat, which was to be expected. She dropped the binoculars so that they hung around her neck again before turning her head to speak more clearly into the comms.

"Suspect is riding solo. He's heading your way, Juno — please try and stick to the plan. Coro and I will handle the rest." Her words were icy — flat and lifeless even; she could intimidate the most seasoned Elementalists who worked with her. But this time, there was a reason for her strict focus. The team was in hot pursuit of an elusive criminal who'd been on the run for a very long time.

"No need to be so serious, Livy. I've got everything under control," Juno said, far more enthusiastically than her counterpart. She made no qualms about her excitement, or her confidence.

Olivia sighed, shaking her head at the nickname. Nobody else would dare to address her that way.

With the first objective complete, Olivia gracefully dropped down from her perch, the long coat of her Elemental Council uniform flapping in the breeze as she touched the ground. She remained silent for a moment before turning to Coro, who stood leaning against the base of the tree beside her.

"We're only going to get one shot at this, so be ready." Her orders were as crisp as the night air.

Coro pushed himself off the tree, his steel hair faintly rustling in the wind. He nodded and said, "Right." His tone was one that rivalled his partner's. He wore the same uniform as his superior, but without the added decorations that symbolized Olivia's rank in the Elemental Council.

Normal procedure when running a stealth operation was to keep all chatter and noise to a minimum. This time, though, that rule didn't apply. Since they were dealing with someone who was stationed in a car, and also far from any main streets, this wasn't an issue to be concerned with.

That said, Olivia and Coro would never be confused with being overly talkative anyhow. Getting words out of them on the best of days was a challenge.

The speeding car itself provided another set of problems. To ensure a more seamless pursuit, and with the citizens of Toronto's safety at the forefront, Olivia and Coro were implementing a plan as far from the main streets as possible. They also kept the team to a minimum with the hopes of keeping the mission quiet from the public.

Luckily for them, after learning of the suspect's travel patterns and seeing a trend of movement in the dead of night, they knew that there would be few obstacles in terms of other cars traveling about.

At all costs, they wanted to avoid any form of high-speed pursuit—it would only lead to more problems. Police were set up at a rendezvous point a few kilometers down the street, but the hope was for them to merely arrive for the arrest and have that be the end of it. If a chase were to take place, it could open up a potential battle. And for an Elementalist of substantial power, the situation was best to be avoided for everyone's safety.

The most likely scenario in such a situation was to simply

let the Elementalist make his or her escape, and hope that they managed a second chance of capturing the wanted criminal. But they knew that this seemed unlikely—after all, the suspect had avoided capture for so long in the first place.

It had taken years of pursuit, but Olivia and her team were finally given a small window of opportunity to act.

The information regarding their mission had been presented to them just 24 hours prior. With Luminosa's new leader Brooklyn still on the loose—and having remained in hiding for well over a month—the EC took their chance to plan proactively. They dug up old leads in hopes of finding information on the villain's whereabouts.

The first time Luminosa had formed, led by their tyrant leader Dusk, their support had reached much further and their message resonated with many. Since their re-emergence, however, it appeared based on reports that Brooklyn was struggling to drum up that same level of support as Dusk's successor.

For the EC, this meant that finding current members was near impossible, but there was a long list of former Luminosa members who'd managed to escape capture from the previous regime.

At the time, those who'd aligned with Luminosa and failed to face punishment either fled or changed their name, opting to live a more secluded life upon Dusk's historic defeat. Records stated that about 80% of those linked to Luminosa faced charges and had been arrested over the years. Most had either served or were still serving time for their crimes, but they all refused to speak.

Despite their silence, that still left a possible 20% of Elementalists directly affiliated with Dusk roaming free. The hope was that after so much time had passed, perhaps some of them would drop their guard, allowing for their capture.

For many long nights, copious EC members searched for all

available records in the EC library. It took some time, but soon they'd produced a list of viable suspects to bring in for questioning.

In the end, their efforts did prove fruitful; old records and reports frequently referred to a man who went by the name "Rush." For most, the name would mean little, but for those around long enough to remember their original battles against Luminosa, Rush was known as Dusk's main informant. He was a master recruiter, feeding on the toxic emotions of the Elementalists and bringing them into Dusk's clutches. He also communicated Dusk's message toward different groups, spreading it throughout the city like a disease.

After Luminosa fell and the EC regained control, for decades there was no sign of Rush. He, like many others, disappeared into obscurity and was no doubt living under another name.

After some extensive digging, a few members learned of Rush's existence once again. Of course, he was still wanted for espionage in the first place, but while tracking his activities they noticed his constant late-night drives far out of the city every few days. They had yet to determine a reason for Rush's goals, but they had every intention of doing so.

That's where Olivia's team came into play. As the cream of the crop in the EC, and excelling at most everything she ever strived for in her life, Olivia was a perfect candidate when preparing the manhunt for Rush. She could adapt on the fly, was always forward-thinking, and had the skill to ensure that nobody would be hurt in the process. Having her at the helm gave the EC the highest chance of success.

But although her talents were extensive, she couldn't complete the mission alone.

When it came to the EC, Olivia wasn't big on relationships — she kept to herself and limited her interactions with co-workers to a minimum. She did have a few people she relied on, though, and so while picking her team, an obvious choice came to mind.

Since first being assigned to help Coro find his father, she'd grown to rely on the young dual Elementalist. She might not have trusted him with her life, but at the very least to be competent. They shared the mutual goal of bringing the now disgraced scientist Dr. Jarrad to justice while destroying his plans to help Luminosa.

Still, at the tender age of 16, Coro was considered too young to join the EC as a full-time member. He was only in his second year of Elemental Academy, and he still had a lot of growth ahead of him. His battles with Luminosa, being abandoned by his father, and the loss of his mother in those battles put him into a unique situation, despite his age. President Zale Osiris of the Elemental Council, after much consideration, chose to grant Coro special permission to continue his role on Olivia's team—as long as long as it directly related to Luminosa and the search for Coro's father.

Some believed that the exemption would be a dangerous slope for the EC to head down, but there were a few reasons why Zale made the decision.

Since Coro's family was all but torn apart, he was mostly left to fend for himself. Fortunately, he was wise beyond his years and displayed logical and rational thinking skills in spite of the tragedies that befell him. And so worrying about Coro's mental fortitude, although a priority, still remained second to Zale's other concern.

Coro's strange ties to Luminosa and his father made him a prime target for the evil group. At first, it appeared that they were hoping to use his father as bait to coax him into joining their cause, but when that failed, they set their sights on elimination. Dr. Jarrad always planned to use his son to boost his scientific genius into another stratosphere, but Coro's refusal to play his part made the doctor even more bloodthirsty for his ambitions. For Coro's safety, it was best to have him around the members of the EC—people who could keep him safe while also teaching him to defend himself in ways that even Elemental Academy couldn't.

The last reason had to do with Coro's own ambitions—he was dead-set on bringing down his father, stopping him from causing any more pain to those he perched high above on his pedestal. Zale believed that if denied the right to pursue his father with the EC, Coro would continue the goal alone. And that was more dangerous than allowing him on any mission.

The stipulation on Coro's contract was simple: he was to remain in EA and continue through until graduation. Besides, the school was a spot where Coro would be safe.

Even so, for Coro, this was *nothing* like his EA classes. It was far more important.

Rush's car sped down the long bend of the highway, skipping past one offramp and hitting the checkpoint for their operation. It was only a matter of time until the trap was sprung.

On the other side of the bend across the highway from Coro and Olivia, the third and final member of Olivia's patchwork team stood at the ready—Juno Barns. Most in the EC knew little about her, except that after graduating from EA, she moved down south and worked there for years until moving back and returning to her roots.

Her personality was the polar opposite of Coro and Olivia's; she often walked around with a nonchalant grin and laid-back demeanor. If she hadn't attended EA with Olivia, she never would've even been on the team.

Juno stood cloaked in shadows, her all-black uniform flailing in the wind. As the car approached closer, she sprung from the dark, her fiery red hair illuminated in the moon's faint glow. She landed on the other side of the barrier, waiting for the car to finish speeding around the bend. When the headlights came into view, her part of the plan commenced.

She smiled as the lights shone on her face, and said with a laugh, "Oh, yeah — it's about time we get this show on the road. Let's rock and roll."

She knelt down like a wild animal, and with her palms flat on the asphalt, she felt the vibrations of the road through her fingertips. They were small tremors, but precise, and thus they resulted in little damage.

Although creating any form of earthquake was considered a basic skill for earth Elementalists to handle, Juno's real power was demonstrated by the distance that she could spread her quakes. Even from well over 50 meters away, shockwaves rippled underneath the road, and she managed to bump the SUV off balance with pinpoint accuracy, forcing it to steer in a panic to avoid crashing into the barriers along the road.

The SUV came to a skidding halt, the tires bellowing out a sharp squeal. The car came to a dead stop horizontally across two lanes of highway, just inches from the steel guardrails.

With phase one complete, the trio jumped into their next move.

The highway remained clear, and officers were keeping the roads free from cars a few miles north, so Coro sprung out from the other side of the forest. With one swift swing of his hand, a ring of fire roared around the halted vehicle, ensuring that escape would be impossible.

Or maybe not. Rush was an unregistered Elementalist, which meant that there was a chance — a *slim* chance — that his element could counteract the flames, and the others knew it. Either way, though, the task wouldn't be easy; Rush hadn't avoided capture all these years by being stupid.

In unison, Olivia, Coro, and Juno converged on the target. When they did, the dancing, pale-blue flames were met with waves of water. Through a gap in the flames, a second stream burst fiercely into their direction.

The three split apart, dodging the water.

"So, which of us had money on him being a Water Elementalist?" Juno quipped as she landed on her toes.

Rush's voice emerged through the crackles of the flames. It was far less intimidating than they'd anticipated.

"Why won't you damn people just leave me alone already?!" Rush shouted from behind the wheel, his window down and hand stretched toward the flames.

Once he realized that his attack had accomplished little, he whipped the car door open and scrambled out.

He made a dash for the forest, but after a few steps his feet were ripped out from under him, tripping and falling face first onto the road. Panicked, he flipped himself around and started shuffling backwards. He smacked up against the metal of the guard rails, staring at Olivia as she marched forward. Rush found himself thinking that she looked like grim reaper.

The elite Elementalist cast her hand toward him, and from her body sprang a string of black whips. They snaked along the road like tentacles and latched onto Rush's arms and legs, locking him in place like a puppet.

Coro and Juno followed behind her, their faces shining blue from the hue of the flames. In the dimness of the night, their group looked like the villains—not Rush.

Juno laughed gleefully as she approached the target. "Why do they always think they can run? I mean honestly, has it ever worked even *once*?"

"Because cowards always run instead of facing proper justice," Olivia rebutted. She stood closest to Rush, eying him as he struggled to free himself from her restraints.

Rush started shouting, "Unhand me you animals! I'm an innocent man—you have no right to treat me like this!"

Finally, like a bull at the end of a fighting match, he began to exhaust himself. When he stopped flailing, he gained a better vision of who were hunting him. One look at the uniforms was all it took for him to become agitated again. "I should've known it would be the likes of you…this is the exact sort of stunt the EC would pull."

"Shut it," Olivia seethed, glaring at Rush with a look that was violent enough to kill. She eyed him up and down, using the flames to illuminate his face. There was no question that he was the target, but regardless, she had to exercise due diligence.

The faint wrinkles on Rush's forehead indicated that he was definitely middle aged. Wispy grey hair clung to the sides of his head, and the rolled-up sleeves of his jacket revealed arms with a half-dozen scars—some tiny, others large and noticeable. He also had a small diamond piercing in his right ear.

All these distinctions matched the description of who they were searching for, but there was another, simpler way to confirm his identity.

Olivia grabbed Rush's pant leg and yanked it up. Underneath was a tattoo of a black snake wrapped around a cross. It was worn and faded into his calf, but there was no mistaking that it was a definite sign that this was Rush.

Olivia turned back to Coro. "Contact the police and let them know we've got our guy. I want him questioned tonight."

Coro could hear Rush grumbling in the background, but he left that for Olivia to handle before walking away and pulling out his comms to make the necessary calls.

Since Coro was tasked with bringing in the police, Juno strode up next to Olivia. "Not exactly on the young side, is he? Guess the last known picture of him was rather dated."

"What'd you expect? He was a first generation Elementalist, and if the records are to be trusted, he's one of the first Elementalists ever discovered."

"One of the first, eh?"

Juno smirked and fixed her eyes on Rush, whose head hung low, his energy all but erased. "Well, why don't we have a little chat with old Wrinkles here ourselves and see what sort of information we can peel from him?"

Without missing a beat, Olivia retorted, "Denied." She ignored Juno's disappointment and instead began walking over to the car behind them. While they waited for the police to arrive from their roadblock not far down the highway, she wanted to do some investigating of her own.

Inside the SUV was a layer of dirt, caked on like frosting. The vehicle itself was grimy and full of muck; Olivia was hesitant to even open the doors. The windows were stained with streaks of dirt looking like they'd never had a fresh cleaning, and the leather seats were full of rips and tears as if a cat had clawed through them. Fast-food wrappers and drink cups were lazily strewn on the floors and under the seats. In many ways, it appeared as if Rush had been relegated to living out of the vehicle.

There was something in the backseat, however, that took Olivia especially by surprise. Mixed in with the pile of garbage on the floor mats were small toys—little plastic trains, some baby dolls, and even a rubber ball. Also strapped into the back was a toddler seat.

Olivia glanced back at Rush, who remained in confinement. She raised an eyebrow and then focused back on the car. She couldn't help but wonder: There was no mistaking Rush's past, but based on what she was seeing now, it appeared that he'd changed his tune—at least on the surface. Without knowing any previous history, Rush could've been pegged as a family man with no ties to Dusk at all. But there was, of course, a chance as well that Rush simply stole the car. In the end though, those were nothing but speculative thoughts, and for Olivia they didn't mean much. As long as Rush cooperated with the EC in their search for Brooklyn, the rest of his life choices were currently of little interest.

Olivia slammed the vehicle's door shut as she heard the sirens from police cars coming down the road.

Meanwhile, Juno grew bored of staring at her target, who did nothing but grumble about the EC. She called out to Coro, "Hey, kid — come take a turn watching this bum. His ramblings are killing my mood."

Coro, who was staring down the road and waiting for the cops, nodded and walked over to Rush, while Juno took her leave.

After getting a reasonable distance away from the commotion, Juno pulled out her device and started typing away. She glanced back at Olivia and then at Coro, and, seeing that both of them were still preoccupied, began typing again. She continued to document everything of note — location, the people involved, the time of day, even the weather conditions. All of it might serve some kind of purpose.

The police only took a couple minutes to arrive and handcuff Rush. He put up little resistance, finally choosing to remain quiet. The police thanked Olivia and her team for their work, and agreed to meet them at the station in hopes that their labour would bear fruit.

CHAPTER 2
NEGOTIATIONS

DEPENDING ON THE THREAT LEVEL OF A CRIMINAL upon capture, two things could happen. First, if they were of little threat, they could be held at the Toronto police station with the help of an EC member, detained and watched until a questioning period took place, when the issue could be resolved.

In more extreme cases, if the suspect was deemed a high-level threat to those around them, there was a small chance that they'd be taken to Penetang jail and held there until further decisions were made.

Placing people in Penetang before any form of trial wasn't an easy task, and a road that most Elementalists dared not go down. Situations like that were best kept for the likes of Dusk, or for Dominos, the shamed leader of the Adenji gang. Not for washed-up hacks like Rush.

But because of his ties to Luminosa, he *did* remain a relative threat, and a simple police station just wasn't considered safe enough to hold him. For that rare scenario, Olivia requested to hold him in the EC headquarters for the night, allowing for some decisions to be made in the meantime. It would also ensure that he could be held at bay, and that nobody from Luminosa would attempt to break him free.

Since interrogation rooms in the EC were used so sparingly, there was only one—but it looked no different than any of the other rooms. The walls were dull and lifeless, and the room was barely big enough to fit three people.

President Zale Osiris, dressed in a lavish black suit with his tie undone and draped around his neck, stood at the one-way mirror. He sipped at his coffee in hopes of gaining energy.

Juno stood at his left, stifling a yawn with her arms crossed. She checked her watch—1:15 a.m.—before turning to glance at Coro, who sat at a table with different folders in front of him. He was locked into his work, paying little attention to the mirror.

Juno turned back to Zale and said, "Should the kid be here this late? I know that you and Olivia are doing him a favour, but this is a bit much, don't you think? He's just a student."

"I wouldn't worry about him—he'll be fine," Zale responded. "Besides, it's not a school day tomorrow, so it's his choice in this case. He hates leaving things unfinished."

Part of Coro's deal when working with the EC was tied to his attendance in EA, but regardless, both Zale and Olivia refrained from acting like a parent. They tried to keep his best interests in mind, but Coro was old enough to make his own decisions.

Dropping the subject, Juno pulled out a chair and put her feet up on the table. She leaned back against the wall and let out a second yawn. "Don't you think we should've had someone...I don't know, a little more sociable trying to get answers out of this guy? Liv might just beat him senseless if the old fool doesn't spill," she quipped.

Zale kept his focus glued to the window. "Maybe so, but if he doesn't speak, then he's of little use to us anyways. Besides, he'll speak. He has no leverage otherwise."

Juno raised an eyebrow, and the comment even caught the attention of Coro', now glancing up from his files.

"I knew Liv was cold," Juno said, "but I guess she's not the only one willing to play hardball, is she?"

"When it comes to stopping Luminosa, I'll do whatever is necessary. I refuse to let them rain destruction on us once again."

On the other side of the glass, Olivia stood at one end of the small metal table, Rush sitting in a chair on the other. His chair had latches that locked his hands in place, but that alone wasn't enough to restrain an Elementalist.

What made the EC convenient for an interrogation like this, besides waves of EC members ready at the drop of a hat, was the technology available. Just like in Penetang, the EC's room (but more specifically the chair holding Rush) was equipped with power-restraining capabilities. If the criminal so much as thought about using their element, a sharp electric shock would bolt through their body. It would never be enough to stop someone, and in no way lethal, but it would disrupt the user's train of thought just enough for someone to act.

Not that anyone was worried about Olivia being taken by surprise; if anything, they felt pity for Rush.

Olivia flipped through a series of brown folders, tossing each one on the table when she finished. Every few seconds she'd glance up, a stoic glare in her eyes.

"Axel Mclean, code name Rush. Water Elementalist and member of Luminosa. Oh, and Dusk's right-hand man. Does that sound right?"

"*Former* right-hand man," Rush bit back.

Olivia paid no mind to his tone, continuing to read through her notes. "Wanted on charges of treason, insurrection, 12 counts of robbery, 15 counts of assault, seven kidnappings, vandalism, and last but not least, helping break out multiple wanted criminals from Penetang." Olivia snapped the folder shut. "Did we miss anything?"

To her surprise, Rush flinched at the crisp sound of the folder, but the restraints kept him from pulling away. He regained his anger and growled, "That was my *old* life…the *old* me. I haven't done a damn thing since Dusk fell. I didn't even join up with him when he returned. You clowns have no right to drag me in here and run some crooked interrogation." He took a breath, trying to keep his face from turning red. "Look…I'm nothing more than a simple family man now. I've got myself a wife and a baby son—I'm not interested in helping Dusk, or this Brooklyn." His tone became hot again. "You and your stupid bosses think they can just do whatever they want to innocent people like me."

"Innocent?" Olivia's eyes became cross, her words cold enough to freeze the room. "So because you went and pro-created, that means you're now exonerated from all the other crimes you never paid for? Is that it? What about the children who died because of Dusk, the parents who were killed in your little world execution? I guess those people don't matter now because you've got a family of your own. Don't kid yourself—you've got enough of a rap sheet here to put you in Penetang for life, and the fact that you've got a family won't change that."

Even from the other side of the glass, chills ran down Juno' and Zale's spines.

Rush slunk back, trying to avoid the harsh gaze of his interrogator. But in the dull, stark-white room, he had nowhere to go. He hung his head, now speaking with a more contrite tone.

"You're right. All the things I did and what Luminosa did back then…the lives we took on behalf of Dusk… I don't need you to remind me about it. I'm fully aware of those times in my life. I live with that guilt every day, wondering how I'd have felt if it were my family being ripped apart by Dusk." Rush glanced up. "But what else was I supposed to do? If I had to guess, you were nothing more than an infant when Dusk rose, if that. It was all about survival then. Everything I did was about surviving. Not only the threats of the world against Elementalists but also the threats of Dusk. Most of us were like that—we feared him as much as anyone. He wouldn't hesitate to strike down those who stood in his way, including his own kind. I saw it happen time and time again. Despite what you might think, I wasn't anything special to him. He didn't care if I was killed or not. For him, I was just as replaceable as the next guy in his army. Seeing Dusk fall to the Hero of Light was the best thing that ever happened in my life. I was liberated from his wrath, free to start a family and live a new life. I've had a clean reputation for years."

Olivia studied her prisoner's words carefully, checking his tone, his facial movements, and examining him for any signs of deceit. Rush was right; she'd been nothing but a child at the time of Dusk's peak, and the stories she knew were only that—stories. It wasn't inconceivable for Rush to have been acting out of fear. After all, many people did at the time. But she still had questions.

"Care to explain then why you've been taking weekly trips up north lately?"

Rush narrowed his brow, his tone guarded once again. "If you guys know about that, then you've been tailing me for quite a while," he said, pursing his lips in thought. "Fine, I'll tell you. But not because I'm on your side in all of this. I simply want to return home to my family."

"The sooner you speak, the sooner we're done here," Olivia responded.

"A few weeks ago, a member of Luminosa contacted me. You probably know him as Bronx. He appears to be a bit of an information gatherer himself for their little band. He requested that I help find him new agents who could be of use to Luminosa. But let's be clear: I didn't go seeking him out. He found me, and then used my family as bait. So I moved them up north where Luminosa wouldn't find them. But because I still work in the Toronto power plant doing the night shift, I have to drive back and forth."

"How exactly did you get a job with your reputation?" Olivia asked him cooly.

"I knew a guy from before my days with Dusk. He gave me a job despite my…history."

Olivia glossed over the last part, narrowing in on one important aspect of Rush's answer. "Have you given Bronx any names yet?"

Rush shook his head. "No, I pulled up some hollow leads just to get him off my back, but I haven't given them to him yet."

Without a word, Olivia walked over to the door, leaving Rush and everyone on the outside confused. When she returned to the other room, she said, "What do you think, Sir? Are you buying any of this?"

Zale tapped the ledge of the window, ruminating on the conversation.

"It's hard to say how honest he's being. His car did have kids toys inside, among other things that indicates he's turned over a new leaf into a family man. The part about acting because of fear—well, I've heard that from a number of people over the years. It's not something that can be dismissed. Dusk tried to rule through strength and intimidation, and many were afraid of him."

"Who cares about his story?" Juno piped in, from her relaxed, feet-up position. "Seriously, Liv—you can't be missing the most obvious piece of gossip." She then became a bit more serious, her stance focused. "Luminosa is trying to drum up members to increase their numbers, and they're reaching out to former followers of Dusk to do it. That could become a major issue if Dusk's old lackeys start coming out of the woodwork to help them."

Coro's ears perked up. There was somewhat of a fascination when it came to what he considered "the old days." He often wondered about those times, which came long before he was born. He, like most, knew they were considered dark days by everyone, filled with war and peril, but most people were hesitant to talk about what actually took place. Even Elemental Academy didn't touch on the subject much, so when he saw the chance to gain information, he jumped at it.

Juno continued. "Luminosa is desperate for recruits — that much is obvious, right? And I think it's fair to say they're not looking for a bunch of past-their-prime Elementalists like Rush to join them. They want young, skilled blood."

"What's your point, Juno?" Zale asked. All eyes were now focused on the new member of the EC. For someone with no proper standing in the organization, she definitely showed a lack of fear when speaking her mind.

"We hand them one of our own. Liv, when you were briefing me on some of the tricks Luminosa has been pulling, you mentioned something about a former member of the EC being flipped and used to gain info on our plans, didn't you?"

Behind them, Coro's face contorted in angst, as painful memories of the traitor who nearly killed him in his father's lab surfaced. He finally jumped into the conversation.

"Yeah, her name was Pascale," he said, "and she tried to kill me." He didn't show much emotion, but even so, he still held the traitor in contempt for her role in his mother's passing. Had she not blown their mission off course, what resulted never would've taken place.

"Right. So then I say it's time we return the favour," Juno said.

"It would never be that simple," Zale rebutted. "Members of the EC are far too public. Luminosa would be stupid to drop their guard solely on a hunch. If we were to send a spy in, odds are we'd just be sending them to a pointless death."

Zale's point was a valid one. Luminosa trusted the EC less than anyone on the planet, and chances for success would be extremely low.

Coro thought about what Juno was suggesting. He missed a chance, and he knew it. Thanks to the connection with his father, at one point he could've infiltrated the group, playing on his father's desire for him to be the ultimate weapon. But not now—not after all the things he'd said. Not after the stance he'd taken to stop his father. In no way would he, or anyone in Luminosa ever believe that Coro would come crawling back to them.

However, as was becoming apparent, Juno already had the perfect candidate in mind—something Olivia picked up on as well.

"You can't be serious. You actually want us to send you in as a spy against Luminosa?" Olivia asked. Her voice was packed with skepticism, but also a rare hint of concern.

Juno shrugged. "Why not? I haven't been in the province for over five years. It seems likely that Luminosa doesn't have any info on me, and there are no records of me working for the EC. It just makes sense."

"What about the other role we had for you?" Zale asked.

"I can use that as my cover." She focused on Olivia, an unusually serious look on her face. "Come on, Liv. You of all people know that this is the most logical course of action. Look at it this way: We know this Brooklyn character is dangerous. He might not have the numbers to launch a full-scale attack, but if he finds a way to get support, then everything could go sideways quick. On the surface, things might appear fine, but we all know that in this city, and even across this country, there's an underground proportion of society that still feels similar to Dusk in a lot of respects. So far, they've only been working for their own self-interests, but if Luminosa were to find a way and unite those groups, then we'd be overrun in seconds. I don't have to go in looking for a bust of Luminosa—and besides, I doubt they'd just let me meet Brooklyn on my own anyways. But if I can even draw out just a bit of information from them as to what their plans really are, then maybe we have a chance."

Olivia and Zale contemplated the idea, but it appeared that Coro was already on board with the proposal.

"Remember," Coro said, "this is now a world where the Hero of Light is no more. Crime has been steadily increasing, particularly with Elementalists who believe they're being oppressed. If Luminosa can get just a handful of those people to join forces, then we need to know about it. And with my father on their side, giving him more pawns to play with is dangerous."

"The kid is right, and I'm clearly the best candidate for the job. So send Olivia back into that room and cut a deal with Rush already."

Everyone exchanged looks to see if a debate would rise. Coro and Olivia wore world-champion poker faces on the best of days, and this was no different.

"I guess we're between a rock and a hard place, aren't we?" Zale said before crossing his arms and nodding. "Fine. If you're sure you can handle this, I'll approve it. However, you better not go and get yourself killed. I'm not sending you to be a martyr here."

"Of course not," Juno laughed, returning to her usual self. "They won't suspect a thing."

Olivia locked eyes with her friend and noticed something different about her convictions. There was another motive from her former classmate. *What is she trying to accomplish here? She doesn't think she can... No. Even she's not that delusional.*

Finally, Olivia said, "Fine. Have it your way."

Without waiting, Olivia swung the door open, each of her steps landing with authority. She glared at Rush, whose head sprung up at the sudden noise.

This time, Olivia dropped any formalities and spoke with a vicious bite. "Here's the deal, Rush. I'm gonna ask you a few questions, and depending on your answers, we might let you go free."

The word "free" caught Rush's interest, but he stiffened and put up his guard. "You swear it? This isn't some dirty trick?"

"Like I said, that depends. You said you met with a man named Bronx and that he wants you to help point him in the direction of new recruits, yes?"

"Yeah…but I've given him nothing, so I can't give you that list."

"That's not what I want. I want you to set up a meeting between him and one of our members."

"Are you insane?" Rush gawked. "If they found out I led them right into the hands of the EC, they'd hunt me down and string me up by my feet. I'm not doing that."

"Fine. Rot in Penetang, then. I don't care."

Olivia turned on her heels and headed for the door. There was no hesitation in her words, and even Zale and the others behind the glass weren't sure if she was bluffing. But before Olivia could reach the door, Rush called out.

"Wait!"

Olivia stopped, her hand on the doorknob.

"If I set this suicide meeting up for you, then I want your word that my family will be safe. I want the full might of the EC protecting them. That's the only way I'll accept this deal."

Olivia kept her hand firmly where it was, mulling over Rush's words. There wasn't a particular way for them to keep one family safe over another's, and they definitely couldn't assign a member or two to watch them at all times. They just didn't have the numbers.

She took her time deliberating what to say next, making Rush sweat. "Fine. You have my word that we'll do all we can to protect your family if it comes to that. However, if you dare turncoat on us, you and your family will know the full wrath of my power." She jarred open the door and walked out, gesturing for Zale and Juno to enter. They could handle the remainder of the process.

The rest of the interrogation went on as normal—Rush helped provide whatever information he could, as well as told the EC how to get in contact with Bronx. He hated helping the EC, but feared what Brooklyn and a new era of Luminosa could bring in its wake. All he cared about was protecting his family.

CHAPTER 3
PUT TO THE TEST

WHILE CORO CONTINUED PURSUING HIS FATHER, Minisc, Lily, and Jules were finally set to make their return to the classroom. Their two-week-long apprenticeships came to an end, and after a few days of much needed rest and recovery, they were ready to continue regular education. What was meant to have been a basic educational tool allowing students to learn from real life experience turned into far more than the three could've ever bargained for.

In particular, Minisc once again found himself in the middle of it all. A battle against the Adenji leader Dominos and learning to harness Celestial Light, his father's famed power, all in an effort to save his new friend and partner at his apprenticeship, Robin.

But it was their efforts as a team that ensured the safety of the new EA grad, who now returned to the care of the elder statesmen of the EC — and Minisc's mentor — Gordon Howland.

Because their internships were two weeks long and the

rescue operation took place on Sunday, the three were given the rest of the week to recover. Besides, they'd gained more experience in one week than any other student could've hoped to learn.

The toll on their physical health had been tough, but that wasn't something to be focused on—it was the mental health of the group that required a break. Much had happened, and allowing their first real mission to sink in illustrated the life that potentially lay ahead of them. It was a lot to absorb, especially when the circumstances involved placing one of their own in immediate danger.

But at least they could rest knowing that Robin was safe and that much of the Adenji gang were arrested. Together, they'd achieved a great thing for society, and that brought more joy to them than anyone could've expected.

When everyone returned to the classroom the next week, relief washed over Minisc. He sat in his familiar spot, staring out his familiar window and resting his head in his familiar hand.

But even though being in school was still a strange feeling after all the disruptions, there was also a sense of joy. The opportunity to learn in a far less pressure-filled situation was always a welcomed change.

With everything going on, it made Minisc wonder how his father had lived the life as the Hero of Light, being in those situations at all times. How did he handle it with such grace? It might've been the most astounding accomplishment on a long list of his never-ending glories.

Fluffy snow lined the windowsill with large white flakes that continued to sprinkle all across the city. For the first snowfall of the year, it came in full force, and so did the cold.

Inside Ms. Wright's classroom, the students sat in their seats dressed in warm sweaters and jackets as they caught up with each other. Two weeks of new knowledge and new experiences were being shared in abundance, creating a prominent buzz through the air.

Minisc wasn't overly talkative in class on the best of days; outside of Lily and Jules, he liked to keep to himself. But today in particular, his mind remained cluttered.

Although provided a few days to mentally recover, a part of him still failed to process the battle against Dominos. He tried to force the repeated thoughts from his mind, but it was no use. The fight remained on loop, utterly controlling his brain.

That week had started with Minisc learning Celestial Light, or at least the basics of it, something he'd struggled with mightily on his own. Mastering the skill was a near impossible task, but to his and his mentor Mr. Howland's surprise, he managed to combine the skill with his full power in an act of desperation. Though it was little more than a blip in time, it was still a miraculous achievement to pull off — especially considering that his max output to that point had been just 8% of his full power, a limit that Mr. Howland made clear he was not to surpass for any reason. Not that Minisc intended to; it had sort of just happened.

As much as the fight remained vivid, so too did the feelings he experienced while achieving Celestial Light. One second, his body was ice cold like the outside winter air, and the next, his insides were on fire — not to mention the way he moved so effortlessly, so freely, almost like he was weightless. And then there was the peace of mind that came over him. He could focus on bringing down Dominos and saving his friends — nothing else in that moment mattered. In a way, the whole mission had been an out of body experience.

Even after a full week, he could still feel the lingering effect of his actions. They were coursing through his body like small palpitations. His arms tingled with a radical sensation that came and went, and his senses felt more in tune than ever before. It was like time itself was slowing down for him.

His senses, however, were far from being perfectly in tune. He stared out the window, oblivious as Jules continued tapping him on the shoulder.

"Hey, anyone awake in there?" Jules asked him.

Sitting at the desk in front of them, Lily was turned around and staring at her friend as well. "Earth to Minisc…anyone up there?"

Though not exactly catching their words, Minisc heard his friend's voices and finally snapped out of his reflective state. He lazily turned around, staring blankly at his confused, maroon-haired friend. "Huh? You need something?" He could tell from the look on their faces that they were still worried about him.

"No," Lily said, shaking her head. "You've just seemed really quiet lately, and for you, that's usually dangerous."

"Oh. Uh, I hadn't really noticed." Minisc forced himself to sit in a proper position and display more attention. "It's nothing, really. I'm just still adjusting to early morning is all. You know me, I hate having to get up." He let out a shallow laugh. Before his friends could call out him out, the bell rang.

A trained silence fell over the room, as anyone not already in their seats scurried back like rats.

From down the hall, the distinct if not terrifying clacking of heels could be heard. They were in quick succession and carried a sense of authority.

In walked Ms. Wright, her copper curls bouncing off her shoulders as she approached the front of the room. When she faced the class, she gave them a flat and unimpressed glare, but unlike in the past, her no-nonsense scowl failed to intimidate anyone.

"Welcome back, class. I hope you've all returned with some form of new knowledge thanks to the lessons at your apprenticeships. Experiences like the ones you gain from being part of the EC will be an invaluable asset going forward, I assure you. Here at EA, although we try our best to prepare you for whatever situation might be presented in the real world, there is no better teacher than practical experience. This will not be the last time you have the chance to learn from others, so I hope you made the most of those opportunities and will use them to push yourselves forward in the coming months."

She looked to her left, staring at the pile of papers on her desk. Each one was a written report from supervisor and student alike, recapping their experiences and the lessons learned.

"That being said, gaining information is only valuable when you know how to properly apply it, which means that I believe it's about time we see what you've learned by putting them to the test. For this morning's lesson, I will be breaking you up into groups based on where you did your apprenticeships. We'll be drawing on your experiences in a practical way." She walked over to her desk and grabbed her black winter jacket hanging off the chair. "You are to meet me in the Academy cityscape in half an hour," she said, pulling on her coat. "Don't be late."

Jules glanced out the window to his left and then back at his teacher, who'd rendered the room otherwise silent. "But the Academy cityscape is entirely outside! And there has to be at least a foot of snow on the ground. We can't work in that," he complained.

Ms. Wright shot him a deadly glare and responded sharply, "Then I suggest you dress appropriately." Not another argument was made.

Once Ms. Wright left the room, Jules slouched back in his chair. "Man, why does she like torturing us so much? I *hate* the cold."

***

Within the domain of Elemental Academy were a multitude of buildings. The most prominent by far was the school itself. Even before its facelift after the return of Dusk, it was home to all classes, and students spent most of their time in its classrooms. Then there was the school's state-of-the-art training facility. Contrary to most gyms and recreational centres around the city, which still had the goal of bringing fitness to the Human race, EA's gym was tailored specifically for Elementalists. The equipment could withstand the intense training periods and provided much more variety for the many different Elementalist types. It was a far more ideal environment to practice, and one that was safer for both Humans and Elementalists. The grounds also featured sparring stadiums that could be filled with different terrain elements, much like the Tournament of Elements.

Minisc and his friends knew that all those spots and equipment were available for first-year students, but that wasn't the case for every facility in EA.

The most notable of the restricted areas was a massive open-roofed stadium that stretched a few miles back behind the school, an area known as the Academy cityscape. As the name implied, and the reason the stadium was open-roofed, was to allow for the towering buildings to peek out from above. When walking down the street, students could often be seen taking a look at some of the monumental buildings. After all, they were hard to miss.

From a bird's eye view, a number of different streets, roadways, and dozens of buildings could be seen inside the stadium. In many ways, it was a small-scale model of their home city, except in terms of functionality, the landscape was little more than a fantasy. The buildings were simply hollowed-out structures with some prop furniture tossed in for authenticity, but when it came to industrial standards such as water lines and electricity running through the buildings, there were none. When training, there tended to be a fair bit of damage created, and so it helped to keep costs down and prevent the school from going bankrupt by making the buildings as easily repairable as possible.

The only building with power was just on the outskirts, and it acted as home base. It also doubled as a classroom. Since the cityscape had all sorts of cameras set up around the various buildings, students could commune in the home base and watch their fellow classmates participate, allowing for valuable teaching moments.

Crucially in the winter months, it provided a warm environment for students to stay as they waited their turn…or at least it *would've* played that role if Ms. Wright wasn't their teacher.

Minisc, Lily, and Jules stood with their classmates in two formal lines. The snow continued to fall at a blinding rate, which left them shivering to the bone. Each of them was covered with extra layers of clothing, but even so, they looked miserable as they waited.

Some students tried to prove their toughness against the elements by opting to ditch the heavy uniforms, seeing it as a sign of weakness, but Jules was of no such mindset.

Usually the first person eager to prove that he could handle any challenge, his knees clacked louder than anyone's. He wrapped his arms around his body and rubbed them up and down like he was trying to start a fire. More than any other student, he was positively bundled in mitts, earmuffs, and layers of his uniform, not that it made a difference.

"I…hate…the snow…" Jules' grumbled through his chattering teeth. For good measure, he let out a couple of sneezes before trying to wipe his nose with a tissue from his jacket pocket.

Beside him, Minisc let out a small laugh, much to his friend's annoyance.

"This isn't funny! I hate winter—it's freezing out here!"

Still, Minisc wasn't feeling much sympathy. "Well, now you know how I feel in the summer when you and Lily always want to go swimming."

"How are those two things even remotely related?!" Jules shot back.

Lily giggled at their feud before kneeling down and picking up a handful of the fluffy white powder. She stared at its beauty before softly blowing it into the frigid air, and the snow fluttered into the air, falling to the ground again like a snow globe. "Aww, come on Jules—it's not all bad. I love the snow. It's so beautiful when it's falling like this."

"You two are insane."

Minisc sighed, trying to get things back on track. "Regardless, whatever this test of Ms. Wright's is, the weather is gonna become a big issue."

"That's true," Lily agreed. "With it being so cold, my water won't travel as far, and with these extra layers and less traction we're all gonna struggle with a lack of mobility. But if I had to guess, that's what Ms. Wright probably wants—to make the conditions as tough as possible."

Jules rubbed his hands together and blew his warm breath into them. "What's it matter, anyway? Shouldn't Minisc just be able to use Celestial Light like he did against Dominos? If you do that, Minisc, there isn't an Elementalist alive who could handle you, snowstorm or not."

Minisc shook his head and frowned. "I wish it were that easy. But Mr. Howland and even my father were adamant that I don't push Celestial Light that far again. For the time being, they only want me using a max output of 12% until it's like second nature for me. What I did against Dominos was strictly out of necessity, and honestly, most of it was luck. If that fight had gone on for even a few more seconds, I probably would've collapsed from the intensity."

"Well, I guess that rules that out," Jules frowned.

"Still," Lily added, "it's a good thing you did use it with all of your power regardless. I can't imagine anyone outside of maybe your father having the strength to stop a monster like Dominos in the way you did."

"You might be right, which is why I need to keep learning Celestial Light as quickly as possible. If I can learn to master it the way my father did, then when Luminosa finally strikes, I'll be ready to stop them."

Lily and Jules both felt the heaviness of Minisc's words. Now that he knew what he was capable of, the pressure for him to achieve such power was even greater. But his friends wouldn't let him go it alone.

Lily placed her hand on Minisc's shoulder. "Just remember, we're not going anywhere, either."

"Yeah, this isn't just on you to stop Luminosa. It's on all of us. We'll be right by your side the whole way," Jules agreed. The sentiments were almost enough to warm Minisc's frozen body.

Not everyone standing out there in the snow shivered and sneezed. Ms. Wright approached from the opening of the cityscape toward her class, but she showed no ill effects of the nipping frost.

Minisc wondered if it was just her hardened demeanor that refused to show discomfort. After all, she was dressed only moderately for the weather. But it was more than that—when she walked, it was with a gliding ease, as if the snow had no effect on her. Curious, Minisc focused on her feet and saw that the snow was melting right off her boots with each step. Then he noticed her jacket—the snowflakes landing on her melted as though they were hitting a sauna.

As one of the elite fire Elementalists of her generation, the intimidating instructor appeared to be heating different parts of her body with such precision; from the soles of her shoes to the bulk of her jacket, she cast the snow away effortlessly. Thanks to this power of hers, she walked down the winter wonderland street toward her class with far more ease.

Ms. Wright came to a stop and stared at the standing lines her students had already organized without her. She had them well-trained for their second year.

No one said a word, but she could see their chilled expressions; her students made no effort to hide their misery. But they knew that any complaints would only be met with harsher training.

The teacher folded her arms and smirked. "All right, the first team to participate in our exercise will be the group of Lily, Jules and Minisc." She locked her focus on the three. "I've kept this in line with your apprenticeships, which means that the three of you will be conducting a search and rescue procedure. Within the main plaza of the city are three hostages, and they will be within one of the apartment complexes. It will be your job to find their location and bring them to the safety zone, which will be marked by these flares on the ground."

From her jacket, Ms. Wright pulled out a small black tube with red stripes. She gave it a shake and then tossed it over the students' heads, close to the entrance. It began to spew red smoke with a bright light, which mixed into the storm of snow. "Now, before we start, there are a few things you should be aware of. For obvious safety purposes, we will not be dealing with real hostages, but that doesn't mean that you can treat them recklessly. The replicas you are trying to save will be equipped with lifelike damage sensors. They can measure any form of physical impact, or other injuries like burns and frost bite, so if you are to fatally harm the hostages or seriously injure them throughout your rescue, you will automatically fail the exercise."

"I guess that doesn't sound too bad," Minisc said, "All we have to do is find the hostages and get them out of here?"

Ms. Wright smirked again, shaking her head. "I can assure you, it won't be nearly as easy as you think. First of all, you will only be given 30 minutes to accomplish the rescue. Exceed the time limit and you will fail. And secondly…" Her face grew more sinister. "It will be my job to stop you. I'll be doing everything in my power to make sure that you cannot reach the hostages. And be warned, I won't be taking it easy. You'll need to use all of the lessons you've learned since starting EA to succeed."

"Hold on," Jules said. "It's going to be just you going up against the three of us? Doesn't that seem…a bit one-sided? I mean, we're not amateurs here."

"Don't you worry, it will certainly be a fair fight."

Like any curious teacher would with their pupils, Ms. Wright kept close tabs on what her students had been doing while working with the EC. Because of her extensive history before becoming a teacher at EA, her connections were vast. With one phone call she could receive updates on her student's activities and their progress. This meant that she knew in relative detail everything her top students endured only a week ago through their apprenticeships. Undergoing the trials that Minisc, Lily, and Jules had, while also learning exactly what being in the EC was about, piqued the teacher's curiosity. She wanted a first-hand experience of what her students learned.

Finally, an air of excitement began to buzz through the group, somewhat replacing their numbing cold. They began chatting amongst themselves trying to figure out what their group's task would be and how they'd succeed.

Instead of being left on the outskirts of a frozen city, the re-maining students were free to watch the test at the home base. They awed as the warmth fill their bodies, taking seats in the chairs placed at the front of the room. They were lined up like at a movie theater, watching over 15 different screens that showed various streets and buildings throughout the cityscape.

Minisc, Lily, and Jules weren't granted such an opportunity to warm up. In fact, they'd have a few other disadvantages, too. Their counterpart classmates would be granted the extra time to discuss strategy and prep, a luxury that the three of them weren't permitted. Then there was the composition of their group. They were best friends and could work through silent communication with ease, but they couldn't change their elements. Because of the inclement weather, having a fire Elementalist was a hot commodity. Like Ms. Wright, a fire Elementalist would be able to move freely through the snow, and also have an easier time fighting in the freezing conditions. None of them fit that bill, which meant that their team would just have to figure out a solution on the fly.

The last disadvantage they faced was that Ms. Wright had split the three up and placed them all over the city. They'd have to find each other as well as the pretend hostages needing rescue—and do it all in a timely manner.

Of course, these factors weren't designed to be entirely cruel to her students. There were real world applications to the disadvantages Ms. Wright had piled upon the three. For instance, when the call for help came, as a member of the EC, they'd have no idea who might arrive alongside them on scene. There could be emergency services like police, fire fighters, and paramedics, along with other EC members there to provide aid, and so the key to being successful was swift communication. In most situations, there was little to no time for any intricate planning—the goal was about being quick and effective. Worrying about failure or overthinking their strategy would only be a detriment.

Some would argue that going to such in-depth lengths on these students who were merely learning from an exercise might seem extreme, and not all teachers would go about it the same way. But Ms. Wright wasn't in the business of setting her students up for anything unrealistic in their lives. They were volunteers who'd chosen the life that lay ahead of them, not hostages being forced against their will. If they'd thought it was unfair, they were more than welcome to leave.

Besides, she already knew the planning skills of her three students, and now she wanted to see how they worked off each other when communication was at its toughest. The mounting snow was just an added feature of the challenge.

***

The entire layout of the cityscape was about a kilometer long and two kilometers wide. Minisc stood at the furthest point near the west end, which also happened to be where one of three safe zones were marked. The small flares sat in the snow behind him, casting a reddish smoke through the dreary sky.

Normally, such a distance would be easily traversed for Minisc, but thanks to the unrelenting snow that continued to pelt his face, he could barely make heads or tails of his direction. His cheeks were bright red and growing more numb by the second.

Aside from the worsening weather, he didn't have the foggiest idea of where Lily or Jules would be starting either. And in the storm, finding them would take a stroke of luck.

Then there were the potentially bigger issues, like Ms. Wright's starting location. She could be anywhere in the city, and with the ease with which she moved, finding the trio before they found each other would make being picked off that much easier. Perhaps with all three of them together they'd be able to handle their teacher under the current conditions, but separated they'd be in serious trouble.

Of course, standing around would solve none of those issues, and so Minisc took a deep breath to calm his racing mind. He might not have been a fire Elementalist, but perhaps the heat generated from his body while using Celestial Light would make his life, not to mention his movement, slightly easier. He pushed himself to 12% power and watched the snow around him become soft and slushy.

One benefit of doing a search and rescue mission, at least in

Minisc's eyes, was that fighting their teacher wasn't the mission. In fact, it wasn't even part of the goal. Sure, beating her would make their job much easier, but as long as they rescued the hostages, they'd still pass.

Through the howls of the wind, Minisc heard a loud buzzer echoing. The blaring sound coming from the home base signified that their mission was a go.

Wasting no time, Minisc started trekking through the droves of snow. He had a rough idea of the hostage building's location, but when his surroundings were completely layered in snow, distinguishing differences was difficult. He could make out a few standard-looking homes all squished together, but none of them were apartment complexes. He followed the roadway and attempted to go east.

Since Lily and Jules would both be hampered in their mobility, Minisc figured that the safe bet would be on him arriving first to the site. He'd have to try and assess the situation on his own for the time being and hope that he wouldn't find his teacher all alone. But if she were to stand in his way, at least he could use the apartment as a landmark for backup. He just had to hope that his friends were thinking the same way as him.

The air grew still, making the crunching of his footsteps more audible than he'd have liked. He tried to move at a solid pace but kept his eyes alert and his head on heavy rotation, hoping not to be blindsided by his teacher. After a few minutes, he turned onto the main street, and his destination was in sight.

He stopped and took a moment to assess his surroundings. The snow on the streets remained untouched, which meant that he must have been the first person to arrive, as he'd expected.

On either side were two connecting streets, both of which were potential locations for his teacher to ambush from. There were also a few homes attached together on the left, while on his right were the apartments Ms. Wright had been referring to earlier. He approached the apartment building with caution. The chipped red bricks were coated with snow, and the windows that climbed the three-story building were all boarded up. It looked fairly abandoned, but Minisc knew that this was only for effect.

He did one final check for any ambush spots, but aside from an aerial attack there was little for his teacher to use as cover.

Even so, he still harbored concern as he stared up at the building. *This has to be a trap. Of course Ms. Wright would head for the victims first and try to cut off any direct route for us. I should try and wait a minute or two and see if Lily or Jules show up...but then again, that could be losing valuable time.*

Minisc tried to recall his experience when saving Robin, as well as the lessons he'd learned from his father and Mr. Howland. *Think: If this were a real scenario, how would they react? What would father do in this situation?*

It didn't take long for him to come up with an answer—he knew exactly what his father's actions would be. He'd seen and heard of the Heroes' unrelenting triumphs so many times before that he'd often roll his eyes when hearing them. But in this case, they were beneficial.

I don't have time to wait around. If lives were really on the line, then every second would count.

With his decision made, Minisc quickly formed a plan. In his mind, the easiest point of entry would've been the front door, as most would suspect. But a seed of doubt about the straight-forward path lingered in Minisc's brain. Perhaps it was paranoia from learning under his teacher, but not for a second did he believe that she'd allow such easy access. If anything, she was likely waiting inside ready to strike. He needed another way.

He looked to the sky, blocking the snow with his forearm. If his teacher suspected a frontal assault, then he'd try another route—the rooftops. Since Jules was the only wind Elementalist of the three and the only one with real flight capabilities, nobody would suspect Minisc to come in through the top floor. With any luck, and thanks to the shallow visibility, perhaps Ms. Wright would be taken by surprise.

Minisc hurried between the two buildings. It was a cramped area, and he was barely able to stretch his arms out fully before touching brick. He checked for a ladder on the side of the building but found nothing, so he resorted to his next best option.

His body began to glow gold as he channeled Celestial Light. The warmth filled his body and he took a deep calming breath, the worries of the mission, the cold, and his friends fading into the background. The building was only three floors tall, and so if he used his strength just right, scaling it with well-timed jumps would work fine.

He crouched down as the power of his element filled his legs, tingling all the way down to his toes. His face contorted in concentration, and golden sparks started to flicker off his feet. With one last look to make sure that his angles were perfect, he launched himself forward without fear. When his feet hit the cold, rough bricks of the building wall, he quickly bounced off them, shifting his momentum back and forth with bursts of energy. He reached the rooftop within seconds, landing in an explosion of snow.

He took a few deep breaths, waiting for the burning sensation in his legs to fade as his body began to return to normal. Yet for some reason, the sensation refused to stop. If anything, his body felt like it was heating up further. His chest began tightening and his head started to feel fuzzy.

He shook his head, trying to knock the cobwebs out before shielding his face from the snow once again. He needed to regain focus now that he was in the danger zone.

No sign of Ms. Wright yet. I wonder if she decided to go after Jules or Lily first. Guess I should take a look inside and see what's going on.

On top of the roof was a small rectangular room with a steel door that led to the floor below. That was his entrance.

Minisc walked up to the door and grabbed the handle, but as he pushed down it refused to budge. "Of course it's frozen," he grumbled, dropping his whole weight on the handle, but even that didn't break the thick ice. Figuring that the only way through would be brute force, Minisc took a step back and lowered his shoulder. Once, twice, and then on the third try he smashed clean through the door, sending it flying open.

After getting inside, Minisc was finally free of the pelting snow. But now he was shrouded in darkness as the stairwell had no lights, not from what he could tell anyway. Luckily, unlike the snow, a bit of darkness could be easily dealt with. A quick flick of his wrist sent a small ball of light a foot in front of him, illuminating the hallway.

But what was supposed to be the simplest of moves, and one he could control in his sleep, began to gleam with far more energy than expected.

Geez, that's bright! He held up his arm to block the rays. *That's not at all what I wanted to happen. Is something going on here? First my body won't stop burning from Celestial Light, and now using even the most minimal amount of energy feels like I was fighting for my life!*

With no other choice, Minisc flung the ball of light behind him and up to the top of the stairs. At least that way, the light would hit his back and beyond rather than blinding him.

Down the hall he walked, and once he reached the floor below the roof, he was shocked at what he saw. The insides of the building were brutally destroyed—walls were crumbling with holes in them, ceiling beams were scattered along the floor, and even the furniture had been flipped over and shredded. For a moment, he forgot that this was a test and was alarmed, but after thinking about it for a second, the room's destruction was probably for decoration more than anything. Just a simple way to increase the stress level. Still, he could sense that something was off. *There's nobody here. Could the victims be on a different floor? I thought they'd be placed at the top, making them harder to escape with…but then again, if the front door was indeed a trap, then they must be closer to the main floor.*

When Minisc started walking into the middle of the room, a strange noise caught his attention. It sounded like crackling sparks. He immediately sensed danger and hopped back from the entrance to the stairwell, when a wall of fire sprung up like a barrier blocking his path. He gawked at the display and then kicked himself for being so obvious. *No! She read me like a book!*

Knowing that he was in trouble and that the path forward was blocked, Minisc hurried back up the stairs to the rooftop for a quick escape. But just as he'd feared, that entrance was blocked by a wall of blistering red and yellow fire. The snow outside pelting the flames extinguished instantly.

Unbelievable. She played me. I didn't even consider that she could use her flames to set up barriers without being around…unless she is around?

Perhaps the flames were merely a façade, he wondered, and with a simple attack they'd fade. He walked close, the crackles filling his ears while he felt the warmth on his face. He shot off a ball of light in hopes of his freedom, but the ball was absorbed by the flames and refused to break through. *Well, that answers that. These flames are too thick to simply break through.* Minisc sighed. *I knew I should've waited for Lily and Jules. Ms. Wright probably expected that in these conditions I'd be the first to arrive, and so she set a trap realizing that I had no way of escaping, unlike Jules or Lily.*

Minisc walked back into the other room and decided to take a look around. Waiting to be saved would defeat the whole purpose of a rescue mission, but his options were thin. He looked at the decaying drywall and felt a burst of cold air filling the room.

I could probably smash through the walls and get back outside pretty easy, or even through the floor, but I'd probably fail the test for unnecessary damage. Plus, if the victims are below, I might accidentally hurt them. There has to be a better way.

He folded his arms in thought, but his escape wasn't the only thing on his mind. Strange, tense pulses still danced in his arms and legs, like something was crawling around inside him.

CHAPTER 4
PUT TO THE TEST (PART 2)

WITH MINISC FIRST TO ARRIVE, AND ALSO THE FIRST to spring Ms. Wright's trap, Jules arrived next, unaware of his friend's predicament.

Since he despised the cold as much as any person could, he forced his way through the weather in hopes of finding warmth in the apartment building. But he knew full well that such hope would be naive. If he could simply waltz into the building and save the hostages, then Ms. Wright wasn't doing her job—something nobody would accuse her of.

Swirling snow continued to hamper Jules' mobility, but he could still rely on his wind for precise movements. For him, the bigger issue was his vision. Seeing more than a few feet ahead was impossible, which meant that flying forward with any amount of speed was not only careless but also dangerous. If Ms. Wright were to spot him alone, he'd be placed in a precarious position. He still wanted to try and reach his friends before they arrived so that they could team up, but he understood that this would come down to some lucky timing.

Before doing anything needless, Jules tried to slow down

his thought process. For once, he tried to heed his brother Yuri's characteristics. That meant taking a moment and thinking through the situation instead of reacting.

Okay, let's think this through logically here…the way Yuri would.

Since the apartment building is located on the east side of the cityscape, chances are that Ms. Wright would start us off on the three furthest directions. I know I started on the south side, which means it's likely that Lily and Minisc started north and west. If I remember the layout, I have the furthest distance to go. Assuming that none of us get lost in the snow, and based on how fast we can travel, Minisc should arrive first. I'll likely be second, and Lily will be third. But that would create a massive disadvantage for Ms. Wright — she knows Minisc would put up the toughest fight, even in this weather. Also, Lily always has the obvious counter of water vs fire, which means chances are that she'll try to avoid Lily and not waste her energy on a losing battle. So I guess that makes me the main target of the mission. If she can take me out of the equation before Lily or Minisc arrive as backup, her odds will skyrocket. I need to be on my guard at all times.

Jules hurried down the street, his eyes constantly on alert. His vision was getting clearer, and the numbing cold in his body wasn't nearly as unbearable as it had been. *Maybe the storm is finally letting up.*

But the storm still appeared relentless in the distance; it was just his little area that seemed a bit calm. A realization started to dawn on him. *Oh, this is bad.*

Jules spun around, but before he could react, a circle of flames sprouted up around him like a fortress. *Looks like my hunch was right. Time to move!*

Since going through the flames wasn't an option, Jules crouched down, and with a ferocious gust of wind he leapt into the air. Unfortunately, he was met with a second stream of fire striking down from above. He forced himself to the left, contorting his body in mid-air just enough to miss the attack.

Phew, she's not kidding around. She could've caused some serious damage with that one. Well, fine by me, I'm not holding back either!

When Jules landed safely on the other side of the fire, his eyes darted around looking for cover. He was in great shape, but the winter air burned his lungs as he tried to catch his breath.

Since the second set of flames dropped from the sky, or at least from that general direction, Jules knew that his teacher held the higher ground. Spotting her through the snow would've been tough enough, but being able to use the thin brick barrier around the rooftop meant that finding her would be next to impossible. He needed cover, and quick.

After another blast of fire, Jules rushed for the closest building he could find. If time had permitted, he would've much preferred making a dash for the building with the hostages, but he was stuck on the opposite side of the street and desperate for shelter. Even if it wasn't the right building, at the least he could buy time for Lily to arrive and act as a shield for him.

But just like Minisc, who—unbeknownst to Jules—remained on the other side of the street, he fell right into his teacher's trap.

Once he reached the inside of the building, a large wall of flames shielded off the entrance just as he was trying to close the door. Thinking quick, Jules leapt back and stretched his arms out. Propulsions of wind ripped through air, causing the fire to dance drastically but failing to extinguish the wall of flames.

You've gotta be kidding me. I can't blow that fire out.

Stuck, Jules decided that now was the right time to explore his hew confines. He was well aware that the clock was ticking, but there was little choice. He'd somehow have to use the building to his advantage.

He made his way to the middle of the room, devoid of windows and featuring only a set of stairs heading up to the next floor. The rest of the room was filled with lifeless walls and dusty old furniture, nothing that could be of any benefit.

But at least he could pause and reset now without fear of being attacked.

It seems likely that she's on the roof, but as long as I can't see her, I'll have to remain on the defensive. Then again, there was no sign of Minisc or Lily anywhere. Maybe I can use that to my advantage. If I can get to the rooftops, I might be able to spot her when she tries to attack them.

Jules hurried up the first flight of stairs, skipping through the barren rooms along the way. Two floors later, and he could see a final set of stairs nearby. There were no artificial lights in the building, but from the top of the freezing cold stairwell he could feel a sense of warmth. He also noticed a strange red-yellow glow casting down from above. He turned the corner up the final set of stairs before coming to a stop.

He sighed, slumped his shoulders, and emitted a defeated groan. He shot off another wind propulsion for good measure, but just like before, the wind cut right through the flames with no effect. *I can't believe her. She's got me completely trapped. This isn't good.*

***

The last to arrive in the area was Lily. Her mobility was severely hampered due to the inclement weather, and she could feel the burn in her legs as she mercilessly forced her way through the foot-deep snow. She didn't have Minisc's use of Celestial Light, or Jules' wind element, so she was forced to rely on leg strength and will power alone.

She rolled up the sleeve of her jacket so she could read her watch. *20 minutes left. That took longer than I thought to get here...*

She looked around and didn't see much disturbance in the land, but off in the distance she noticed two telling signs. There was a strange circular burn mark only a few feet away from her, which was a clear indication of a fire attack. There was also a faint cloud of smoke in the same area rising from the two mirrored buildings, one of which was the search and rescue site and the other a prop. But that seemed strange to Lily. *Why would there be smoke coming from a prop building unless there were also people in there?*

Ms. Wright might have been a tough teacher, but there was no question that she was also fair. At the outset of the test, she'd made it clear that the only bodies requiring rescue were in the north apartment building. They'd all seen what it looked like beforehand, so there was no confusing it for another location.

Of course, that left Lily wondering if Ms. Wright happened to be in the other building facing either Jules or Minisc. But if that were the case, she couldn't figure out why there would be two trails of smoke.

Before Lily made her decision, she felt a strange sense of danger. Instinctively, she cast a shield of water around her body like a dome of protection, and from the corner of her eye she saw a flicker of sparks. Flames rained down around her but failed to penetrate the liquid barrier. Lily extended her arms, pushing the barrier out and keeping the flames as far from her as possible. *Why would Ms. Wright go after me? She knows with my water I'd be the worst match for her. Even in this snow it wouldn't make much of a difference. I can still defend myself one on one against whatever she throws at me. Shouldn't she be going after Jules? Although if he and Minisc arrived before me, that must mean that she's already beaten them? No, that wouldn't happen so easily.*

Then it finally dawned on her: *Unless she trapped them somehow.*

The flames around Lily tempered and she glanced to the rooftops, keeping up her defenses. She caught a glimpse of a shadow on the rooftops, like a rat scurrying away, but she didn't know for certain if it were human. The shadow evaporated into the swirls of snow, leaving Lily with a choice.

Both flames came from the east, which means that Ms. Wright can't be guarding the victims from there. Maybe if I can find a way inside, I can end this quickly.

Lily rushed to the east building's door, hoping that her plan would work. But as she tried to crack the door open, she quickly realized it was locked. Slamming her shoulder into the wood, she bounced off of it like it was a trampoline. *Great, it's locked and frozen.* Out of fear, she spun around ready to protect herself from incoming flames, but they never arrived.

For a second she was disappointed, but she understood why her teacher wisely wouldn't attack. Whether the door coated in ice was by design or simple circumstance, any form of fire element would weaken the ice and make it breakable. With that, she could likely smash down the remains of the door. It would be too easy.

That left Lily stuck in the middle of the street, the sound of the clock ticking in her mind. There was still no sign of Minisc or Jules, but she was confident that they'd already arrived, and so they must have been around. She made up her mind, refusing to second-guess as she made a run for the other building. She hoped to find her friends stationed there already, which would give them a clear advantage. With united strength, they could handle their teacher much easier.

Changing course, Lily decided that the smoke rising off the building across the street would be her guide. Once she was within view, she realized that the door was barred by flames. Luckily, unlike her friends, walls of fire weren't anything she couldn't handle. She flicked her wrist and with a swish of water, the flames were doused, and then she ran inside and started calling out for her friends.

"Minisc! Jules! Are you guys in here?" She waited a moment in the main room, keeping her eyes and ears peeled for any danger. She could say with confidence that Ms. Wright absolutely wasn't in the building based on the location of her previous attacks, but that didn't prevent other traps from lying about, just waiting to spring into action.

After a few deafeningly silent moments, Lily finally heard the first call that brought her comfort.

"Lily?" Jules rushed down the stairs toward her. "Man, am I glad to see you!"

"You're telling me! Ms. Wright tried to attack me and I couldn't get into the apartment with the hostages, so I decided to follow the smoke trail in hopes of finding you or Minisc."

"Quick thinking. I was trying to get shelter from Ms. Wright too, but she must've been planning it from the start. She forced me to use this building as shelter so that she could trap me inside." Jules paused and then asked, "I don't suppose you've seen Minisc at all?"

Lily frowned. "No sign of him yet. It seems pretty obvious that Ms. Wright had no intentions of taking us on as a team. Her whole goal is to divide and conquer while waiting out the clock." She rolled up her jacket and checked her watch again. The seconds were ticking away.

"Well, there's no way Minisc wouldn't have been the first of us to arrive, and since Ms. Wright was free to focus her attacks on us, that must mean that Minisc likely fell into a similar trap as me," Jules concluded.

Lily recalled seeing smoke coming from both buildings. She'd found it strange at the time, but now things were adding up. "Minisc must be in the building with the hostages. But the front door was frozen shut, despite trying to bait Ms. Wright into thawing it for me. Which means that he must've found another way in."

"Another way in…" Jules lingered on the thought, trying to place all the pieces together in his mind. "He must've tried the rooftops somehow. Did he run into Ms. Wright while he was up there? If that's the case, I think I have an idea."

A mischievous smirk formed on his face, one that made Lily worry. "What are you planning?"

"Come on—we need to get to the roof."

Jules led the way, ignoring Lily's question. Time was of the essence, and every second they spent being indecisive shrunk their margin for error.

At the top stood another fire blockade, and just like before, Lily washed it away with ease. They busted through the door and were met with an intense flurry of snow. Lily lifted her arm, trying to shield her eyes from the blinding forces of nature as the wind howled past her. "This is ridiculous! I can't see a thing!"

"No kidding!" Jules agreed, following Lily's arm. "Ms. Wright picked one heck of a day to do outdoor training!"

Jules pointed north, noticing the faint dark smoke cloud. It was rising high but became lost in the blotchy clouds so quickly that it was hard to tell if he was staring at a mirage.

"That's the building where the hostages are. And with any luck, Minisc as well." Jules said.

Jules rushed to the lip of the roof, crouching down behind the foot-tall brick wall built around the building.

"I've got a plan. I'll fly us over there, but I need you to watch out for Ms. Wright. I won't be able to defend us while we're in the air, so it's all on you."

Lily joined her partner in squatting just out of sight, but was more focused on the plan than staying hidden. "You're kidding me, right? That's your great idea? You can't even fly for that long—and besides, we can barely see past our hands, let alone far enough for me to protect us." The disapproval in her voice was glaringly obvious.

Jules, on the other hand, remained undeterred. He smiled with confidence and said, "I know, but don't worry about it. I trust you. Now buckle up. Time is ticking."

Before Lily could spit out another debate, she felt Jules wrap his arms around her waist, squeezing her in tight. "Whoa, hold on a second! I didn't agree to this! I swear — if you drop me, I'll kill you!"

With a gust of wind forming below them, Lily felt her feet lift from the ground, and her body became light as a feather as she began to float. The wind blew her hair in all directions while the snow illuminated her cheeks with a pink, frozen hue.

For any wind Elementalist, the biggest advantage their element provided was the ability to soar through the air like a bird. It allowed for better maneuverability and flexibility in both battle and in life. But most struggled to grasp that power — the strength it took to fly freely was immense, and it was also draining. Even after practicing for years, Jules had only recently mastered his own ability to fly.

Though never willing to rest on his laurels, he decided to up his training, using Minisc and Lily as added weight. After all, flying was nice, but if he could carry people to different locations as well, that would change the whole dynamic of the situation.

Lily tried to keep staring ahead, but looking down was a foregone conclusion. Under normal circumstances, she loved the feeling of floating freely in the air. The sensation was like floating on a bed of water, drifting along with no worries in the world. Feeling the wind through her hair and the change in perspective staring at the ground below her was always exciting, even if in previous instances they only hovered a few feet off the ground. It often made her wish that she was born a wind Elementalist so that she could learn to soar through the air like a bird.

From this height, she was debating those wishes. They'd never tried flying from such a height, and if Ms. Wright managed to get the jump on them, it was a long way down. At least she'd have some snow to cushion the fall.

"Jules, can you hurry this up?!" Lily whispered, hoping not to draw any attention.

"I'm working on it, but you're not the lightest thing I've ever tried to carry you know!" Jules quipped.

"Excuse me?!" She punched Jules in the chest.

"Ow! Relax, it was a joke."

"Joke or not, the sooner I'm back on solid ground, the better."

"Just keep your eyes open, okay? Let me handle the flying."

The technique of flight, at least in the way Jules was applying it, took far less strength. Because he'd started on the roof, he only needed to travel parallel. The real toll on a wind Elementalist's strength was when trying to ascend. Ascending with another person was still something Jules hadn't yet achieved.

The ride was the longest 15 seconds of Lily's life. Regardless, her faith in Jules would pay off as they reached the lip of the opposite building.

As the view became clear, they saw smoke ferociously rising from the walls of fire.

"Thought so — it looks like Minisc fell for the same trap that I did," Jules said.

They were only a few feet away from their destination and ready to land with ease, when Lily yelled, "Jules, look out!" She freed her left hand from Jules' chest and cast a wall of water to her left. The air filled with steam as the fireball, like an incoming asteroid, splashed into Lily's defenses.

The goal of the shield was protection. In that sense it worked to perfection. But the force from the impact sent the two sprawling off course.

Jules gritted his teeth, fearing they'd shatter; he felt like a pilot losing control of his plane. With all the energy he could expend, he lifted Lily and himself up a few feet, praying that as they came crashing down it would be enough to land on the rooftop safely.

With part luck and part skill, they narrowly missed the lip of the roof. Lily and Jules squeezed out muffled screams as they crash landed into a thick pile of snow, stumbling to a halt. The snow piled in on them as they coughed out whatever they'd inhaled on their landing.

Lily lay face first in the snow, mumbling, "You could've stuck the landing a little better there, Jules." But with no time to complain, she pushed herself up. Other than some small aches from the bumpy crash, she felt no worse for wear, and neither did Jules as he got to his feet to dust off the snow seeping through his clothes. The chill on his skin only made him curse the weather that much more.

"Well, I wasn't planning on Ms. Wright having the force to push us off track like that," Jules grumbled, "But still, we made it, so let's hurry. Minisc must be trapped inside."

They nodded, and Lily washed away the flames blocking the door before they rushed down the stairs.

***

Still trying to come up with an effective yet safe escape route, Minisc paced back and forth. His arms were folded and he surveyed his surroundings. The fire in front of him continued to sway, taunting him. He could hear his teacher's voice in his head, chastising his mistake. He didn't have any way to check the time, but he knew that it was running thin and there was still no sign of Lily and Jules. Were they being attacked by Ms. Wright? Had they fallen for the same trap as him? Obviously, Lily could escape, but Jules would be in the same precarious position as himself.

Minisc took one last glance around the room, then gripped his fist. A faint sparkle of light danced around his fingers like lightning bolts.

Even though the test was supposed to simulate a real-life scenario, or at least as close as the school could get, there was no getting around the differences. This was not real life. No hostages were in danger. There was no Robin to be saved at all costs. Try as he might to ignore it, that fact did change Minisc's approach. In a real crisis, he'd max output Celestial Light and shoot through the floor, taking his chance that nobody below would be caught as collateral, then take the hostages to safety. Of course, he was sure that his teacher would have something to say about that risk, which would hurt their evaluation.

But it wasn't just about some grade. In a way, that sort of reckless abandon would be betraying the trust in his friends. Just because he carelessly fell into his teacher's trap didn't mean that they would, so he chose to wait a little while longer. At least until the time started to tick down to desperation levels—then perhaps he'd risk his idea.

From above, Minisc heard a loud thud, like two boulders crashing. He jolted upright, raised his arms, and braced himself as cracks of dirt fell from the ceiling. For a panicked second, he wondered if the building was falling, but once the echoing sound from above subsided, everything became quiet again.

He then heard the sounds of water splashing, and he sighed with happiness as his friends finally arrived to bail him out of his careless mistake.

"Minisc! Are you down here?" he heard Lily call out.

"Yeah—but Ms. Wright blocked all the pathways with fire," he shouted back in response.

Lily and Jules came hustling down the stairs, and Lily immediately washed the flames away, granting them an entrance. She spun around to face the others and said, "We need to hurry—we're running out time!"

There was no time for explanations or updates. They were a

reunited team on a time limit, and if Minisc and Jules knew any-thing about their best friend, it was that she hated failing tests.

Once the three ran down a few flights of stairs, they eventu-ally reached a large space that looked like a hotel lobby without the furniture. More wooden structures were collapsed on the floor, and even small fires burned around the room. Directly in the middle of this war zone were three, large brown bags of sand — all adorned with wacky clothing and notably absurd wigs. These bags had been dressed up to look like people — or, in other words, the fake hostages.

"Come on — grab them and let's get out of here!" Lily urged. "I have a feeling Ms. Wright will be here any second."

They all took a peek around for Ms. Wright, but realized they were alone.

Jules rushed over to the bags, hoping to pick them up with ease, but when he knelt down and tossed his arms around one, he let out a grunt. "Seriously, these things must weigh a hun-dred pounds. Shouldn't hostages be able to walk of their own accord? This is ridiculous."

"Hold up, Jules — we also have another problem. The front door is frozen shut," Lily reminded him. She reached down to pick up one of the hostages and tried to toss it over her shoul-der. Lily was thin and athletic, and she had the muscle to carry her share of the hostages, but the weight felt like it would pop her shoulder out at any moment.

Minisc joined them. "Okay, I'm pretty sure I have a plan," he assured them. "We know that Ms. Wright will be prepared to at-tack the second we bust that door open, but that also means that she'll have to reveal herself, too. When she does, we'll have our best chance. I'll take her head-on — as long as I can see where she is, I think I have the best chance of holding her off. I'd suggest Lily, but through the snow I think it would be tough. So if you two can take the three hostages to the safety circle, we can win."

Lily checked her watch again and said, "Well, honestly, I don't think we have time for another plan anyway, so I say we go for it."

Jules bent down to one knee and said, "Minisc, give me your hostage. I'll carry one on each shoulder."

Minisc loaded Jules up with the sandbags, and Jules let out a grunt as he got to his feet. "You better make this quick, though — I'm already losing feeling in my arms."

"Everybody ready? Here we go. Celestial Light, 12%." Minisc increased his power and his light shone brightly. But something felt strange this time — something felt worse. He was usually comfortable with the power and in tune with all the different sensations that tended to happen alongside it. This time, though, he felt his body heating up in unnatural ways.

But Lily and Jules were staring at him and waiting for action, and so he shook off the discomfort and refocused on his task.

"Okay. Let's do this."

They nodded, and Minisc rapidly shot forward. He crashed his shoulder into the frozen door and busted through cleanly, nearly blowing the hinges off. Skidding to a halt in the middle of the street, waves of snow swirled around him like a snowy tornado. Even he was shocked at the power he displayed; it felt far more extensive than what he was used to at 12%.

Lily and Jules followed up at the rear, taking a sharp left and running in the opposite direction. Lily hesitated for a second as she noticed Minisc standing still, paralyzed. Then, from the corner of her eye, she saw their threat.

"Minisc, to the west!" she shouted.

The words smacked Minisc out of his head, and he whipped around in the direction indicated. Leering over him from the rooftop was Ms. Wright. She was eying him specifically, a fierce stance at the ready.

If there was anything he knew about his teacher, it was that the gift of time only served to aid her. If she was able to view her opponent's strategy early, and was provided time to analyze it, there was almost no chance of winning.

Knowing this, Minisc chose to take the attack to her. He just needed to buy some time for Lily and Jules.

He opened with a Lum Bomb in her direction. It screamed out with fury—along with an intense burn in his arms and chest. The sting took his breath away, but that wasn't the biggest issue. It was his aim. Something he'd done so many times that it was nearly a reflex, and he'd never thought about the ball of light having a mind of its own. Except, this time the Lum Bomb spiraled out of control before smashing into the left side of the building, missing Ms. Wright by a good ten feet.

Seriously, what's going on with me? Minisc braced himself as the front end of the building started to collapse right before him, as he happened to see his teacher sailing toward him like a blur. She kicked off the falling debris and shot herself forward. Minisc dodged the assault, narrowly missing a strike from her fist.

Minisc bolted for Ms. Wright, leaving a trail of light behind him. He tried to guess where Lily and Jules would be at that very moment, but his mind wouldn't function. His head became fuzzy, his vision blurry.

Suddenly, he felt frozen. His face was flush and he stumbled forward. Before he could counter his teacher, he started to see three…no, *five* Ms. Wrights. The teacher was good, but never before had she displayed illusion skills.

In addition to the dizziness, a bout of nausea filled his stomach. He kept swinging at the multiple Ms. Wrights but continued striking air. He could tell that something was wrong, and he stood no chance against his teacher in his condition. Instead, he chose to be the martyr. Every second he could add to aid Lily and Jules in their escape would give them hope.

As expected, when his attack ceased, he saw what looked like his end. The scorching heat from walls of fire encircled him, and before he could make a sound, his face was crushed into the snow. He struggled to free himself, feeling a strange tightening around his hands, and hearing a click and then a beep. His fight was now over. He'd been "captured" by his teacher.

In a real-world situation, Minisc could've easily broken free of the cuffs binding him. Then again, in an actual scenario, he most likely would've been burned to death instead of tied up. To play by the rules, he kept his mouth shut and left their fate up to Lily and Jules.

"You three had the right idea," Ms. Wright told him. "Being the most dangerous in terms of strength, sending you as a distraction while Lily and Jules escaped with the hostages could've worked. But now that you're out of the way, the rest of this test will be over quickly."

Meanwhile, unaware of what was going on behind them, Lily and Jules sprinted through the snow, doing what they could to keep trudging forward. Through the relentless storm, they could see hope. A small, red flare was releasing smoke, signaling their destination. They were only 100 meters away.

Their biggest obstacle was Jules lagging behind. Thanks to twice the weight—and already being exhausted by flying Lily from one building to another—he could feel his legs throbbing. Each step sent shocks up his thighs, his face contorting in angst. But he refused to stop; if he did, chances were that he'd sink right into the snow, a prospect he hated more than the pain.

But hope, like snow in the sun, often melts quickly. Walls of fire sprung up a few feet in front of them, as if they were the gates of hell.

"What?! There's no way! Minisc couldn't have lost that quickly!" Jules gawked as he and Lily came to a sudden halt.

He waited for Lily to clear the path, but he could tell that her focus was elsewhere. He turned around and saw more balls of fire sailing in their direction.

"We've got company!" Lily yelled.

Thinking quick, Jules dropped the sandbags, letting them sink into the snow as he threw his hands forward. Jet streams of wind came to their protection. The propulsions connected with the flames, managing to change their course just enough to keep them safe.

"Lily, put out the fire!" he ordered.

Jules held strong, making sure that the flames were dispersed as Lily ran up beside him using her free arm to wash away the flames. But it was too late—Ms. Wright was practically on top of them.

They both braced themselves to fight back, but their teacher continued walking toward them with an almost devilish grin. She didn't immediately raise her hands to attack, but after a few steps she stretched her arm parallel to the left. A small flicker of fire danced from her palm, heading a few feet away from Jules and into a pile of snow.

It whooshed as it landed, and a loud buzzer began ringing from the snow.

"Wait…what?" Jules sputtered.

"Uh, I think we just failed…" Lily said woefully.

"Maybe, but…oh, no! The hostages!" Jules freaked, suddenly realizing what Lily was referring to. He sprinted to where he dropped his sandbag people before becoming fully aware of his mistake. He immediately extinguished the feeble fire, but the damage was done. All that remained was the charred burlap sacks and faint strands of fake hair.

"She played us," Jules said, sulking.

***

After the test finished and everyone returned to the warmth of home base, Minisc, Lily, and Jules stood at the front of the class with the monitors playing footage of the events that had taken place. Ms. Wright stood in front of them, launching into her evaluations.

"Obviously, since the hostages were critically injured, you three failed your mission. However, I believe that there are lessons that can be learned from this little exercise."

She spoke in a flat tone. Whenever she did that, her students wondered if she was disappointed or trying to be encouraging.

"Despite Minisc and Jules both being trapped in buildings," she continued, "Lily, you acted quick and managed to deduce where your partners were. Keep those instincts sharp and let them guide you. As for you, Jules — the idea of using your wind to fly from rooftop to rooftop admittedly took me by surprise. If I'd expected a plan like that, it would have been quite easy to shoot you down, but since it was unconventional, you deserve some credit. You assessed the situation well and I dare say that your plan would have worked out if not for a small executional flaw." She glanced in Minisc's direction.

Minisc shook his head, knowing what she meant. "Sorry, guys. I don't really know what happened. All of a sudden, I just started feeling dizzy and nauseous. If I'd put up more of a fight, we would've passed."

Despite Minisc's self-blame, neither of them cared to fault their friend. Instead, they looked at him with concern. Jules didn't care much about grades, and nothing was more important to Lily than the health of her friends, so they both easily disregarded any angst about a failing grade and instead focused on him.

"Are you okay? Did you get injured earlier?" Lily asked, lifting his arms up and down running her own makeshift medical exam.

"It's nothing like that, I'm sure," Minisc said, trying to wave off his well-intentioned friend. "I think I might just need some more rest is all. It's been a long couple of weeks." He was lying through his teeth, but perhaps it wasn't just for his friend's sake.

He was experiencing strange feelings in his body, and it was causing a bit of fear in him. But with his day now over, he could take a few minutes to relax and plan his next steps.

CHAPTER 5
RISK VS. REWARD

CLASS FINISHED UP AS IT USUALLY DID. EACH GROUP had completed their respective tests with varying degrees of success, but Minisc's mind refused to pay attention to any of that. Each prickle in his body, each wave of nausea made him pray for his own bed. Unfortunately, he knew that he'd have to wait for that.

His mind was fixated on the cause of his pain. There was no concrete evidence, but he had a strong suspicion that these symptoms were somehow caused by Celestial Light.

The obvious choice was to call his father, and he did — the second class ended. But, surprisingly, he received zero clarification from him. His father couldn't recall having any similarities to what Minisc was experiencing when first learning Celestial Light. Then again, he was far older and much more adept at using his powers. As his mentor Mr. Howland would describe it, he was a natural, and no one else could even compare.

Minisc, although talented and perpetually working to improve, still had much to learn. Especially when it came to mastering such a dangerously powerful technique. He could only dream of reaching the heights his father had.

With both of them curious for answers, they turned to the only man who would know best.

Minisc arrived at the EC first, as the school had a direct bus to its headquarters. Since his father wouldn't arrive for a tad bit longer and the snow was still falling heavily, he headed inside.

Since rescuing Robin and being granted a few days of rest, Minisc had put his Celestial Light training on hold. But with the lingering discomfort, he couldn't wait until training started up again to learn more about what was happening in his body.

Up the stairs to the third floor and down to the end of the hall, Minisc arrived at Mr. Howland's office. He came to a stop, reached for the door handle, and hesitated.

As Minisc had learned through painful, first-hand experience, walking into Mr. Howland's office was unlike walking into any other room in the EC. His mentor's training methods were rather unconventional at times, and the intimidating experience of approaching his imposing office was just the beginning. When Minisc saw the door handle, he felt nothing but dread.

Normally Minisc would prepare himself for a clever trick or two and head on inside without fear, but with his body in its current condition, that seemed dangerous.

While he debated his next move, he heard a strange, repeated sound on the other side of the door, like around ten pieces of wood falling to the floor, one after another.

"Oh no! Mr. Howland's going to lose his mind!"

Minisc heard the voice and suddenly forgot about any potential threats, swinging the door open.

Mr. Howland was nowhere to be found. Instead, he spotted a young man with wavy green hair and the brightest smile Minisc had ever seen. He wore a striped polo shirt and white shorts with random shapes on them. He was a shade taller than

Minisc, but his face was quite young, although Minisc knew firsthand how deceiving looks often could be.

"Robin?" Minisc asked, surprised to see his new friend in the office.

"Whoa! Minisc, what're you doing here?" Robin replied, just as surprised, "I was just trying to clean up a new experiment Mr. Howland was working on."

Minisc peeled his focus from Robin to see a bunch of building blocks toppled on the ground.

Robin knelt down, plucking a few of them off the ground and cradling them in his arms.

"Are those toy blocks?" Minisc asked.

"Yep. Mr. Howland has me trying to use my element as a catalyst for holding things. Us being light Elementalists, we don't have the same advantages as, say, ice or earth. They can create platforms that allow them to keep people safe, and reach new heights, too. So he has me working on focusing my light and using it to create platforms, hence the blocks. Here, watch!"

Robin tossed the blocks up high into the air, and they quickly started to give way to gravity. Robin whipped his hands forward repeatedly, and tiny saucers of light like discs flew out, floating in place while the blocks landed on them. The first four blocks landed with a slight give on the discs, but the fifth one crashed straight through and ricocheted off the ground. When it did, the other four saucers gave way as well.

"Man! Almost had it." Robin snapped his fingers in disappointment. "I really have to keep my focus while doing it. One disc isn't a problem, at least with small objects, but the more I try to hold up, the strain is just too much—at least right now. But I'll figure it out."

Minisc smiled. "I'm sure you will."

"Do you want to try? We can start with only one until you get used to it?"

Minisc rubbed his arm, knowing with his power being intermittent at best that he better not. "Thanks, but actually I just came from class and I'm pretty worn out."

"Of course, no point running yourself ragged! Especially after the week we just had." Robin started picking up the blocks again. "So what brings you by Mr. Howland's office, anyway? There's no way that you could've known I was here, so you must've come to see him, right?"

"Yeah, actually I did. He said be here at 5, but I guess I'm a little early."

"I figured as much. So does that mean you're gonna come join us again and work under Mr. Howland? We could really use your help around here. Since your father retired, things have only gotten busier."

"Not quite…" Minisc trailed off; he hesitated to mention Celestial Light around Robin. Somewhere in his heart, there was still a strange bit of belief that the young EA grad should've been the one learning it in his place. The one without simple genetic luck should've been learning Celestial Light and preparing to face Luminosa. He was more than up to the task, of that Minisc was sure. Also, his shinning personality was perfect for the spotlight, something that Minisc vehemently hated.

"What's up then? Did something happen? He didn't forget to fill out your report, did he? He's awful about that sort of stuff, you know. It took me over a year to get my paperwork from him."

"Uh…sort of. I just wanted to talk to him about the report is all." Minisc rubbed the back of his neck.

Luckily for Minisc, the phone on Mr. Howland's desk began ringing. Robin picked up, nodding his head as the voice on the other line went on about something, but Minisc couldn't hear what was going on.

When Robin hung up, he said, "Sorry, Minisc—I've gotta go. Mr. Howland forgot to hand in some documents about our raid of the Adenji gang, so I need to hand it in for him." Robin grabbed the papers, and with a big smile headed for the doorway. There was nothing that Robin didn't love about his job.

Robin waved goodbye to Minisc, then left him to wait for his father and Mr. Howland's arrival.

***

The setting sun cast a pink hue through the window of Mr. Howland's office. Minisc sat on one side of the couch beside his father Don, with Mr. Howland sitting across from them. As usual, Mr. Howland had a cup of tea in hand, the sweet lemon scent wafting its way through the room.

Between the three of them, Minisc was hopeful that he'd find a rational explanation for the sensations inside his body. The class exam took place hours prior, and yet a lingering, uncomfortable feeling still gripped at his chest. He was getting a headache, too, but he had other things to concern himself with at the moment.

Mr. Howland took a sip of his tea before lowering it to the table. His snow-white beard gave him the hardened face of a veteran, but his rounded glasses made him look like a teacher.

He spoke with controlled measure. "So — do I understand the situation correctly? Lately you've been feeling a strange, almost burning sensation when you try to use your element? Even without the use of Celestial Light, the feeling persists, and matched with that feeling is a lack of control over the input of power in your element, correct?"

"Yeah, that pretty much sums it up. I'd say it's been an on-again off-again feeling for the past few days. But then today in a simple training test at school, it was like my body had a mind of its own. Even the most basic use of my element felt like I was combining it with Celestial Light at 100%. Then when I actually *did* try to increase my strength as it was needed, my body gave out. My vision became blurry, I felt sick, and before I knew it, I'd collapsed in the snow. Honestly, it was sort of scary, which is why I came here. I wanted to know if this was something I should be worried about."

Don spoke next. As the only person who could possibly relate to the strains of Celestial Light, he wanted to lend his perspective.

"I certainly recall feeling the burn in my body at times," he relayed, "and there's no doubt that Celestial Light is taxing, but I don't recall ever having any sort of control issues. You don't suppose it could be something unrelated? Mr. Howland, do you remember any of this stuff happening while I was learning?"

Howland remained in thought, digesting the symptoms in order to form an explanation.

"I doubt that all this is unrelated, but allow me to ask you a question, Minisc. Can you recall when these symptoms first started? I know you've been taking some time to recover, but did these issues start happening before or after your fight with Dominic?"

"After, for sure." Minisc massaged his arms; there were a number of tender bruises that he was covering up with his jacket. "I'd say that this only started a few days ago, but I sort of just chalked it up to fatigue. Today was the first time I'd really put full effort into an exercise, and that's when I noticed just how bad things were."

Mr. Howland stroked his beard and took another sip of tea. "And in this training, were you using Celestial Light at 12% as instructed?"

"Yes, I kept it strictly to 12%. I didn't dare go over my limit. Not again."

Minisc remembered his battle against Dominos, at the end of which he made the risky move of using as much power as he could in order to defeat the tormenter. Using Celestial Light at 100% would've been a death sentence if he'd continued that state for a second longer, but he lucked out.

"Interesting," Mr. Howland said, stroking his beard again. "Without running some tests and getting a larger sample size of these effects, it's hard to be precise in any assessment. That said, I do have a mild guess regarding the issue you're currently facing. On the surface, it appears to me at least that you're paying some repercussions for your actions when fighting Dominic." Mr. Howland paused and took another sip of his tea, allowing time for Minisc to think about how he'd disobeyed his mentor's direct orders, even if it had been for good reason.

Mr. Howland continued, "Your body appears to be stuck in its own heightened state and is struggling to return to normal. Almost like a pseudo form of Celestial Light."

Minisc was confused. "So what does that mean? That I'm actually using more power than I think I'm using?"

"Something like that. Think of Celestial Light as a switch. When you flicked that switch on at full power, the strain it caused seems to have broken it. And now your body remains stuck in its heightened state long after its use is necessary, albeit in a fairly weakened form because of how little energy remains in your body. This is one of the many reasons I told you not to go over that 12% threshold. Your body is still growing, and with it, so too is your element."

Mr. Howland looked up at Minisc, and then to his former pupil Don. He swallowed hard and his voice became a little bit lower. Suddenly the room became tense, and Minisc felt a cold sweat forming on his forehead.

"Look, Minisc. I know you did what was needed to save Robin, and in no way should you be punished for such heroics. But when it comes to the effects that Celestial Light can cause on an Elementalist, I believe that these symptoms and the issues your body are currently dealing with proves that it's too much for you at this time. With your body still growing, and with you still learning to harness the full depths of your power, I believe that continuing forward would be too risky."

Minisc's eyes grew wide. He choked, "What do you mean, Sir?" His heart was beating rapidly, a lump forming in his throat.

"Do you recall what I told you when you started training to use Celestial Light? I told you that eventually, using the technique would burn up your element altogether—just like it had done with your father."

"Yes, I know that. And I said that I was willing to accept those consequences." Minisc's voice became more frustrated—he understood what was coming next.

"Minisc…" Don whispered, trying to ease his son's angst.

Mr. Howland replied, "I understand that, Minisc, and it's a noble sentiment, but you have to look at this rationally. Right now, you are doing more harm to your body than good. Stuck in this state, even with minimal effect, I'm sure that you're burning up your element far quicker than even your father did. Had I foreseen this happening so soon, I never would've agreed to train you."

"But…no, wait—we can't just stop! Father, tell him I can do this!" Minisc's eyes pleaded with his father, but Don lowered his head and sighed. In a way, this was his fault, and he knew it. He'd put Minisc and Mr. Howland in a tough position, and now he was left with a choice. Do right by his son, or do right by society.

Don swallowed hard and locked eyes with his son, gearing up to tell him the honest truth. "Minisc…it's not that I don't think you can do this, but I don't know…you have your whole life ahead of you. To see you destroy your body the way I've destroyed mine, but without getting to live the quality of life that I did…I'd be failing you as a father to allow that…"

As Don trailed off, Mr. Howland stepped in to finish his former pupil's thoughts.

"I understand your frustration, Minisc. Like your father said, we're not saying that you're incapable of mastering Celestial Light. In fact, from what I've seen, there is little doubt that with the right training and commitment, you could usurp the power of even The Hero of Light. I think we all recognize that. However, the problem remains: you're just too young. Your body hasn't finished maturing yet. And because of that, we don't know what sort of issues could arise for you. The damage caused could be catastrophic."

Minisc sat stunned, fighting to find any form of argument. He opened his mouth, but the words refused to come.

Mr. Howland continued, "For one such as yourself to achieve Celestial Light, it takes an extraordinary amount of focus and a sound mind. That is something that a young teen, even one such as yourself, can hardly be expected to sustain. I was hopeful that by gradually getting your body accustomed to the rigors little by little and getting a taste for the power, it would offset some of these sorts of issues. But thinking back, I believe that I made an error in judgment based on wishful thinking. Even the power you've displayed thus far exceeds what someone your age should be using. We can't go on like that."

Minisc didn't know where to begin. He glanced at his father and waited for him to intervene, only to be faced with silence, which frustrated him more. It was his father's idea in the first place, so why was he suddenly going back on his belief now? Nothing else had changed. Luminosa was still alive and ready to fight. Had everyone just forgotten about them?

Although Minisc believed in the cause he was fighting so hard for, he admittedly did fear the dangers that awaited him. How could he not? After all, he'd watched the shining example of those consequences right at home every day. Celestial Light took a massive toll—that was an indisputable fact. His father was a shell of the Elementalist he used to be. No villain would fear him, and no civilian would put their safety on his back.

Of course, with that fear also came confidence. The full power of Celestial Light was god-like, and he was untouchable with such strength. Luminosa, the Adenji Gang…nobody could stop him. The potential was limitless, and the world his to shape. He could help usher his mother's dream into reality.

Perhaps that's why he was so adamant about sticking to the process. Until he experienced the power for himself, he never realized just how vital the technique would be to achieving peace. He needed to master it, and there wasn't time to wait.

Minisc gripped the couch, on the verge of ripping a hole into it as he shifted his eyes from Mr. Howland to his father and back again.

They appeared to agree on the subject, but that wouldn't stop Minisc from finally forming an argument.

"Was it not you two who agreed I was the only one capable of learning Celestial Light? That despite my age and despite other Elementalists being more talented than me, I was born to learn this? Luminosa is still out there. They haven't gone anywhere, and they're not going to just disappear. We know that they're planning something right now, and it's only a matter of time until they strike again. I was supposed to be the only one to stop them, and now—just like that—you two of all people are telling me to give up?"

"It's not that simple, Minisc…" Don tried to interject, but Minisc was far from finished.

"And what about Robin? What would've happened to him if I'd never started using Celestial Light? Not only would Dominos have likely killed him, but the repercussions of that battle could've affected far more than just him. And now for doing that, for giving it my all, I'm being punished? We're all being punished for it?"

Minisc took a deep breath, trying to keep his wits about him. Simply yelling wouldn't convince anyone, least of all Mr. Howland, to change his mind.

"Look," Minisc started again, this time with more measured control. "I understand that what I'm doing is dangerous. I do. And I know that the risks could be greater than what I can even imagine. But honestly, if my options are pushing myself far past what's safe or just sitting around doing nothing while people like Robin or Lily or Jules are out there being attacked by groups like the Adenji Gang and Luminosa, then I'd much rather at least try. Right now, without the Hero of Light, people are scared. They know that things are changing and all they can do is pray that someone will be able to keep them safe from monsters like Dusk and Dominos. There's too much at stake to just throw everything away. If I have the power to stop that pain, then I have to use it."

Mr. Howland glanced at Don and sighed. "He really is your kid, isn't he? Right down to being as stubborn and strong headed as you."

But Don remained unconvinced. Obviously, he'd been the one to push Minisc into learning the technique, but he'd also assumed that it would be just like when he himself had learned it—tough, and certainly grueling on the mind and body. But not nearly as concerning because he'd been a fair bit older; he was matured, and his body had been ready. But Minisc had his whole life ahead of him, and it was Don's job as the boy's father to make sure that he got to live that life, fate of the world be damned.

Finally, he broke his silence. "I get how you feel Minisc, I really do. And everything you said is true. But had I realized the potential danger it could cause to your body, I would've given it a second thought. I never had these issues, so I never knew that such things could happen."

"But you did know that it would erase your element, didn't you? You knew that the consequences would be irreversible, and yet you still chose to learn it."

"Yes, but it's not the same. At that time, it was more of a speculation on what *could* happen. And the state of the world was far worse off than it is now. In the end, I had no choice but to learn Celestial Light—it was a matter of survival. There were people who I could only protect using that power. For their safety, the cost didn't matter."

Minisc stared into his father's eyes, refusing to look away. He hated going against him, but what he'd just explained was the exact reason Minisc felt that he must.

"Well, there are people I can only protect using that power, too. Lily, Jules, Robin, and so many more. We know that Luminosa is going to strike, and when they do, it'll be me they're after. Everyone knows the Hero of Light is retired, but Dusk is the only one who believes that I have the capability of learning Celestial Light—you said that yourself. I'm target number one on his and Luminosa's hit list, which means that he's going to come after me regardless of whether I'm learning Celestial Light or not. That fact is going to put everyone I love in danger. And I can't hide behind you anymore to protect them. It's up to me. So I know the consequences, but the flipside of that could be a lot worse. If anything were to happen to Lily or Jules and I couldn't save them, I'd never be able to live with myself. Please, Father—this is something I have to do."

Finally, Minisc was getting through to the two men. He had a valid point, specifically when it came to Luminosa's goal.

Don recalled a meeting between him and Dusk in the jails of Penetang after he'd defeated the Luminosa leader. The words were cryptic, but the message clear. Dusk knew of Minisc's potential through their fight, and recognized that he'd be the one to stand in the way of Luminosa's plans—not to mention he knew that taking the life of Don's son would be the ultimate payback on his nemesis. There was no way to protect Minisc from that.

Don lowered his head. He was scared — scared of all the different scenarios. And without his own power to keep his son safe, he felt helpless. There wasn't much else he could do.

"All right...if you're really this determined to see things through, despite whatever consequences may come from it, then I'll be by your side the entire way. But this means that you're gonna need to work even harder and prepare your body to be capable of drawing on your full power. That also means that you need to listen to Mr. Howland and do *everything* he says. But, most importantly, if you're having any strange feelings or problems like this again, you're to tell us right away. No hiding it for fear of being forced to stop. You're still my son, and your health and safety come first above all else. Got it?"

Minisc nodded with a smile. "I understand. And I promise, I'll do this and I'll do it right. I'm going to master Celestial Light and stop Luminosa once and for all."

Don glanced toward Mr. Howland and gave him the nod of approval. He could see in his master's face that they were both thinking the same thing. Neither wished for any kind of doomsday scenario to come, but in the end, perhaps there was no way around it. The biggest factor remained: Luminosa would come after Minisc — of that, they had no doubt — and Celestial Light might be the only way for him to not only stop Luminosa but to defend himself from them as well.

But something else occurred to Mr. Howland. He knew his former protégé well, and he was slowly learning the similarities between him and his son. Refusing to take no for an answer was one thing, but the elder statesman had reason to fear saying no — a reason with Minisc's own health in mind. If Minisc was so dead set on harnessing such power while already getting a taste of it, it was likely that he'd attempt to learn it on his own, and that would prove extremely dangerous. In the end, the can of worms they opened couldn't be put back—no matter how uneasy it made him feel.

Mr. Howland took another sip of tea, the look on his face a little ambiguous "If this is truly what you wish, then I will not object further. However, we will need to put the use of Celestial Light on hold for a few days and make sure that your body rests. After that, I believe it is best that we drop you back down to 8%. You will train with your father to get your body strong enough to endure the stress, and I shall train you after school each day in Celestial Light. You will have to dedicate all of your free time if you want to do this properly."

Minisc bowed his head. "I understand. Thank you, Sir. I know I can handle this."

"We believe in you, too. I wouldn't waste my time otherwise," Mr. Howland reassured him.

Minisc knew that his task would be a massive undertaking. There were only two people who'd ever managed Celestial Light, and they were far older and carried more experience than him. On top of that, he'd be lying if there wasn't some seed of doubt that came with the odds of destroying his body, but all those worries seemed trivial to the big picture—the image of Robin's jovial smile, loving life…walking through the park with Lily in the summer, laughing as she smelled the roses… sparring with Jules as his friend tried to come up with new techniques—all things he cherished and refused to lose.

CHAPTER 6
THE 8 PROJECT

TIMES WERE STRANGE IN THE CITY OF TORONTO. THE Hero of Light's sudden retirement sent shock waves through the city. Most found the news hard to swallow, while the Hero's biggest supporters struggled to even imagine him as mortal. And how could they? Their iconic figure had spent so much of his time portraying the mythos of a deity, an Elementalist who couldn't be felled by darkness. Having that staple vanish like a cloud in the night left many with fear. Where did they go from here? What dangers were lurking and waiting to pounce now that they had their chance? Those thoughts left everyone on edge.

It wasn't just from hearing the stories on the news, either — the entire city had a dreary vibe. The Hero, Don Premier, might not have been physically dead, but most people continued to treat his retirement like a funeral.

But a segment of devastated fans was far from the only issue. Don's retirement had left a massive hole in the EC's forces, and on that front, the impacts were immediate. He'd only retired a few months prior, but already the crime rate continued to climb. Robberies, elemental attacks, and other crimes involving Elementalists were beginning to flood the streets in ways not seen in decades.

There was an emboldened feeling amongst certain Elementalists who were no longer forced to fear being brought down by the Hero. With his absence, they were free to push the boundaries on what they could achieve while simply daring the EC or anyone else to try and stop them.

The EC might have been powerful, but the larger they grew over the years, the rumors that quality members were diminishing only increased. Many criminals believed that most in the EC were little more than rank amateurs that they could handle if need be.

And in many ways, that couldn't be disputed. But that didn't mean that the Elemental Council was going to throw in the towel—they knew that hope was coming with the next generation; they just needed to be patient. Until that time, new measures would be required, a solution that would alleviate the burden of a single hero, unlike the way they'd operated in the past.

But Minisc wasn't focused on that. He kept working on his own solution to their future issues. He was doing all he could to tune out the noise around the city, focusing solely on Celestial Light.

A few weeks had passed since Mr. Howland agreed to continue his training, and with it came a rigorous schedule. Both physically and mentally, the work was enough to make anyone his age break. And it wasn't just the training—the schedule meant that he lacked any time with his friends, the exception, of course, being school. At least he knew that they understood. The sacrifices were tough, but they supported his goal and grasped the importance of it, even if they were just as disappointed.

Fortunately for Minisc, that Friday after school, Mr. Howland had abruptly canceled their training. Minisc wasn't given a reason, but it was his first break in weeks and he greatly appreciated the time off.

Minisc, Lily, and Jules walked through the Christmas market of Toronto, admiring the city's decorations for the holiday season. The different store owners on the street had lined their fronts with bright lights and colorful tinsel, while in the middle of the Christmas market stood a towering tree adorned in pomp and glitter to the heavens. The festive lights flashed bright in all different colours, and on the top was a large, golden star. Each branch was covered with ornaments, from round glass orbs to small carved toys, like a train or an animal. Anyone could put a decoration on the tree, allowing it to represent as much of the city as possible.

"I love the Christmas holidays so much!" Lily cooed. "The city is just bursting with life, and everyone is so happy and excited! It's the best time of year!" She smiled brightly, admiring their surroundings as they walked. Every few steps she paused, wanting to snap endless pictures to commemorate the decorations she found so delightful.

"Yeah…I just wish it wasn't so cold already," Jules groaned, rubbing his hands together.

There was only some light snow in the air and the sun was beaming, making the weather far better than what they'd endured during their training exam.

The trio's ultimate destination was the Scotia Coliseum, which was playing host to a massive announcement today.

Only a week ago had the EC made mention of big news on the horizon. It caught the city by surprise due to recent events, but nobody knew exactly what the announcement could be—only those in the Elemental Council were privy to such information, although even some of them remained unaware.

At first, Minisc didn't think much of it, focusing instead on his task, but his father made the suggestion that he and his friends join him in attending. Given that Minisc had the afternoon off, and that school was out for their winter break, the three decided that they could spend the afternoon walking around the Christmas market and the shopping district before making their way to Scotia Coliseum only a short subway ride away.

Lily led the charge, going in and out of every store, checking the different displays and assessing her options. She was on the hunt to find the perfect present for everyone on her list, while Jules and Minisc simply tried to keep up.

After searching a handful of stores, Minisc started to notice something strange, a trend he'd been picking up on lately. It was clear in each store they entered that there was almost no merchandise of The Hero of Light anywhere.

Minisc asked, "Does anyone else find it strange to not see the Hero of Light front and centre during the holidays?"

Jules came to a stop in front of a large window. All sorts of decorative displays were on offer for the eyes, but like Minisc said, there was nothing to do with the famed icon.

"Now that you mention it, I guess it is a bit weird," Jules added. "I can't remember a Christmas where all the Hero of Light mugs, signed posters, and action figures weren't right out in the open, at least for the stores that hadn't sold out immediately."

"But it's not only that," Lily said. "I've noticed it everywhere lately. The trains, the billboards, even commercials—everywhere I used to see his face, he's just not there anymore. It's like they're trying to get people to forget he existed."

The three walked across the street before stopping to look up at a billboard that hung high above the north part of the market. For years, that billboard had been a staple of the Hero's legacy, if not his latest endorsement deal.

Not this time, though. This time, there was a man being lifted by a large crane standing on the edge of the billboard. He had a giant roller, and like painting a wall, he ran it back and forth on the board, sticking a new advertisement onto it. But underneath, a small strip of the previous ad could still be seen — and it was the single eye of the Hero of Light. Like his persona, nothing but a fragment remained. The man started rolling over another long strip to finish the ad, and in just a brief second the Hero's presence was erased from yet another spot.

"It's definitely different now," Jules agreed. "But honestly, Minisc — I thought you'd be relieved in a way. I remember plenty of times as kids when you used to hate seeing all your father's stuff at Christmas."

"I guess," Minisc muttered. "This just isn't quite how I pictured things going. You're right, it did bother me. I mean, every Christmas growing up it was like I saw him on merchandise around the city more often than I actually saw him in real life. I know that I'd always dreamed of the day when he'd retire, when the fame would stop and people would slowly forget about him. I'd finally be able to live a nice quiet life with nobody bugging me about him anymore…but now that it's actually happened, I don't know."

As was often the case, Lily tried to bring a bit of positivity to the situation.

"Maybe this is a good thing, though. Not that we should forget about what your father did for us all, but his absence has really been tough on the city's morale as a whole. I understand why so many felt dreary and depressed when he retired, but remember what he said at his press conference? 'It's time for me to move over so that a new generation can rise up and continue what I've tried to achieve.' I guess that businesses are really taking that to heart and trying to get a jump on the next generation."

"It could also be an 'out of sight, out of mind' thing," Jules added. "The sooner they scrub away all the representation your father had, the sooner those that follow in his footsteps will be able to shine, right?"

Minisc rolled his eyes. "You mean *you*, don't you?"

Jules sheepishly rubbed the back of his neck, trying to hide his grin. "I never said that, but still, that's not the point. The point is that now that your father's no longer watching over the city, everyone needs to step up and help take his place. There are tons of incredible Elementalists around. Sure, they don't have the level of power that he did, but we can still hold down the fort without him."

Lily tossed her arm around Minisc. "Jules is right. We won't let anything happen to our city, even without your father there to back us up!"

A warmth filled Minisc, and he grinned. He knew full well the burden placed on him, thanks to his father's retirement. And it's a burden that he was more than willing to accept. But even so, knowing that he had friends ready to stand beside him and face the challenges ahead brought him great comfort.

Minisc and Jules were thoroughly exhausted after chasing Lily from store to store. Finally finished, they worked their way to Scotia Coliseum with their remaining energy and prepared to witness the mystery announcement that Minisc's father alluded to earlier in the day.

Known citywide, the marvelous Scotia Coliseum often hosted the biggest events of the year, including the Tournament of Elements. Though unlike back then when the sun was shining bright and the heat was scorching, the building now looked entirely different amid the winter chill.

One thing that stayed the same year-round, however, was the waves of people pouring through the gated entrances. Security guards were scanning people with metal detectors before ushering them through, but no tickets were required for the event— they'd just go until the venue reached max capacity and then shut things down from there. There was an air of anticipation, and people seemed on edge as lots of rumors permeated the crowd.

The last time an impromptu press conference had been called, The Hero of Light was announcing his retirement. Obviously, nothing of that magnitude could be on the agenda again, but that did little to quell the lingering worry in people's minds.

But not all the rumors were negative or laced with fear. Minisc had heard one rumor circulating around school that the EC would be introducing a new Hero of Light, but he and his friends all agreed that such an idea seemed unlikely. There wasn't enough of a basis for it. Trying to replace his father from a heroic's point of view was one thing — he'd inspired more than his fair share of Elementalists to work hard and shoot for the moon. Minisc himself was already working to accomplish the near-impossible task himself. But trying to replace the symbol he represented to not only Elementalists but also the city and the entire world was an entirely different challenge. People would see it as an act, a meritless gesture with no weight behind it.

Another theory making the rounds was related to stricter laws regarding Elementalists. The city already kept a tight grasp on Elementalists and the freedom to use their powers, but with the current situation, people debated if lawmakers needed to take things a step further, like some other cities had done in the past. Minisc and Lily had even read an article that morning about what sort of laws they might be: placing a curfew on Elementalists, upping the age to attend EA, and even the complete outlaw of Elementalists being able to use their powers in the workplace. Most right-minded thinkers considered those laws a drastic response, steeped in misguided fear of Elementalists. The group also agreed that the odds of those restrictions coming into their city were slim. Also, such laws would be pushing the advancements in society backwards while only punishing the Elementalists who were already obeying civil order and simply trying to live their lives.

The real issue was the growing strength combined with the

emboldened bravery of a small subset of Elementalists. They were equipped with power and molded with a desire to negatively impact society. What they *really* needed was a way for Humans and Elementalists alike to feel at ease in their city. To know that if danger called, someone would arrive to help.

Upon entering Scotia Coliseum, the three could tell that it had undergone quite the transformation.

Not so much in structure but in decoration. When the Tournament of Elements was being hosted, another trophy case was on display everywhere they'd turned. Massive, lifelike banners of previous winners loomed large, and the energy in the building was palpable. Now all the displays were removed and replaced with Christmas decorations. Scotia Coliseum hosted a yearly toy drive, and from all the canned food and boxes of toys under various small trees, Minisc guessed that they were doing quite well.

Down the main hall they walked, following the signs that led them to the stadium's centre. Even it appeared to be different, though Minisc had expected it.

Scotia Coliseum had an octagonal hollow in the middle of the stadium's roof, but with the winter season in full throttle, that space was sealed up by the roof's retractable functions. Inside, where the long rectangular battlefield had been surrounded by artificial grass, was now covered by elegant tiles like a ballroom floor, and right in the middle was a massive stage, displayed on the jumbotron located at the south end of the stadium. There were also hundreds of lights all shining like stars and illuminating the stage with elegance.

Despite all the changes, there was still an uneasy feeling for Minisc now that he was returning to the building. He didn't give the events much thought on a typical day, but there was still no forgetting the attacks at the Scotia Coliseum. After all, it was the day his life had changed, the day when Luminosa had announced their return to relevance, placing the world in a state of peril once more.

He could still vividly picture the scene like a movie he'd watched hundreds of times. It started with him fighting Coro in the tournament finals, then Luminosa arriving, and ended with his father saving them all in heroic fashion.

Minisc shook off the lingering memories and followed Lily and Jules to a nearby section of seats. The grandness of the event was starting to sink in, which all but confirmed what he already knew: stricter laws were not coming into effect.

There was no way that the EC would go to such showmanship just to slap everyone in the face with a few arbitrary laws purposed by Humans. That would cause an uproar—not to mention a media storm—for weeks, something that nobody wanted to deal with.

With that rumor dispelled, it left room for another one: they were there to see a new Hero of Light being introduced. Minisc still didn't buy into the thought, but the sort of hype and spectacle surrounding such an impromptu event did match the level of his father's other engagements.

Jules led them through the row of seats before waving. "Hey! I was wondering where you were!" he greeted, working his way over to his brother.

As usual, the elder Embroider brother was far more punctual and had been there for a while already. Yuri, who dressed far nicer and with an air of professionalism about him, was holding down a few seats for his brother and his company. But it wasn't just Yuri they knew in the row. Sitting next to him with his hands in his lap staring straight ahead was Mr. Howland, much to everyone's surprise because, much like Minisc, Mr. Howland hated large events.

Yuri moved over, letting the three take their seats between him and Mr. Howland.

Since Mr. Howland was around, Minisc expected to see Adelle and Robin close by as well, but they were nowhere to be seen.

More of the crowd poured in and filled the upper bowls of the stadium. After a few minutes of tense energy, the lights gradually dimmed. The buzz in the stadium picked up for a moment before going silent; it was like a concert was about to begin. Down below, two men walked out from the same tunnels that Minisc and his friends had passed through for the Tournament of Elements, only this time they were sealed with long, red drapes.

The President of the Elemental Council, Zale Osiris, walked out first to a chorus of applause, exuding presidential aura as he walked. The way he dressed, the way he spoke—all of it indicated his importance in the Elementalist community. He gave a small wave of acknowledgment as he approached centre stage.

Don walked beside him, but unlike Zale he was dressed a little more casually, in a sports jacket and jeans. It was strange for everyone to see him in street attire—the Hero of Light's suit was one of the most iconic uniforms in history, and it was a given that he'd wear it at almost any public appearance.

Even so, the retired hero still received a deafening applause, but his response was far more subdued. He followed Zale's lead and gave a simple wave.

Of all of the public speakers Minisc witnessed over the years, nobody spoke as eloquently or commanded a room as skillfully as Zale. Even his own father often had such hype around his appearance when speaking that the crowds would go nuts, but not here; when Zale spoke, the room remained quiet. His title came with respect, but his public persona was one of being in complete control. Those close to him knew that wasn't exactly accurate at all times, but he always believed in putting on a front to avoid public panic.

Zale took to the stage and approached the microphone on the podium. When he started speaking, the applause died down, as everyone was keenly interested in what he had to say.

"Hello everyone, and thank you for coming out today," he began. "I would like to start by saying that I know these past few months have been tough. The sudden retirement of our champion, The Hero of Light, has left many feeling on edge, fearful, and even lost. I share in these feelings, I assure you. Since that day, we have seen rates of crime involving Elementalists continue to climb, with acts of violence and power grabs at the forefront. We recognize that if we do not act now, our days as a merged society will be numbered." Even though Zale spoke the truth, his words certainly deflated the energy out of the building.

"That said, I didn't come here today to spread the gospel of doom and gloom. Rest assured that as long as I remain President of the Elemental Council and call this city my home, I will not stand for these trends to continue."

Minisc glanced to his right, seeing Mr. Howland listening intently. Then he looked to his left and saw Lily fixated on the president as well. Their faces both shared the same tense focus.

Knowing that he'd created a rather uncomfortable atmosphere, Zale continued. "Much like yourselves, I have heard all the rumors swirling in these recent weeks, which is why I have chosen to gather you here today. We would like to put those rumors to rest and pave our new way forward." Zale turned and looked to his longtime friend and closest ally, now speaking in a more somber tone.

"We all know what the Hero of Light represented to our society, and we also know that one soul could never fill such lofty shoes. However, after numerous internal discussions with the Human Government and leadership within the EC, we have decided to take steps in filling that void as a collective—a new force that will help bridge the gap as we prepare the next generation of Elementalists for what is to come. We have dubbed this venture The 8 Project, and we will be putting it into effect immediately after this conference is over."

An audible whisper travelled through the room. The energy was returning, but this time more confused.

"Now, as this is the first you are hearing about our new initiative, I'm sure that you have many questions, so allow me to elaborate. Over the past year, we have been working to create a new system within the EC. This system is known as the elemental growth initiative, which will be led by The 8 Project. After careful consideration, we have decided that as the threat from dangerous Elementalists continues to climb, we must be equipped to handle them. It is unacceptable to place law enforcement and our younger, less experienced Elementalists in situations that could be potentially perilous. So to mitigate those risks, we have chosen to create an elite fighting force to work as a team and take these threats on. In order to make sure that they are ready for any situation, we have selected one Elementalist from each of the eight types. At the start of each calendar year, the EC will select the eight Elementalists we feel are most suited for the missions ahead. These are the best of the best, and they will be helping ensure that our city remains safe and prosperous for all. So with that said, it is my honour to introduce the members of The 8 Project."

The spotlights in the stadium illuminated the red drapes on both entrances, and out from behind the drapes walked eight people—four on the left and four on the right. Each one wore a tailor-made uniform, allowing them to stand out from the crowd. Some were more colourful, others more subtle, but all of them had the usual EC armband.

Gradual claps turned into more boisterous cheers as each of the men and women waved to the crowd. Some of them were even playing into the attention just as The Hero of Light often would.

As a collective, most of the group were unrecognizable to Minisc, which was to be expected, but the last two on his right gave him a bit of a shock. He blinked, wondering if his eyes were playing tricks on him, but when Mr. Howland joined in the clapping and nearly cracked a smile, Minisc knew that he wasn't seeing things.

With easily the brightest smile, Robin was waving back to the crowd, looking up at Minisc and Mr. Howland specifically. His white uniform had gold and yellow accents, as well as a large light element symbol on his left shoulder. In a group of stand-outs, he still managed to rise above the rest.

"No way! Robin is part of The 8 Project?" Minisc asked.

"And look, Adelle is with him, too!" Jules added.

Following up behind Robin was Adelle, but unlike her friend who revelled in the spotlight, she remained more reclusive, giving a small wave and staying close to her friend's shadow.

Both of them were top graduates of EA and already working under Yuri and Mr. Howland respectively, so their skills were unquestioned. But it was their ages that raised eyebrows. Robin and Adelle were fresh-faced youths, and being handed such a large responsibility and a great level of prestige was nothing short of astonishing.

That said, Minisc knew that they were up to the task—he and everyone else in the EC could attest to that. Without their help in the pursuit of the Adenji gang, they never would've put Dominos behind bars.

The last to join the team onstage was a woman the group knew little about. Her blonde hair flowed down her back while shading her left eye, and her uniform was a mix between plain purple and midnight blue. If not for her previous dealings with Coro, then Minisc never would've known her name. But since the two had chatted on occasion, he was aware of the stone-cold Elementalist known as Olivia. The way she was described to him—her imposing walk, her aura of power, her deadly glare—couldn't be mistaken. Her rise through the ranks was meteoric and her skills were incredible. But more than that, her intellect and logic gave her an edge against almost any opponent she faced.

She was the only one in the group who refused to wave. There was no acknowledgment to the crowd at all, which, from the way Coro had described her, made sense to Minisc.

When all eight members lined up on stage, Zale returned to the podium. He waited a moment for the applause to dissipate before speaking again.

"I'm sure that some of you are familiar and may have even worked with these outstanding Elementalists in the past, but for those who are less familiar, allow me to make introductions. I'll also let them say a few words on behalf of their new role in the EC. I can assure you that we have picked the best of the best, and with their help, we will work to ensure a safe and prosperous future for our city and all Elementalists who live in it." Zale turned to face the first person to his left, and the spotlight followed.

"Starting off, we have our chosen wind Elementalist, Sora Monroe."

He handed the microphone to a woman with midnight black hair that was curled to her shoulders. She looked a fair bit older than most of the others on the stage, but that only signaled her experience. She wore a fitted, dark-green jacket that flared out at the bottom, with white pants covered in floral designs on them. On her one arm was a band with a symbol looking like gusts of wind, while the other had the usual EC band.

The woman took the microphone from Zale and stepped forward with a regal wave as everyone gave her a round of applause. She proved herself to be well-spoken.

"Thank you, President Osiris. And hello, everyone. Thank you for coming out to celebrate this incredible honour with us. On behalf of all the great Elementalists that I currently share the stage with today, and to all those out there watching, let it be known that we will do everything in our power to keep you safe. Humans and Elementalists alike deserve the peace of mind to know that their city has nothing to fear. Those who seek to cause harm will face swift justice. As part of this appointed group, I will make it my sworn duty to uphold the peace that our previous champions have. I, and those by my side, do not take this role lightly, and in time we will prove to you that we are here to help make our city a safer one, once again."

Sora's speech caused an uproar of applause. In these uneasy times, her words were exactly what the masses wanted to hear. Whether they were words that could be backed up by action was yet to be seen, but they'd no doubt be put to the test quickly.

Going down the line next was the earth Elementalist Juno Barns. Most didn't recognize her, as she'd just returned to Toronto after a few years away, but she spoke with flowing charisma and infectious confidence that filled the stadium with hope. She even put Luminosa on notice, making it clear that they would be stopped once and for all.

After that came a young man with a charming smile and devious eyes. His name was Etro, and he was the electric Elementalist in the group. Beside him stood the fire Elementalist Hugo. He was a bulky man and also the tallest of the bunch.

Next up was a young woman who Lily was familiar with — a freshly graduated student the same as Robin and Adelle but with less fanfare, the water Elementalist Rose. She and Lily had faced off against Bronx when Elemental Academy was attacked during the rise of Dusk, and from there Lily could see that the young woman had not only incredible talent but also the leadership and personality to help bring about an era of peace.

Beside her stood Adelle, who simply said thank you for the applause and adoration and moved things along. Then came Robin, who smiled and waved to the crowd before saying that he was proud and honored to be given such an opportunity.

The last to be introduced was Olivia. When Zale handed her the microphone, an uneasy look crossed his face. He knew that she wouldn't mince words—if she even spoke at all.

But it appeared that Olivia *did* have something to say. She took the mic and held it to her lips, the silence in the room lingering.

"As of today, we face a turning point in our society. There are many threats we deal with on a daily basis, but they all pale in comparison to the current state of our city. There is no denying that Luminosa is back. And as long as they remain free and attempting to gather sympathizers, no one can feel safe in this city. They will stop at nothing to ensure the destruction of everything we've strived to build, and what those in the future will continue to improve upon. That is why it is paramount for all of us to work toward maintaining the legacy built by those that came before us so that the world can strive with those that will come after. I, along with everyone else standing on this stage beside me, take the oath that we will bring an end to these dark days. And when we do, we shall move together. As one."

The crowd hesitated, not sure if they were to cheer or be fearful based on Olivia's icy tone. Sure, it had been a call to action and for unity, but she certainly pulled no punches about the perils ahead.

More whispers circulated through the room, and so Zale took the mic back in an attempt to wrap things up on a warmer note.

"Okay, then. Thank you…thank you for that, Olivia. Starting today, these eight Elementalists will be patrolling different parts of the city, and over time, working as a group on missions deemed worthy of such an elite force. We hope through these actions that our city can once again be the safe haven we know it to be. And on that note, that is all for today's announcement. Thank you for taking the time to come out today — and to those watching at home as well. We appreciate your continual support. Stay safe."

The group started walking off the stage and the fans were ready to leave the stands, but Minisc and the gang wanted to congratulate their friends.

"If we hurry down to the main lobby," Jules said, "I'll bet we can still catch Adelle and Robin before they leave. Come on!"

Minisc stood up and, as a courtesy, turned to his mentor. But Mr. Howland, without missing a beat, said, "Go on without me. Robin must return to the office tonight anyways, so I will congratulate him then. I've got a few things to attend to in the meantime."

Minisc shrugged, knowing all too well that asking anymore questions would lead to even less answers.

Minisc, Lily, Jules, and Yuri returned to the main lobby, where there were a number of smaller crowds beginning to form. Some of The 8 Project's Elementalists were laughing and talking with friends and family, or even potentially fans, while others were signing autographs. It appeared that they were becoming quick celebrities in the city.

"I don't see them," Jules said, scanning around but finding neither Adelle nor Robin nearby.

"You don't think we missed them, do you?" Minisc asked.

"No, I messaged Adelle telling her that we were waiting for them, so they must be just taking their time getting out," Lily said.

Just then, Robin and Adelle came emerging from the tunnel, as if on cue.

"There you guys are!" Robin shouted, walking up to Minisc and his friends. Adelle followed, looking more relieved than anything.

"Why didn't you tell us you guys were going to be part of this 8 Project thing?" Jules asked immediately.

Robin grinned sheepishly. "Well, actually…President Osiris stopped us from telling anyone."

"Huh?"

Adelle nodded in agreement. "He asked everyone who was announced to keep the whole thing a secret. We haven't even told our families yet. He didn't give much of a reason other than to make sure they picked the best people possible with no bias, I guess. If word started to spread too quickly, then maybe other Elementalists would begin lobbying for the position. It's just speculation, but it's the best I can think of."

Yuri added, "I guess that makes sense. I do remember being asked to fill out evaluations last month on Elementalists I'd worked with over the last year. Perhaps that was part of the decision-making process. But either way—congratulations, you two! I'm extremely proud of how far you guys have come in such a short period."

"Thanks, everyone. I'm just glad we can finally talk about it. I've been dying to tell you guys!" Robin said.

"How long have you two known?" Minisc asked.

"About two weeks," Adelle responded, "but I guess things have been growing worse around the city because we were supposed to be waiting until after Christmas for the announcement to be made official. Then suddenly they decided to move things up just last week."

"Well, with my father retired, the EC knows there's no time to waste, I guess," Minisc added. "But hopefully this will make everyone feel a little safer, and maybe even lift the mood of the city before Christmas"

The group agreed, sharing in smiles and more congratulations.

CHAPTER 7
LINGERING IN THE SHADOWS

THE TIMES OF DECADES PAST WERE BELIEVED TO BE just that—the past. An era when chaos ruled the streets, and when Elementalists and Humans were at war with not only Luminosa but also themselves.

People who lived through those days hoped that they were long in the rear-view mirror, and that a more tolerant society was on the horizon. But those hopes were once again uprooted when Dusk returned to claim his vengeance. Even after he'd suffered his defeat at the hands of The Hero of Light, his intentions were slowly coming to the forefront. With his actions, the lives that had been taken, and the flames of fear once again stoked, Dusk had left an indelible mark in history.

At the time, Dusk's call to action involved surrendering three Elementalists who'd been deemed traitorous. Such demands were used to create a layer of divide, cracking open a door into the hearts of society so that he could bring out their worst.

A healthy number of Humans were naive enough—and perhaps fearful enough—to believe that by turning the three Elementalists over to Dusk, they'd be granted both their lives, and also their freedom in Dusk's new Elemental Kingdom. Of course, that only served to generate resentment in the hearts of Elementalists, who were less than thrilled to play the role of sacrifice—and certainly not as the first option.

Over the next few months, even with a united belief in The Hero of Light as he defeated Dusk for a second time, tension between Elementalists and Humans remained on the rise. Because of this, there were a number of Elementalists who decided to back Dusk's motives and use them to justify their own evil acts. They might not have been Luminosa members in their loyalty to his apprentice, Brooklyn, but they were certainly ready to make their presence known. Those circumstances followed by the individual acts committed were what forced the Elemental Council to begin increasing its protocols.

That said, those individual threats could be quelled. There was knowledge of most criminals, accessible at every database in the city, that could be used to create quick investigations, and those in The 8 Project would be strong enough to handle such lawbreakers.

The real problem, as viewed by the EC, wasn't increased crime—that was only an effect from the real problem. The real threat was Luminosa.

Though most knew Dusk as the leader of Luminosa, the EC was acutely aware of the tyrant's successor, Brooklyn. Unlike Dusk, Brooklyn mostly remained a mystery. Their only source of information came via Dusk, who spoke in riddles through the bars of his Penetang prison cell.

As for any sort of family, it seemed safe to say that Brooklyn had none—at least anymore. There was no concrete evidence, but based on his ties to Dusk and the lack of information around him, it stood to reason that Brooklyn's family were either deceased or long abandoned, something far too common when it came to Elementalist children.

The EC could also gather that Dusk was guiding most of

Brooklyn's actions. But with Dusk behind bars and no longer in control, at some point Brooklyn would be left to decide his own fate. That in itself was a concern.

They also knew that he had help with a few close allies, but in the limited interactions with those who faced him, it wasn't clear to see how he became the leader of the group. He simply wasn't ready to stage an uprising the way Dusk was.

All signs pointed to Dusk pulling the strings, which perhaps told of Brooklyn's lack of maturity, or lack of preparedness.

The last thing they knew was that Dusk favored Brooklyn's strength, a power that could bring down humanity as it was constructed — or so they were forced to believe. That created a lot of questions, and a number of worries from the EC.

Days after The 8 Project was announced, there was already quite a buzz throughout the city. Humans and Elementalists were optimistic; if nothing else, people viewed it as a step in the right direction.

Quelling fears above ground was one thing, but putting the underground society on notice was even more of a message. Through the creation of The 8 Project, it was time to let the sewer rats of the city know that they wouldn't be taking over without resistance.

As more days passed, people gradually got used to seeing members of The 8 Project rushing around the city. They were making swift work of small crimes, helping lower the numbers until they could approach bigger tasks.

But not all of them were present and accounted for — Juno was preoccupied with other tasks. She'd chip in on occasion, helping those who were already nearby, but she mostly tried to remain isolated from all association with the EC.

This was made easier due to the majority within the organization not knowing her name or recognizing her face. Still, some precaution needed to be taken to avoid unnecessary questions.

After a week of The 8 Project's emergence into public consciousness, Juno went walking alone down the streets of Toronto. Normally, the only thing guiding her path would be the florescent streetlights shining down every few meters, but it was the holiday season, and so a number of stores still displayed eye-catching lights, further brightening the starry night sky. Even the steady snow twinkled in all sorts of colours as it gracefully landed on the pavement.

Juno tightened the belt around her winter coat. It wasn't her usual uniform, and was made to look as discrete as possible. Her long white boots blended in with the snow, and her hair was wrapped in a braid to avoid bouncing in the wind. It wasn't a powerful disguise, nor did she need it to be, but she'd assumed that it was enough to keep her from being pegged as an EC member.

She kept a steady pace with her head down, trying not to look eager or in a rush. But butterflies fluttered in her stomach, her breathing growing heavier as she approached her destination. She tried to shake off the unease, burying it away. Their enemy could smell fear, and she was heading straight for the shark's den.

When she reached the street corner, she glanced to her left and then to her right. The roads were silent, no cars and no pedestrians—a rare sight for the city, but Juno was closer to Toronto's outskirts at this point. There wasn't much around, just a few grungy buildings and a large parking garage.

Juno was headed to the North Toronto Train Station. People from further out of town often drove to the station, parked their cars in the garage, and then caught their train into the city. However, Juno would be doing nothing of the sort tonight.

Once she confirmed that the coast was clear, she walked around the corner toward the garage. It was three stories tall, with multiple ramps running parallel to each different level.

There were two barriers used to block cars from coming and going, but they'd do nothing to prevent her from walking in freely.

From left to right, she was surrounded by walls of concrete, and hundreds of cars parked in lines along the walls. The garage was lifeless — not a soul around — so Juno walked down the middle of the path without hesitation. She took one ramp down and then another. The cars were becoming more scarce the further underground she traveled, the shadows of the parking lot growing longer and longer.

Most people would be far from comfortable in this kind of environment at night, but Juno's mind was preoccupied. She started heading for the corner of the garage where, in the shadows of a small alcove, she noticed a silhouette. The lanky shadow leaned up against the wall with his arms crossed, wearing a long black hooded cloak. Nobody in their right mind would think of approaching this sketchy character, but Juno took a calming breath, said a silent prayer, and casually strolled toward him.

The man looked up at Juno but continued to slouch along the wall, showing little interest in her. But then he pulled off his hood to reveal a long silver ponytail and a deep scar over his left eye. His pencil thin frame was deceptive to his power.

He rolled his eyes and said, "So, you actually showed up. Gotta admit, I seriously didn't think you'd be stupid enough to come here without at least a little backup."

Juno shrugged. "What can I say? I was curious if you'd show your face, too."

She stared down the Luminosa member, someone she'd been sworn to bring down at all costs. But instead of acting on those duties, she maintained a relaxed front, not that she wasn't aware of her surroundings at every turn.

Hours before arriving at the meeting spot, she'd checked out the other floors, looking in cars and inspecting all that she could find, while making sure that no ambushes would be taking place. She did have an emergency beacon in the lining of her jacket that could be activated if need be, but none of those were ideal options.

For the EC, taking out one of Luminosa's members was enticing. With Bronx so close to their clutches, they could've easily staged an attack and attempt to bring him in, but the chances of that working seemed slim. They'd managed to apprehend him before, and that lasted for only a short stint, along with a number of lives being lost during his breakout. It would also put Brooklyn on high alert, which was the exact opposite of their intentions.

This time, they were taking another approach. If the EC could monitor Bronx while keeping any potential threats to a minimum, and in turn inch closer to Brooklyn, they'd be in a far better position than just taking out one of the group's core members.

Bronx stared at Juno, beginning to show more interest. He made a smug face and said, "Well, when one of Dusk's right-hand men and number one informant go through all the trouble to arrange a meeting with one of the prestigious 8 Project members, I couldn't possibly say no, now could I?" His voice dripped with sarcasm.

"Is that so? And you didn't suspect any sort of a trap from this 8 Project member?" Juno matched Bronx's tone but chose her words wisely.

"A trap? Don't take me for a fool. I know damn well that I'm not the one the EC is after. My life would be a poor trade-off for straying further away from Brooklyn. Besides, knowing that I was set up would be useful information to have."

Bronx's words reeked of arrogance. Something about his aloof demeanor suggested that he could've handled a trap just fine, and he would've been granted the bonus of knowing that his informant betrayed him.

Juno noted the words and tried to extract a little more info. "So you'd actually lay down your own life just to help rid the world of Humans? Seems like a bit of a waste, don't you think?"

"Who said anything about laying down my life? I have no reason to fear the EC."

"Confident now, aren't we?" Juno baited. She could tell that Bronx was in a boastful mood, and she wanted to see if she could draw any tidbit of information out of him before he caught himself.

"The EC reeks of desperation right now — it's so obvious. They know that they've become lazy since hiding under the shelter of the Hero of Light for so long. Their members lack any real skill. That's why they created The 8 Project in the first place, but I'm sure you're well aware of all that. They want to show that they still have control over Elementalists, but anyone with open eyes can see it every day. The more Elementalists begin to rebel and fight for their freedom, the more fearful the EC becomes. And when that roadblock is removed, wiping out Humans will only be the beginning."

Juno thought about what Bronx was saying for a second, and she could see what he meant. If they were able to take down the EC, it would turn into another case of anarchy, in which the most ruthless would win. Elementalists willing to kill for power would soon take over.

In a way, The 8 Project did appear — even to her — as a bit of a knee-jerk reaction to the Hero of Light's retirement and, possibly, also as a publicity stunt to make people feel safe. But she knew that those chosen were strong and of the right mind to help fight against the likes of an uprising.

Unfortunately, Bronx's spouting of such news was far from a revelation. They all knew, in some shape or form, that those were the plans of Luminosa. The EC and anyone who'd put Humans under their protection through laws and obstruction on what was deemed freedom was *always* the target.

Juno bit her tongue, fighting the urge to debate, and instead said, "So you see it too." For added effect, she rolled her eyes and put her hand to her head. "I tried to tell them…it was painfully obvious from the start what they were trying to do. Nothing but a vain attempt to exert power."

"Oh, yeah?" Bronx refused to blink, staring at Juno. He wanted to watch her squirm. "If you could see though such a pathetic facade, then what business would you have joining up with them? You actually want me to believe that someone who was just deemed one of the eight strongest in the EC, placed in some new superhero role to protect the status quo, suddenly wants to join our little rag-tag team of Elementalists? How stupid do you think I am?"

Juno kept her wits about her, noting Bronx's relaxed posture. His tone was becoming snarky, but he showed no signs of attacking, something she needed to be weary of.

"My motives have nothing to do with Luminosa or the EC. I'm just more perceptive than most. People need to face facts. With the Hero of Light no longer in the picture, we as a society are at a tipping point. One way or another, Humans and Elementalists will begin to try and take over. While the Hero of Light existed, there was at least *something* to unite us all as people—a desire for peace. But not anymore. War is coming, a war between Elementalists and Humans who want to keep the status quo, versus those that sense an opportunity to seize power and mold the world the way they see fit. In the end, I simply want to make sure that I'm on the right side of things when the dust settles."

"You actually expect me to believe that garbage?" Bronx began to raise his arm, and a tense energy filled the air.

But Juno refused to be goaded into a fight. She knew it didn't play into Bronx's best interests, either.

"You don't have to believe my motives…that's not really relevant," she goaded back. "But since I'm in those 8 Project meetings, I know about your circumstances. You don't currently have the resources to do any real damage. You lack recruits, and unless you can manage to unite everyone in the underworld to join your forces, you won't be doing much now, will you? We both know that there are thousands of Elementalists in this city alone that are sick and tired of being oppressed, but that doesn't necessarily mean that they have any interest in siding with you. I dare say that it might even be beneficial for them to let the EC hunt you so that they can free themselves up. Face it—everyone is against you guys."

Bronx lowered his hand and leaned back against the wall, twisting his mouth and thinking her words over. The cold chill of the air mixed with the silence of the garage left Juno wondering if her speech was taking effect.

"I'd be careful about any assumptions you dare make. We're not so desperate as to let a member of the EC waltz in and learn all our plans." Bronx stepped away from the wall and prepared to leave, his interest in the conversation seemingly gone.

Watching her opportunity slip away, Juno frantically thought of a way to stop him. She reached into her jacket pocket and pulled out a long brown envelope. "You play a hard game, but fine. Here—it's all yours. I think you'll find this to be more than a fair peace offering." She tossed the envelope to Bronx, who snared it in his clutches.

Ripping off the top, he slipped out a piece of paper and then glanced at Juno. "You've gotta be kidding me."

"Watch it for yourself—it's all right there. You can monitor the activities all week long. They'll be accurate, I can assure you of that."

Bronx mulled over the document, reading it line by line. "This isn't enough to prove your loyalty, but maybe you can make yourself useful. Look, I'll cut you a deal. Meet me on the rooftop of Scotia Coliseum in one week's time. And you'd better come alone."

"Have it your way," Juno shrugged.

Bronx turned the corner and disappeared from sight, after which Juno took another look around for good measure. She'd passed the first test, which was not scaring Bronx off or starting a war in the streets. But her curiosity about the rooftop meeting bugged her. Why Scotia Coliseum…and what could he be intending?

Once she exited the garage and returned to the snowy night, she went over the meeting in her mind. But not because of what had happened; there wasn't a lot to analyze there. Her intrigue had solely to do with Bronx himself.

She pulled out a small pocket watch and popped it open, where there was a picture of a much younger version of herself. On either side of her was a young boy and a young girl. Both had their arms around Juno, and likewise. They all looked like the best of friends.

"I know you're somewhere out there, and I'm going to find you. I swear it."

CHAPTER 8
FESTIVE CURIOSITIES

DAYS AFTER THE ANNOUNCEMENT OF THE 8 PROJECT, times were busy, but everyone needs a break once in a while. Especially with the Christmas festivities just around the corner.

On a rare day off, and in desperate need to do some Christmas shopping, Adelle and Lily took a free Saturday to accomplish just that.

Normally, Lily would've gone with Minisc or Jules, but shopping for them while they were with her wasn't exactly an option, no matter how oblivious they could sometimes be.

Though there was a faint flurry of snow dancing through the sky, the weather remained unseasonably warm for the day. Sidewalks were still caked with a level of the white powder that made a satisfying crunch with each step, but full winter gear wasn't entirely necessary.

The shops along the street were packed with crowds, and all the local booths were swarming with business. It was their busiest time of year, and all hands were on deck to keep efficiency high. The energy through the square was electric, bringing enthusiastic smiles to Lily and Adelle.

As they walked down the busy pathways, they admired the wonderful sights in front of them. Like usual, Adelle was more reserved, taking in the atmosphere with a controlled enthusiasm, while Lily reveled in the adventures ahead.

Down the brick path they walked, and as they approached the Christmas market's centre, Lily's eyes began to glimmer—the towering tree decorated for the season kept drawing her eye. It was a magical sight that abolished all the stresses over the past few months.

"You know," Adelle said, "I've never actually been to the Christmas market before."

"What!?" Lily couldn't believe what she was hearing. "But it's the best place to be this time of year! Everyone's so happy, and it's filled with all these great little presents you can get for people."

"I know, I've just never been very big on Christmas. The Adenji gang weren't all that into gift giving."

"Oh…right. I guess I never thought about that." Lily frowned for a second before snapping her fingers. "Well, then—we'll just have to make sure that you get the full Christmas experience! We'll take pictures with Santa, get some gifts, and drink hot chocolate! A perfect girl's day for us!"

"That does sound kind of nice." Adelle said, only with slight hesitance.

"And we have to throw a big Christmas party with everyone invited! I'm sure that Minisc will let us use his house."

Adelle raised an eyebrow. "Are you sure? Minisc doesn't seem like the type to want parties thrown at his place."

"He's not," Lily laughed. "But when I ask, he'll say yes." She winked and strutted away with a snicker.

Their first destination, at Lily's request, was the towering Christmas Tree in the centre of the square. She loved getting pictures of the different ornaments, and she also wanted a pic-

ture of her and Adelle in front of the tree, which she successfully captured amidst the throngs of people.

The next hour saw the two take stops at every small booth in the area, each filled with different unique trinkets and knick-knacks. The choices were endless — small figurines of babies, trains, angels, and much more. All of the options made Adelle's head spin, but she managed to pick out a couple small trinkets for her friends. They weren't much, but they knew that it wasn't about a price tag — it was about the thought, and nobody put more thought into their gifts than Lily.

However, after so much walking, even Lily's generally high energy levels were dropping. It always amazed her how Adelle's temperament never showed any wear and tear through the day.

After leaving their final booth, Adelle said, "Maybe we should take a break for a bit and get some food?"

"Yeah, that sounds like a good idea. My feet could use a rest."

Near the south side of the Christmas market were a quartet of little shops at which to grab a bite, and the best part was that they were also indoors.

The girls selected the quietest cafe they could find — there were only a handful of people scattered about the many booths lined along the walls. The cafe had a bohemian vibe, with strange art on the wall and a much more modern feel about it than a traditional java hut. Lily and Adelle sat in a cushioned booth with sandwiches and cups of hot chocolate

For a while they sat in a content silence, sipping away and taking a moment to rest. Even if Lily had Adelle running all over the place due to Christmas fever, it felt good. She was content with the morning's adventures, getting to experience even more of life outside of the Adenji gang's clutches.

Adelle blew the steam from her cup and let out a comfortable sigh. "It's so nice to finally have a day off. It feels like we've been working non-stop since The 8 Project started."

"I still can't believe the EC is actually doing this," Lily said, sighing as well. "Not because I think it's a bad plan, but I guess I just haven't gotten used to the idea that we're now in a world where Minisc's father isn't leading the charge for everyone. It's strange."

"Honestly, me too. Nobody was more surprised than Robin and I when President Osiris called us into his office. I suppose that since Minisc's father had worked with so many others in the EC over the years, they knew one day it would end—though maybe not like this. I certainly wish that he were here to lead the charge forward, but I guess we deal with the cards dealt to us."

"Even still, this is a huge honour for you. And who knows—maybe one day I'll even get to be the water representative. I'm sure Jules will be dreaming day and night about being the wind representative," Lily said with an eye roll.

Adelle laughed. "But Minisc is gonna be in for a tough one with Robin already at the helm for the light spot, though. And if I know Robin, he'll do everything in his power to hold that title for as long as he can."

But Lily shook her head with a knowing smile. "I don't think Robin has anything to worry about on that front. I know Minisc as well as you know Robin, and the Minisc I know would be the last person asking for that sort of spotlight placed on him. It would drive him insane. I bet even if he were to be nominated, he'd turn it down."

Lily took a bite of her sandwich, sidestepping the fact that Minisc's role in the EC would soon be far bigger than any single representative in The 8 Project. That wasn't her secret to tell, so she kept the subject focused on Adelle.

"It must be really cool though, getting to work with all these great Elementalists? It must feel like it validates all the effort you put in, right?"

Adelle paused, giving her friend's words a chance to sink in. There hadn't been much time to think about such personal introspection, but she was right. Adelle smiled and softly said, "Yeah, I guess in a way it does. But it's even more than that for me. Really, what being selected did was validate the choices I made. The day those Adenji jerks, who I thought were my friends, left me to be caught by the EC changed my life. Even now, sometimes I wonder how things could've been different. What if I never met Robin, and what if Yuri never took me under his wing? I know it was a risk for the both of them. It's not like I had a great reputation to back myself up, and yet they knew my past and still chose to take a chance on me. That's really what this validates to me—that I made their risk worthwhile."

"You have a good heart, Adelle. You never belonged with the Adenji gang. I think you've proven that. I know Yuri, and he'd never risk mentoring you if he didn't already know that, too. Besides, it's much better to have you on our side."

The girls talking and catching up over their meal was like two sisters chatting away. One of the many things Lily had always dreamed about when growing up was having another sibling. Since that opportunity never came, she wanted to take full advantage of her relationship with Adelle, which often felt like the next best thing.

Minisc and Jules were her best friends—there was no debating that. What they'd done for her and the adventures they'd had together cemented their bond; it was an unbreakable one. But there was something that Minisc and Jules were simply not fit to be a part of. To have a sister to confide in, even if not by blood, was something that couldn't be replicated.

Once they finished up in the cafe, there was one last thing on Lily's list: a classic Christmas picture with Santa Claus.

They were standing in line at a makeshift workshop, decorated to make it look like the North Pole. People were dressed in red and green elf costumes, and at the end of a snaking line was a throne fit for the king of Christmas himself. Behind that was a lovely Christmas tree, even though it paled in comparison to the one in the centre square of the market. Underneath was a bunch of presents of all shapes and sizes, and hanging to the left was a sign that said CHARITY TOY DRIVE. Based on the amount of boxes strewn about, it seemed that they were having a great turnout, so much so that every minute or two one of the elves would pluck a few presents and take them to the back room so that they could fit more underneath.

Adelle and Lily waited in the winding line, mostly comprised of parents and children, but a few groups of friends were around as well.

Adelle was slightly embarrassed; she knew that she an Lily were a bit too old for this kind of thing. But it was also a moment she'd been looking forward to. Since she'd ran away from home at such an early age, there were no memorable photos of her on Santa's lap. No enduring memories or long-standing traditions. This was her first step in hopefully changing all that.

The line moved quickly enough, and soon the girls were up next.

"Ho, ho, ho! Merry Christmas!" the girls heard the festive big guy boom as they approached. His bigger-than-life-laugh made Lily grin brightly, while Adelle just smirked at the entire experience.

He stroked his long, obviously fake beard and said, "And what can Santa get you two young women for Christmas this year?"

Lily opened her mouth, ready to reveal her biggest wish, but then heard a strange beeping. It was incremental but continued to grow faster and at a steady rate.

Something felt off, and Lily glanced to Adelle, who hopped off Santa's knee and stepped a few paces away.

Lily attempted to do the same, but her reaction time wasn't

as fast as Adelle's. Then she heard a loud bang. A second bang followed, and then a third.

Immediately, Lily covered her ears, trying to lessen the piercing sound. She worked her way through the crowd and over to Adelle, grabbed her around the shoulder, and pulled her to the side.

They could hear shouting and terrified cries for help, all while the room filled with white smoke.

Smoke bombs, Adelle thought. *What's going on here?*

Then they heard someone shout, "They're stealing all the toys!"

The smoke didn't last long—which clearly meant that it wasn't from an Elementalist,—and when it began to clear, most people had scattered.

"Lily, get everyone to safety," Adelle ordered. "Whoever's responsible for this, we don't know if they have other threats up their sleeve. I'm going after them!" She was already in full sprint, chasing down the lumbering Santa himself.

Just as one would expect from an 8 Project member, Adelle was out the door without a second thought, leaving a shocked Lily to try and handle a bewildered crowd.

Lily knew that whatever threat was posed, Adelle could most likely handle it on her own, but if it were Luminosa, then trouble was on the horizon. She couldn't just let her friend go at it alone.

After Adelle took off, Lily heard another voice from a shop owner next to them. He started hollering to those still in the area, "Everyone, it's Shadow's Light! Hurry, come hide in the back!"

Lily heard the shop owner's words, but they took a second to register. She knew about Shadow's Light, or at least had heard the group's name before. If Luminosa and the Adenji gang were the most well-known threats to the city, Shadow's Light would be a distant third. Lily wasn't sure of their motives—or even their strength but a co-ordinated attack had the potential for trouble.

But her main priority, as instructed by Adelle, was getting people to safety, and so that's the task she tackled first.

She rushed over to the shop manager, who was holding his door open and continuing to shout at the crowd. Because the smoke was fading, Lily cast her hands out wide and cleared a lot of it away with a bubble of water.

"This way, everyone! You can hide in here until the threat is dealt with." Her voice carried far, and people were gradually hurrying in her direction.

She then turned to the shop keep and said, "Can you call the EC and the police and send them this way? I'm gonna try and help."

The shop keep nodded, as the last of the crowd was getting in. Lily took off, following Adelle's path through the back door and entering the snow-filled streets.

She assessed her surroundings and saw that the square was now empty. It looked like a stampede had rolled through—all the booths were flipped over and the wonderful displays were smashed. This was a Christmas scene upended by evil intentions, the perpetrators even stealing presents intended for needy children.

Lily's heart sank when she noticed the shattered glass ornaments. She could only imagine the sadness felt by those who'd put so much work into making them.

Unfortunately, she didn't have the time to be concerned about damaged trinkets. Right now, her focus needed to be on finding Adelle and the Shadow's Light members.

Come on—how hard is it to miss a giant man running away in a Santa costume. They couldn't have gotten that far ahead of me, but I can't even hear them anymore.

She picked up her pace and headed in the direction of the towering Christmas tree, which she could use as a landmark.

Meanwhile, Adelle had nearly been swallowed up by the crowds as people attempted to abandon the market. They were franticly on the move in an attempt to find safety. She could see the remnants of other smoke bombs that had gone off around the market.

Spotting a streak of smoke in the distance, she hurried toward it. But as she popped out the backside of the crowd, her senses began to tingle.

She whipped her hand across her body and formed a trail of cool blue wind. A streak of ice formed in mid-air, just wide enough to block the incoming shadow ball.

The explosion cut through the square, causing a cloud of smoke to engulf them. Effective, but through the commotion, Adelle heard the voices of two men:

"Unbelievable! She blocked it?"

"I don't care! Just get rid of her so we can get the money and scram. If The 8 Project shows up before we're out of here, we're as good as dead."

The first had a more measured voice, almost like he was enamored with her skill, while the other was far more callous and hard-edged.

Perfect, so we've got a couple of holiday thieves looking for a quick payday. And they're willing to steal from children to do it. Why can't these people ever leave well enough alone? Adelle thought. A blast of arctic air whooshed out from the smoke, dispelling it quickly.

All the bystanders were able to flee, which made Adelle's life easier but she still had yet to lay eyes on her adversaries. She stayed on her toes, her eyes peeled and ears focused.

Hearing a high-pitched whizzing sound in her vicinity, she leapt to her left, dodging a ball of light that sunk into the snow before causing an eruption. The snow and light nearly blinded Adelle, and she dove behind a toppled booth for protection.

So we have one light and one shadow Elementalist. Both attacks came from my left side, which means that maybe I can cut the field in half. Adelle dug her hands into the snow, and barriers of ice began sprouting up to her right, stretching along the path for a solid distance. Hopefully it would seal off half of her potential battlefield, which would allow her to dial in her focus.

"Look, girl," she heard the callous-sounding man yell. "We don't have any business with you. Stay out of our way and we'll let you live."

Though placing the voice was difficult, it was more than enough indication for Adelle to move. She got to her feet and slid from one destroyed booth to another, narrowing down her blind spots but also her hiding spots. At some point, she'd need to place her eyes on the two men if she were to stand a chance. She also needed to pray that there weren't more Shadow's Light members headed her way.

Her mind swelled with ideas but her options remained limited. There was also a sense of growing worry, though she pushed it aside. This is what being in The 8 Project was all about—and this is why she, a former Adenji gang member, was selected. She needed to prove that she was worthy of the faith bestowed upon her, even if it meant placing herself in danger.

Getting to her feet, she knew that the only bait she had was herself, so she decided to use that to her advantage.

With the calm composure one would expect from the young ice Elementalist, she planted herself in the middle of the snow-covered pavement and braced for an attack. Allowing a heightened focus to control her body, when the attacks streaked toward her, she reacted without hesitation. She spun around, whipping her hands diagonally. Just like before, the blasts collided with her walls of ice and an eruption of snow and smoke absorbed the air.

"Can't say we didn't warn you," mocked the callous man.

When the dust settled, nothing remained but a small pothole in the ground. The two Shadow's Light members appeared from their hiding spots, one merging himself in the branches of the Christmas tree while the other stood high up on a street-light. Both jumped down to the collision spot.

"Callum!" the gruff man wearing the Santa suit bellowed. "Hurry up and grab the cargo—I'm sick of carrying it!"

"Uh…right. Yes Sir, Mr. Bauer," the much-less confident teen, who was clearly Callum, said. There was a significant age gap between the two. In contrast to Bauer's Santa-perfect physique, Callum was a toothpick with glasses and messy black hair. His wiry frame didn't look like it had ever seen the inside of a weight room, and the way he walked displayed a distinct lack of confidence.

Callum headed for the decorative Christmas tree, where the bag of presents had been stashed away while the men were dealing with Adelle. But their over-confidence played right into the hands of The 8 Project's ice member.

Since Adelle knew that she was at a disadvantage while the attackers remained hidden, her goal was to lure them out. But the only way to do this would be if they thought that they'd eliminated her.

"Gotcha!" Adelle sprung her trap, sending pillars of ice to imprison the two.

They both saw Adelle standing on the light pole, but before they could react, they were trapped in an icy prison. She dropped down, keeping her guard up as she approached the cold white bars. She examined the two men. Since they were wearing an elf costume and a Santa costume respectively, identifying them was simple.

"A couple of those people you scared said that you were part of Shadow's Light. If that's true, what are you guys doing around here? This isn't your usual territory."

Adelle knew more about Shadow's Light than most others in the EC, particularly from her Adenji days. The two weren't fond of one another, and that could often lead to thick tension.

There was a reason the Adenji stuck to the Toronto waterfront, while Shadow's Light was more known to be on the east side.

Callum, the younger of the two, was about to speak, but was met with a glare from his superior, forcing him to shut up.

Instead, Bauer grumbled, "We don't answer to the likes of you. Now if you don't mind, we'll be on our way." He grabbed the bars of ice, and purple sparks of energy surged like a power amp.

Adelle hopped backward, bracing herself as the ice shattered. Her prisoners were now free.

Of course, she wasn't naive enough to believe that her trap would hold them for long, but that was never her intention.

The distress call had been sent. Which meant that an 8 Project member — if not multiple of them — would be joining the call for action. This changed the goal of her battle. Winning wasn't the priority — buying time was. But now she also had the added benefit of having eyes on her opponents, which always makes any fight significantly easier.

What's taking them so long? Someone should have been here by now! Adelle thought, beginning to worry.

Once the dust settled again, Adelle braced for impact. A glowing ball of light burst through the smoke, crashing into her chest. A cry escaped her lips as she sailed through the air, landing in a pile of snow.

The sting in her chest left a small mark, but she got to her feet and brushed the snow off her arms. "Okay, *that* hurt," she grumbled.

It was her turn to go on the defensive, using ice to coat her body as she blocked the barrage of light and shadow blasts. Each one stung, making her wince as she battled through the pain. The sound of her armor cracking rang out far and wide, and trouble was just around the corner. She dropped to her knees, unable to hold up her defenses.

"It's nothing personal, but next time you shouldn't interfere in other people's business." Bauer's voice reeked with contempt as he raised his arm and shot off the final blast.

But before Adelle could brace for impact, she heard a familiar, comforting voice call out her name.

"Adelle!" A stream of water sailed past Adelle, deflecting the shadow ball and forcing it off course.

"Lily?" Adelle suddenly forgot the pain in her body and spun around to see her friend rushing down the street toward her. But she was alone — no 8 Project members with her.

"Are you okay? I came as fast as I could," Lily said, glaring at the two attackers, who merely scoffed. At least they held off on another attack.

"Yeah, I'm fine thanks. Is it just you, though?"

"One of the store clerks is sending the police and EC our way, but it shouldn't take too long." Lily said, helping Adelle to her feet.

The Shadow's Light members were apparently distracted with their own conversation.

"Well, this isn't good," Bauer complained. "If we don't get the merch back to the boss, he's gonna flip his lid." He cracked his knuckles and grabbed the sack beside him. "Change of plans, kid — you're up. You hold them off while I run."

Callum's eyes grew wide, his voice shaky at the suggestion. "Wait, what? But I don't stand a chance against two of them! And what if others show up to help?"

"That sounds like it's not my problem. Now hurry up, or I'll toss you back onto the streets where you came from."

He shoved Callum, who stumbled forward weakly; his legs shook and his face began to lose colour at the challenge ahead of him. Bauer grabbed the bag of gifts and took off.

"We can't let him get away," Lily said.

"Leave this guy to me — I'll make quick work out of him. You keep eyes on the other one and I'll meet up with you," Adelle said decisively. Lily obeyed, taking off after Bauer.

"Hold on — I'm not gonna let you go that easily," Callum said, though there was no strength at all in his voice. He prepared to strike Lily but he'd forgotten all about Adelle, which left him vulnerable. He took a shot to the shoulder, a chunk of ice like a snowball that dropped him to the ground.

"You're not so tough without the big guy around, are you?" Adelle shouted. "Well, then — why don't you just spare us the time and we can call it a day." Now that she was on an even playing field, and despite her depleted energy, she overpowered Callum greatly.

Hoping for a quick resolution, Adelle slung blocks of ice at Callum, putting him on the retreat. She could see that he was agile — the way he moved and anticipated attacks was clearly a learned trait. He also packed some level of power, judging by the hit he'd landed earlier. But he also looked conflicted. Something was on his mind, and Adelle had a feeling she knew what it was.

"It was a bad move having that loser you call a friend run off to save his own skin. Not much of a partner, if you ask me."

"What? How dare you!" Callum bellowed. "That's not what Bauer did at all. He left me here because he trusts me! He knows that I can stop you!"

"Is that so?" Adelle picked up her pace, turning the tide of battle quickly. She had Callum at her mercy, and she knew it, but for some reason, she wanted to pull her punches.

"The name's Callum, right? You don't look very old. What…14? Maybe 15? What are you doing with a group like Shadow's Light?"

"Why do you care?" Callum shot back, showing more bite than previously.

"Why do I care? Because I've seen people like you before. That look in your eye, the sound of your voice…You want to please that partner of yours so that you can gain his admiration."

"What do you think you're talking about?"

"Let me paint you a picture of a disgruntled young Elementalist, lost in the world, feeling shunned and abandoned with nowhere to go. No family to love them, no friends to support them. It's a debilitating experience, for sure. And then a group like Shadow's Light shows up and gives you a home. They give you everything you felt you were lacking in life, and in turn you do whatever it is they ask of you. But let me tell you something—it's all a lie. They're not your family."

"That's not true! You don't know the first thing about me, or about Shadow's Light!" Callum yelled, firing a barrage of light blasts. They circled the street like satellites moving into the sky, before each one began firing off rays of light like laser beams. "Shadow's Light has given my life meaning! They've done everything for me. Without them, I'd be nothing!"

Adelle swiftly weaved in and out of the lasers, shooting off flanks of ice to break the orbs of light.

"I'm telling you, they're just feeding you lies. I've seen it before. The second the going gets tough, Shadow's Light won't be there for you. You're nothing but a tool for their arsenal, replaceable at the next turn. But it's not too late. If you abandon this path, you can still become so much more."

"How would you know what I'm capable of? Before I joined Shadow's Light, nobody cared about me. I was nothing more than a wannabe kid who everyone picked on. Shadow's Light gave me purpose. They gave me hope. That's what they do for people, they give them hope."

There was a sadness in Callum's voice, an anguish that was rising up from years of pain. It was something Adelle was all too familiar with.

She shook her head and sighed, "Fine. Have it your way. But don't say I didn't try to warn you."

Callum flailed wildly with attacks, but alone he was of little threat. He furrowed his brow, entranced in Adelle's movements until something dawned on him. She wasn't wearing an 8 Project uniform, but he knew of her prestige. He was sure of it.

"Wait a second. I've seen you before…you're Adelle, the ice Elementalist of the 8 Project. Did Bauer know that? Is that why he left me here?" He began to tremble, taking a step back. His eyes shifted around, looking for an escape route. Fighting was out of the question.

Adelle smirked. "Glad to see our reputation is spreading. Hopefully gangs like Shadow's Light will take notice and go crawling back to where they came from."

Her confidence scared Callum even more. He was distracted and worried, and with that lapse in concentration, his attacks slowed and lost any strength they might've had.

Adelle swiftly sidestepped the beams of light and darted in. She spun around the teen, leaving a streak of ice in her path. Before Callum could react, he was left with layers of ice wrapped around his body.

"Look, I get it," Adelle sighed. "Trust me, I really do. So take my advice—don't get wrapped up with guys like them. They might pretend to care about you, make you think you have a family, and even give your life some sort of purpose, but none of it's true. What they see is someone with some skill who's vulnerable and would make for a good scapegoat when the going gets tough. You've already seen it for yourself—they'll abandon you at the first sign of trouble if it means saving their own skin. Just think about what they've done already." With her parting words, Adelle took off, following hot on Lily's trail.

Meanwhile, since Adelle had chosen to deal with Callum, that left Lily to deal with Bauer.

"Get back here! You're not getting away with those toys!" Lily yelled as she slung blasts of water toward the fake Santa. Unfortunately, thanks to his head start—as well as the cold air slowing down her water—reaching Bauer was tough.

For a big guy, Bauer was deceptively fast. He ran with a thundering crunch under his feet, his bag of toys pounding against his back. Every few steps, he'd cast his left hand to his side and release small balls of shadow. They were minimal but locked onto Lily like turrets, shooting out more small pelting blasts. By no means lethal, but enough to slow down anyone on his path.

In a full sprint, Lily turned her attention to the blasts, waving her hands like a conductor to meet each roadblock head on. She refused to break stride, all while managing to close the gap.

Bauer took a glance behind him and saw Lily, hot on his heels. *Damn it, this girl's fast! Just my luck.* Realizing that his lead was shrinking, he stuck his foot in the ground and came to a sudden halt, swinging the heavy bag of toys into the unsuspecting Lily.

She flew through the air, hitting the ground hard as she groaned, "Those obviously aren't plush toys in there." But there was no time for checking her injuries; the attacks came at her fast and she hurried to the defensive, blocking the barrages with orbs of water.

"You made a *big* mistake showing up here, girl." Bauer dropped the sack of toys and cracked his knuckles. Lily could hear the disgusting echo of his bones breaking. "Just 'cause you've got some kinda pretty face doesn't mean I won't stomp on it." He stretched his hands outward and smoke poured out from his sleeves, dancing like fire and taking the form of different creatures. One was a lion, the other a bear, and the third a snake. They were lifeless husks covered in smoke, but it was like nothing Lily had ever seen before.

Well, that's new, she thought, pushing herself up. Again, she had little time as she leapt away from the bear as it slammed a claw down and rumbled the earth. When she landed, she heard the roar of a lion, which charged at her. Even if it was nothing more than a smoky illusion, its menacing fangs were hard to ignore.

Like a reflex, she shot her hand out and blasted a stream of water though the smoke. It evaporated the lion for a moment before reforming in its original place.

"Oh, great—it comes back to life." But in her confusion, she felt a gross sensation; it felt like something was slithering around her leg. She glanced down and was met with the snake wrapped around her thighs, binding her. She tried to jump back out of instinct but instead fell into the snow.

"Neat trick, isn't it?" Bauer mocked. "One of the great things about shadows is that they can create almost anything. I'd be careful not to struggle too much—snakes are known to tighten their grip when people try to fight free."

Lily did as suggested and stopped squirming. Though she could feel her body being squeezed tight, she knew it was nothing more than an illusion; the snake was just a manifestation of Bauer's element, which meant that there had to be some sort of gimmick to it. Knowing this, the gears in Lily's head started to spin. She glanced up from her stomach, seeing Bauer just standing there, his "pets" suddenly docile. It made her wonder: *Why isn't he running away? If I'm really bound by his element, why doesn't he just pick up the sack of toys and run?*

Though it was hard to formulate a strategy with so many unknowns, Lily tried regardless. *If these things are just manifestations of his element, that must mean that they can't work independently — that's why he's not running away. Okay, I think I'm beginning to understand how this little trick of his works. He creates these fake creatures, and then takes turns pumping them full of his element to bring them to life. To keep me trapped, he has to keep using the snake. But that means that for him to constrict me more, he has to use even more power.*

She had a plan, at least one to buy the others some time to arrive. She resumed her squirming, trying to shake free of the snake.

Bauer laughed again, hearing Lily cry out in pain as her muscles compressed further. "Don't want to take my advice? Fine, then have it your way," he laughed, shrugging.

But Lily knew exactly what she was doing. She could see the concentration in Bauer's eyes, and he was struggling to hold his grip. After a few bone-crushing seconds, she finally broke free, spraying water everywhere in the process.

Crap, she figured it out! This is bad…I need to get a move on, Bauer thought to himself. He glanced around and then grumbled, "Damn it, girl—you're becoming a real pain in my ass!"

Bauer cast his creatures toward Lily, who was struggling to keep her balance. She crossed her arms, bracing to absorb the blow of the bear, when pillars of ice whipped past her and crashed into the bear and lion, destroying them like a cloud of dust.

"Hands off my friend!" Adelle ordered, marching into the battlefield. She grabbed Lily's arm, lifting her to her feet.

"Thanks! You came just in time," Lily said.

"Just returning the favour," Adelle smiled.

Bauer glared at the two, his face becoming red and a vein in his forehead starting to bulge. "I should've known that stupid runt was gonna be useless. Didn't even make for a decent roadblock," Bauer grumbled.

Adelle turned to face the Shadow's Light member and said, "You know, I really didn't wake up this morning thinking I'd be fighting a crooked Santa Claus, but here we are. So now you've got a choice. You're either gonna give back all those toys peacefully and I'll let the police deal with you, or you can take your chances with me and see how long you last. Your call."

"Fat chance, girl. There's a few thousand bucks stashed in that bag, and we can make even more on the black market. I'm not giving *anything* back."

Lily sighed as she and Adelle glared disdainfully at Bauer. "This has to be one of the lowest things I've ever seen—kids are out there just trying to have a joyful Christmas, and this dummy has to go and screw it all up. Don't you even care that you're robbing poor children of their smiles? All so that you can make a quick buck? That's disgusting! And I'm not letting you get away with it. You're giving those toys back."

Bauer lifted his hands to the sky, smoke rising from his sleeves. "I was hoping I wouldn't have to play hardball today, but you girls have left me no choice. Now cower in fear as my shadow creatures devour you!"

Smoke spewed out from his red coat and spread across the snow, and over a dozen different animals formed, all resembling smoky, foggy ghosts.

"I guess he keeps an entire petting zoo up his sleeve," Adelle joked. There was no fear in her voice, which encouraged confidence in Lily, too. They were plenty strong enough, and both wanted to ensure that everyone would be given the Christmas they deserved.

"Ready when you are," Lily smirked as she cast small orbs of water into the sky. Adelle lifted her hands, a frigid air freezing the water. Then, like shooting stars, the newly formed chunks of ice shot off in all directions, vanishing Bauer's brood of pets in seconds.

"Oh, yeah — *way* easier to deal with those things as an ice Elementalist," Lily joked.

"What can I say? Winter is my time of year," Adelle said with a smirk, taking her turn to go after Bauer. Just as she'd done to Callum, she sped through the snow and took Bauer by surprise. She circled around him, coating his legs and arms in ice before coming to a stop behind him.

"This time, you won't be getting out," Adelle spat.

Bauer's eye started to twitch, and the vein in his forehead nearly exploded as his blood pressure rose. "Damn it! Why did they have to give me that stupid kid as a partner?! This is all his fault! We should've never let such a sniveling brat into Shadow's Light…he's a disgrace to Elementalists everywhere."

"What?" a familiar, shaky voice suddenly piped in. "But you were the one who wanted me to join. You asked to be my mentor. You said we were family…"

Bauer cranked his head to the left when he heard the familiar voice, and saw others approaching behind him as well. When he noticed who was heading in his direction, he grew even more irritated and spat at the ground.

Lily and Adelle both sighed with relief as they saw their backup approaching. Two more 8 Project members were on the scene—Juno, the earth Elementalist, and Sora, the distinguished wind Elementalist. But, surprisingly, between the two of them stood Callum. His head hung low, face drooping with dejection. He'd chosen to trade in his icy prison for a pair of handcuffs, tight behind his back.

"Juno and Sora?" Adelle was shocked.

"Sorry we're late. We were the closest in the area, but finding you guys was a bit of a struggle," Sora said calmly.

"At least until we ran across this poor sap trapped in some ice," Juno laughed. "A few questions later, and he sang like a canary."

Upon hearing this, Bauer lost his mind at Callum. "You idiot! You were supposed to buy me time, not lead them right to me! What the hell is wrong with you?! You couldn't even do *that* right!" Bauer could no longer keep up with his phony act. With his plan up in smoke, his annoyance and anger were clear.

Callum raised his head and weakly responded, "Yeah, I guess I *am* an idiot. Because I trusted you. I thought you guys were my family."

"Trust? Family? You actually bought that garbage?!" Bauer taunted. "Give your head a shake, kid. We're not family—you were just a pawn. You think that Shadow's Light would ever let a sniveling child like you into their ranks?"

"That's enough out of you," Juno shouted at Bauer.

It didn't take long for more members of the EC to arrive. They took Bauer away, leaving the stolen presents in the hands of Lily and Adelle. There was no shortage of damage to clean up in the Christmas market, but everyone was safe, and that's what counted.

Just as Lily checked to see the contents of the bag, she heard more people approaching. Most of them looked like parents, and some even appeared familiar from earlier when they'd been standing in line for photos with Santa. One by one, Lily handed back the presents, fully embracing the Christmas spirit.

After some of the commotion died down, Lily and Adelle went on to explain the situation to Sora and a handful of police officers.

Juno approached them with her hands behind her head, gave a whistle, and gestured over to a nearby police car. "Hey, you two—looks like your pal over there wants to have a word with you. Don't worry, as long as he's got those cuffs on he's not of much concern." She gestured over to Callum, who was sitting in a police car with his head cast downward.

Lily shared a puzzled look with Adelle, who shrugged and said, "I've got this…it won't take long."

Lily nodded, and Adelle made her way over to Callum.

"You did the right thing," she said as she approached the cuffed criminal. "I know that right now it might feel like you betrayed your family, but you didn't. Trust me—I'd know better than anyone here."

Callum looked up and sighed, dejected, slumping his shoulders and shaking his head. "I guess this is what I deserve. All I wanted was a place to belong. Somewhere I could be accepted. To have a family." He dropped his head again.

"I know the feeling. I know it all too well, but that's what people in Shadow's Light prey on. Don't get yourself confused, Callum—you're not one of them. And that's a good thing."

Callum sniffled, holding back his emotions while Adelle continued. "Look, I was once in the same place you were. Alone, abandoned, and desperate for any sort of acceptance. I was heading down the wrong path—the same path you were on. But before I got in over my head, someone saved me. He gave me a second chance in life. Without him, I'd never be in the position I am today. And if I deserved that chance, then so do you."

She could see Callum's eyes filling with hope.

"I want to give you that chance, Callum. Your life is far too valuable to rot away in Penetang with that scumbag partner of yours. Yes, you made a mistake, but I don't believe that's who you are. Nor do I think that you should believe it, either. So here's what I'm gonna do for you. I'm gonna talk to President Osiris of the Elemental Council, and explain the situation to him."

"Really?" Callum's eyes grew wide in disbelief. He was nearly trembling at this lifeline being thrown his way.

"Yes, really. But that doesn't mean that you'll be off the hook for this little stunt. Every choice has its consequences, and there'll still be a price to be paid for this one. But it'll probably just be some community work. I do think, though, that it would be a good chance to pair you up with someone in the EC who will make you feel much more welcome. They can give you everything you wanted from Shadow's Light, and you'll know that you're doing good for the world as well. They did it for me, and now I'm here where I belong. So let me do it for you."

Callum sniffled, looking into his saviour's eyes. "Thank you. Truly."

CHAPTER 9
CALM THE MIND

WITH SCHOOL NOW ON BREAK FOR THE WINTER holidays, avoiding use of Celestial Light was quite easy for Minisc. His body eventually returned to normal, moving out of its fight-or-flight state and allowing him to regain some level of control.

For the time being, Mr. Howland wanted to remain working on the mental aspects of Minisc's technique. Now that everyone knew that he was fully capable of channeling Celestial Light, and even able to use it in small doses on command, he needed to make sure his mind was fortified before he could move forward. After all, if he spent all his time worrying about what lingering effects would happen from using Celestial Light, then what was the point?

So even though he continued to let his element rest, his training carried on.

The inside of the EC training facility was pitch black. Minisc let out a yawn and dragged his feet as he cracked open the door, making his way to the change rooms to put on his workout gear—all on auto pilot by this point. His hair was disheveled and his eyes drooping with bags, but he walked over to the sink, splashed some water on his face, took a deep breath, and told himself, *You can do this. One day at a time.*

When he left the change room, he took a second for the eerie silence to quiet his mind. The place was deserted — and a bit spooky since most of the lights were shut off. But that level of fear was nothing compared to facing the wrath of his mentor.

Just like every other morning for the past week, Minisc saw Mr. Howland through the glass window that peered into the weight room. He was going over some notes, although based on the sweat dripping down his brow, it appeared that he'd already begun his own workout regimen.

The dedication was admirable. Minisc had always wondered where his own father had gained such a disciplined routine — training every day, always staying in tremendous shape, and ready to engage in battle at a moment's notice. But now he was beginning to understand. Clearly, much of it could be attributed to Mr. Howland programming it into his brain.

Minisc entered the weight room and was met with a crusty glare. Most people would flinch, but Minisc was accustomed to it. He flashed a disarming smile, but Mr. Howland ignored it. It was all business.

"How does your body feel? Any abnormalities recently?"

Minisc stretched his arms to the ceiling and then did some basic toe touches. "Nope, I feel good actually. I think I'm finally back to normal."

His comments were somewhat of a lie. The continual strenuous workouts did leave his body feeling sore every night, and oftentimes he spent most evenings with more ice tapped to his muscles then he knew what to do with, but he refused to complain about such trivial issues. Those pains were just typical soreness, unrelated to any strange feelings with Celestial Light.

Besides, he knew that if Mr. Howland detected even an inclining that something felt strange, he'd immediately cease teaching Celestial Light. That wasn't an option Minisc could afford to entertain.

"Good," Mr. Howland said. "And what about your element? No more flare ups? You have everything back under full control?"

Minisc shook his head. "Nothing strange at all. In fact, ever since that day, I've felt great. Not that I've really used my element much since then—just small tests here and there to see how I'm feeling. But even now, I feel so much stronger with it." Minisc held his arm out and formed a small ball of light in his palm. It gleamed as bright as the sun, potently sparkling in his hand.

"Hmm, interesting," Mr. Howland observed. "I dare say that your body has taken your Celestial Light state and allowed it to gradually seep into your everyday strength."

"But wasn't that the issue?" Minisc asked.

"No, not exactly. Your issue was not being able to tone down that level of power. But right now if I told you to lower the potency of your ball of light, I would guess that you could do it with ease. Is that correct?"

Minisc nodded, and with a simple effort he shrank the ball to half its size. The brightness dulled and the sparks of energy faded.

"Okay, I think I'm beginning to understand. Unlike before, this is all of my own doing, not my body acting on its own."

"Correct," Mr. Howland affirmed. "It's also a good sign. It means that your body is slowly adjusting to the use of Celestial Light. Doing so will allow you to grow stronger without the need to tap into so much power, which obviously allows you to handle the rigors of the technique more effectively."

Mr. Howland guided Minisc to the training facility's stadiums. While they walked, Minisc took one final look around. He knew that nobody would be present, but he liked to make sure—not so much to hide Celestial Light but because of the damage he was known to cause.

Even when he first began training with Mr. Howland, using Celestial Light at 8% would put the building's high-tech barrier system under considerable stress. In some cases, the blasts could barely be contained. One time, he even managed to short circuit the entire building's functions. Luckily, nobody would dare chastise Mr. Howland, which kept him free of any repercussions.

At the opening of each field on the inside wall was a simple control panel. Mr. Howland walked over to the panel, swiped his access card, and activated the barrier system.

Every time Minisc saw the array of rainbow colours flood the various satellites positioned in the room, he was mesmerized. It brought back memories of his time in The Underground, hiding from Dusk and training through the use of Reynn's new artificial intelligence system. He was hoping that this training would go far better than that session did.

With the room set, Mr. Howland turned to Minisc, "All right, let's see what you can do at 15% power."

"15%?"

"Yes, now that your body has returned to normal, and since your body is growing accustomed to the power of 12%, I want you to try and go further beyond. If the strain becomes too much to bear today, then we will tone it back to a lower power. But at the moment, I would like to gauge where you are currently at."

Minisc shrugged and said, "I guess it's worth a shot." His face suggested a casual perspective on what he was attempting, but it was all a farce. Increasing his power caused a small degree of nerves in his stomach. He hadn't used Celestial Light since those strange feelings had controlled his body, and if they popped up again he'd have to concede defeat. And pushing the power further seemed like a fairly quick way to force those feelings to creep up again.

Regardless, he pushed through, taking a breath and exhaling

the stress from his body. All the negative thoughts, all the fears of Celestial Light and its repercussions were being shoved to the back of his mind until a calm emptiness filled the void.

The warmth, a sensation that made his blood tingle, flowed through his veins. Weight lifted from his shoulders and he could hear his heart pumping, like a throbbing between his ears. Below him, the dirt shook as he reached what he presumed was 10%. He took a second breath and focused on increasing his power yet again. Sparks began to form at his feet like little bolts of lightning, and once he hit his destination, he opened his eyes.

He saw strange, thin swirls of light around him, just like when he'd unleashed Celestial Light at 100%.

He glanced down to his feet, seeing cracks starting to form in the dirt. He was shocked at how light he felt. It had only been a short time since summoning such power, but the sensation of having his senses so in tune with his surroundings brought about a strange feeling, a different feeling than before. The air smelled stronger as his vision focused in on Mr. Howland.

"This is incredible. I knew the increase from 12% to 15% would be different, but I feel light as a feather. In a way, it feels like when I was fighting Dominos."

He walked forward, easing into the weightlessness of his steps. There was no resistance, as though he was unaffected by gravity. He lifted his arms to the sky and then started to swing them in a boxing motion. He cut through the air with a powerful whoosh, strong enough to make the arena's barrier flinch like they'd been hit.

But after only a few short moments, as he should've suspected, he could feel the tension setting into his muscles. His legs constricted and although he felt light, the pain was sharp. He fought off any signs of distress and kept a front up as he locked eyes with Mr. Howland. His teacher was assessing him to see if he could handle the power, and Minisc refused to show

weakness; he could endure any sort of pain that came with the increase. He'd just have to be cautious and monitor things for himself. As long as he remained aware, nothing would get out of control.

After a brief stare down, Mr. Howland finally nodded and said, "Good—it appears that making the jump this time came a fair bit easier for you. It shows that your mind and body are improving. But remember—the more power you call upon, the strain will also become exponentially more, so if this is too much, you need to speak now."

Did he know that Minisc was putting up a front, or was he simply reiterating his point? Either way, Minisc brushed off the lifeline and started stretching.

"I can feel my heart beating a little faster than it did at 12%, but other than that, I feel fine."

Mr. Howland accepted the answer, taking a seat across from Minisc. He crossed his legs and put his hands into his lap. "Just remember—the more you tap into this power, the stronger your will must be. Without that, you won't be able to keep it under control." He shot Minisc a glare that meant business, indicating that he'd better heed Howland's advice.

Minisc obliged, more than a bit confused.

Once seated, he asked tentatively, "Sir…what exactly is it we're supposed to be doing?"

"We are focusing on easing your mind. We already know you have the physical capabilities, but the more of that power you tap into, the tougher it will be to keep your body feeling at ease. You must practice mindfulness, learning to remain calm and in control at all times. Now follow my lead and take a deep breath. Feel your chest expand, and then exhale."

Mr. Howland began giving a demonstration with his eyes closed, taking in deep breaths through his nose and exhaling through his mouth. He looked like he was about to enter a trance.

"Okay..." Minisc mumbled, knowing better than to disobey his teacher.

"Focus on your breathing and remember to push out any other thoughts. Empty your mind of those worries, and begin realizing that you have control over how your body feels. Concentrate on the power flowing through you, not on the tension continually rising in your muscles."

Minisc continued following Mr. Howland's lead, and before long he could feel the stress in his body decreasing. The pounding between his ears died down, and his heart fell into a more comfortable rhythm with every breath. His fears were slowly fading away until he was in a state of peace.

"I think it's working," Minisc told his mentor.

"It's important to remember that your mind controls everything. What you let into your mind will impact the feelings in your body. Allow it to feel confident in its use, and your body will respond appropriately."

"My mind controls everything? I don't think I understand."

Mr. Howland, his eyes closed in contemplative thought, explained. "Think of it like this. Your body has a fight-or-flight instinct, right? In many ways, Celestial Light works under the same premise. When you are in that state, letting your body overflow with power, you could say that you go into somewhat of a fight state. However, when your mind perceives imminent danger and it can't handle those threats, it switches to a flight state. This puts your body into overdrive. That's where things can become quite dangerous."

Minisc was taking in every word that Mr. Howland, still with his eyes closed, was imparting.

"When you were tapped into such a small amount of power, the effects were nothing more than an elevated heartrate, and maybe it was a little tougher to catch your breath. But as you gradually increase the power flowing through you, the effects become that much stronger, too. It can become extremely dangerous if fear were to take over, if those internal mechanisms were to run out of control. This is why it's paramount that your mind becomes hardened to fear and stress, so that you may keep your body under control at all times."

Minisc thought back to his previous uses of Celestial Light. Then he remembered his father's demeanor whenever faced with danger. "Oh, okay—I think I get it. It also explains why my father was always so calm despite the threats he faced. It was so that he could control Celestial Light."

"Yes. Your father was an expert on the matter. What he managed to accomplish on that front surpassed even my own expectations. His ability to hold a strong spirit when faced with overwhelming odds is what allowed him to defeat Dusk."

Minisc mulled the words over. His knowledge of the Elementalist Wars was limited, mostly the outcome and some other small tidbits. It was one of the subjects his father wasn't very fond of bringing up, and one that Minisc never cared to talk about. But with his growing education about Celestial Light and how his father's legacy began, he was becoming curious.

"Sir, if you don't mind me asking...I know that you invented Celestial Light, but how? I mean, I know that my father was desperate to stop Dusk, and the state of the world was in peril...but what made you think that Elementalists harnessing a heightened state was even possible? And why did you choose to teach it to my father?"

Mr. Howland finally opened his eyes and pondered the question, choosing his words carefully. "It came from years of research. Those days were dark, and there was little in the way of Elemental research. Yet year over year, we kept seeing Elementalists growing stronger, becoming more adept at using their powers. This, of course, would eventually come to a head with the rise of Dusk. At the time, I and a group of Elementalists were trying to research the effects of the elements on our bodies, seeing what made us so different from our human counterparts. Though many of those studies came up empty, we did gradually uncover some of the mysteries pertaining to what we now know as the elemental cells."

"Elemental cells?" Minisc asked.

"Yes, the cells in our bodies that provide us our powers. Over time while pushing the elemental cells as far as I could, I began to discover the capabilities of our bodies. Through the use of accelerating those cells, one could, in theory, be able to produce incredible power. But not for a second did I believe that doing so would become what your father turned it into. All my research indicated that such a state could only be maintained in small spurts because of the strength required to activate it. Think of it like a sudden and temporary power boost. One could hypothetically use Celestial Light to multiply their power in short increments and channel it through their element before returning to normal."

Mr. Howland rolled his eyes. "Of course, however, that wasn't good enough for your father. He was determined to find a way to master the technique to the point that he could use it at all times, and to his credit, he managed to pull it off. He trained all hours of the day, doing whatever he could to protect those he loved. As for why I chose your father to learn Celestial Light...I'm not sure. I had no intention of teaching him, or anyone else for that matter. The power was too strong, and also untested. We couldn't predict accurately the effects that one could face from its use. But with Dusk managing to gain more sympathizers, and learning to weaponize them as an army, we knew that it was our only hope."

Minisc watched as his usually stoic instructor smiled ever so slightly. "I knew that my father trained intensely to beat Dusk, but I guess I never really understood just how big a risk he was taking at the time. And all that work just to lose his element in the end…I mean, it's a shame that's what it all resulted in."

Though Minisc accepted that he'd be reduced to the same fate as his father, it was still a hard pill to swallow. The consequences had yet to really sink in, and it was already a heavy burden. But his father had carried that same burden on his shoulders for years—the idea of having such a large part of his identity stripped away without mercy—and yet he never wavered. He simply did what he believed was right, all in an effort to see the world move forward in a positive light.

"I do wish that there was another outcome," Mr. Howland said thoughtfully. "One that made the sacrifices more tolerable. And perhaps one day there will be, as we Elementalists continue to grow and evolve. But for now, an Elementalist's body simply cannot withstand the strain. Celestial Light turbo charges the cells far past what is reasonable, so much so that they disintegrate instead of reverting back to normal. Which also means that after you master Celestial Light, its paramount that you only use it when absolutely necessary. Unfortunately, your father used it so much that he burned up his element faster than even I anticipated."

"How long should he have had?" Minisc asked.

"Based on my early metrics, he should have sustained reasonable use of Celestial Light for a good 10 to 15 years longer. So again, I will reiterate: when the day comes that you have this power at your command, you should only ever be using it when it's completely necessary."

"I understand," Minisc said.

"All right, then. I believe that is enough about the past for one day. Back to the training of your mind. Begin with your breathing again."

The two worked on different meditative exercises for an hour, releasing any stresses currently occupying Minisc's body. The confidence on his face was easy to see.

Mr. Howland pushed himself to his full height and asked, "Do you believe you are ready?"

Minisc opened his eyes from the meditative state. "Ready for what?"

"To begin training at 15%. It's one thing to remain calm while in a meditative state, but keeping your emotions in check during a fight is quite a different task."

"Oh, right—I guess that's true. Then yeah, I'm ready to train." Minisc stood up and loosened his body with some quick stretching. This was the real test of his recovery.

"Good, then come at me," Mr. Howland said, a sly smirk playing on his pale lips.

Minisc could feel the taunting in his teacher's voice. In terms of strength, they were an obvious mismatch. Perhaps in their base forms, the two would be nearly even, but Minisc knew that he was far superior as it stood currently, not that he'd risk going all out and injuring his teacher.

Still, it's not like he saw another option. Mr. Howland stood defensively, beckoning Minisc to move.

Minisc gripped the dirt with his feet, ready to rush in so that he could test his increased speed. Since he felt so light, he assumed that he must've been faster as well.

He instantly dashed forward, leaving an explosion of dirt and ripples through the air in his path. But as he prepared to strike Mr. Howland, he realized his teacher was five feet behind him. He came to a jolting stop, spinning around to stare at him. Minisc blinked twice, furrowing his brow as he tried to process what had just happened. When he looked to the ground he saw thin lines in the dirt, and he realized that they were from him.

Had Minisc moved so fast that even his teacher couldn't keep up? That seemed unlikely. So did that mean that Mr. Howland was even quicker? That didn't seem likely, either.

Finally, it started to set in for Minisc. Mr. Howland knew that he was in no danger; the man was far too calculated.

Keeping his back turned to Minisc, Mr. Howland said, "Your body moves quite fast in that state, but as you've just learned, your actions struggle to keep up. That is also part of training your mind."

Minisc took the subtle criticism in stride and said, "Right, there's no point in moving that fast if I can't even react to my surroundings." But then he thought for a second. "Wait, when I fought Dominos, I was using all my power and I had no issues reacting. So why does 15% feel so weird then?"

"If you recall the way you described your final encounter with Dominic, you were only focused on one aspect at a time. First you focused on movement, dodging the vines chasing after you. Then you focused strictly on attacking to deal the final blow. When broken down like that, you were able to succeed. Now you must put both those aspects together. Master this level of Celestial Light, and you will have surpassed nearly all Elementalists in this world."

The two ran through some simple drills for Minisc, which involved a mix of physical tests as well as elemental training much like he did in school. But unlike class, these exercises were significantly amped up in difficulty.

The exercise that brought him the most angst was his explosive reaction test. Mr. Howland placed ten small lights on the ground, spread out in a star shape, and every few seconds they'd light up green. Minisc would have to dash toward the green light, tapping it with his foot before the next one would light up. He'd engaged in similar things while doing target practice with his element, but this was at a far faster pace. He only had a split second before the light would flip from red to green and then back again. And if that wasn't enough, once Minisc began to improve on the basic aspects, Mr. Howland would start tossing in small bolts of lightning, making him react to those attacks as well.

After 45 minutes of continual back and forth, Minisc dropped to his knees in a heap. "This…is…insane…" he panted—no amount of breathing could slow his pounding heart after such a workout. The light shining from his body evaporated like smoke, and the swirls of wind around his feet dissipated.

"46 beeps in 120 seconds…not bad." Mr. Howland said, tapping a stopwatch.

Minisc rolled onto his back and tried to sit up, the sweat dripping off every inch of his body. His workout clothes were stuck to his frame.

"Do I even want to ask what my father's time was when he did this?"

"It would be unfair to compare where he was at to where you are in your development, but he was often in the triple digits."

Minisc sat up, his eyes wide, "Triple digits? There's no way. I don't care *how* fast his reaction time was, it's not possible!"

Mr. Howland cracked a smirk at the comment, making Minisc wonder if he was just messing with him or telling the truth. When it came to his mentor, there was simply no way to tell.

Mr. Howland said, "Even so, that last attempt was your best effort by far. But you're still thinking too much when it comes to your reactions. You need to let your body take over your movements, using your mind to focus on calmness. However, our time is up. We shall continue this tomorrow."

Minisc pushed himself to one knee. He wiped the sweat off his hair, splattering it onto the dirt floor in small puddles. His heart felt like it was trying to escape his chest, and his leg muscles were throbbing as though they were about to rip through his skin, but he forced the pain back. Inhaling with as deep a breath as he could manage, he got to his feet, stared at his teacher, and said, "Wait. I want to go again." He gritted his teeth and the warmth in his body returned. "I can keep going. If we wait until tomorrow, then we're just wasting precious time."

His tone was forceful, just like when he needed to convince Mr. Howland to keep teaching him. "Luminosa is just waiting to strike again, I can feel it. And if I don't master as much of Celestial Light as I can before they strike, we may never recover."

Even through The 8 Project had been created to take the pressure off what Minisc was trying to achieve, he knew that if Brooklyn managed gain the same power Dusk bragged about, then no matter how strong Robin, Adelle, and the others were, they'd be no match for the monster. The only way to stop Brooklyn for good would be by mastering Celestial Light. It was a race to the top, and Minisc refused to slow down.

"Minisc…you're overdoing it," Mr. Howland advised, but Minisc paid him no mind.

"I'm fine, really. Let's keep going."

Mr. Howland sighed in defeat. He could see Minisc's passion and desire, both traits straight from his father. No matter how many times he collapsed to his knees, he refused to lose the determination that got him this far. If Minisc said he was fine to keep going, then Mr. Howland had no choice but to believe him.

"Well, then let's continue." He tapped his stopwatch again, resetting it as Minisc got into position.

CHAPTER 10
UNDERLYING ISSUES

THE CITY WAS GROWING MORE FESTIVE WITH HOLIDAY cheer as Christmas crept around the corner. It was only a couple of days away, and people were taking advantage of the sudden warm patch in weather.

Since there was more commotion taking place in the streets, that also meant that The 8 Project needed to be ready.

Though the initiative was still in its infancy, the early returns had been prosperous. Data already showed a decline in element-related crimes, and the general sense in the city was a feeling of positivity.

Also, because The 8 Project would be nominating new representatives every year, it gave some Elementalists a different set of goals to strive for. Normally, there were those who sought fame, those who were out to prove they were the best, and those who felt it would be the best way for them to make a difference. But no matter the motive, they were all left in the shadows of their hero.

As much as people wished to replicate the Hero of Light's legacy, such a lofty goal was nearly impossible. But being a nominee of The 8 Project was a far more reasonable and attainable goal for those entering the EC.

Whatever the motives, it was a warning to all criminals in the city. Their short-lived freedom was coming to an end.

It was a non-eventful Friday, and Coro and Olivia walked side by side down the quiet streets. Though there was a cheerful atmosphere picking up through the city, neither Coro nor Olivia was interested in embodying such feelings. They were working and only cared about making sure that everyone else could go about their day without worry.

Coro wore a winter jacket over his EC uniform, while Olivia wore her new 8 Project gear. Most days, the two would prefer to remain in the shadows and work in private, but such methods would be considered counterproductive.

When it came to The 8 Project, the biggest component of the role was visibility. It was well known, when the Hero of Light was present, that criminals knew he could be around any corner at any time, ready to bring them down. That acted as a great deterrent. The EC's hope was to replicate the same sense of fear by letting people know that they were also around at all times. And for the public, it signaled that help was always nearby. All they had to do was ask.

Still, like on most days, Olivia and Coro were hopeful to avoid any cries for assistance. Not to shirk their responsibilities — after all, nobody took such matters more seriously — but so that they could focus on their real task.

Through another conversation with Rush, the former Luminosa informant, they received a tip that Luminosa had plans of an attack somewhere within the area. Even though the words of a former Dusk sympathizer could only carry so much weight, they had nothing to lose by at least preparing for a potential threat.

The tip *did* have some merit — it wasn't a stretch to assume that with the creation of The 8 Project, Luminosa would be looking to make a statement. And what better way than to un-leash mayhem in an area chockful of Humans?

Another problem was the lack of description they were giv-en with this mysterious threat. Any of the hundreds of people around them could be deemed a suspect.

It wasn't just the sidewalks that were packed—even the streets had cars jammed bumper to bumper, and the traffic was never ending. Just another one of the issues of patrolling while people attempted their last-minute shopping.

The current area under investigation was the Eaton Centre, the city's biggest and most popular mall. It was located in the southern part of Toronto and, thanks to the holiday season, it was seeing about triple the traffic in and around the area. This meant that any attempted attacks committed by Luminosa had the potential to be disastrous.

Even though visibility was important, so was keeping up their strength, and so Olivia led Coro to a small, hole in-the-wall restaurant. The place was near empty, but the smell of grilled fish was hard to ignore. However, Coro had other things on his mind.

"Why didn't you tell me about The 8 Project? If there's a group of Elementalists dedicated to bringing down Luminosa, I should be a part of it."

Olivia turned her harsh gaze on the teen. "Remember—you're not part of the EC. You're only here by my request."

Unlike most, Coro didn't flinch from her glare. He under-stood his role and knew that Olivia would never budge on her facts, but even so, he'd done more work for the EC and put more on the line than most members could ever dream of. If there was a team searching out the group that his father now belonged to, he wanted to be involved.

Olivia calmly began explaining things to Coro. "It's true that The 8 Project was created with the intent of counteracting Luminosa. The way things were progressing, it was necessary for such a force to be created. But that is far from the only reason. We now know that most Elementalists refused to side with Luminosa when Dusk made his return—some believed in his cause, but most showed no interest. We can tell by the way Luminosa has still struggled to gather support. However, there's still a not insignificant portion of Elementalists who are simply sick of being part of this mixed society. Most of those that harbour dangerous thoughts continued to marinate in the shadows, refusing to show their hand while still believing that the Hero of Light would once again bring down Dusk. Of course, they were proven right in the end. But because of that, criminals were forced back into the shadows, again waiting, their anger festering under the surface. What they need is an opportunity."

"An opportunity like the Hero of Light retiring."

"Indeed. The EC and the police do what they can to quell everyday threats, but don't let what you see on the surface fool you. There's an underworld to this city filled with those who've felt disenfranchised, forgotten, or outright abandoned by those who walk freely. And now that we lack the blanket of protection known as the Hero of Light…well, you can see the direction the city is going in. Criminals are ready to revolt and bring the underbelly of this city into the limelight once again."

Coro looked at her questioningly. "Once again? You mean like when Dusk first rose to prominence?"

"Precisely. Let me ask you, as someone born after those days: How much do you know about the history of Elementalists in this city? Or around the world, for that matter?"

Coro shook his head. "Honestly, not much. I spent most of my childhood in a laboratory with my father, and history wasn't really something he talked about."

"Right. Well, the history of this city isn't something I'd say that most people your age know anything about. There is a reason for that, though—it can be difficult for less mature students to wrap their heads around."

Coro detected a small pain in his partner's voice, something he hadn't previously heard.

"I know it was bad…but was it really all *that* awful?" Coro asked.

Olivia took a sip of her coffee. "It was. And it wasn't just limited to the city of Toronto—many cities all around the world faced similar issues. The first generation of Elementalists were far less cohesive than the Elementalists of today. Many of them were torn, with some feeling they had the right to master their powers and use them as they saw fit, while others simply wished to be integrated into society with Humans. Of course, the same way Elementalists were split, so too were Humans. They were confused by a phenomenon they didn't understand, and they were also scared. It was a growing power they couldn't control, and that increased the fear. Things quickly spiraled out of control, and those divided groups became at odds with each other. And, as is often the case, those with violent intentions used their powers, knowing there was little in way of Human resistance. All over the country, leaders of what we consider the underworld oozed out from every corner and began taking over. It didn't matter if you were Human or Elementalist—crime was rampant for both. That period of time lasted for more than a decade, with death rates skyrocketing. Tons of people tried to flee the city looking for shelter, but as things grew worse, there were fewer and fewer places left to run."

"Wait, does that mean Elementalists and Humans have been at odds well before Dusk made his attempt at extermination?"

Olivia nodded, tightly gripping her mug of coffee. "I'm afraid so. What made the rise of Dusk different is that he came with power and a goal. He set out to create a world for Elementalists, his kingdom. There were others before him with similar strength, but they had no such intentions. They grew so nihilistic that they only sought destruction. Some refused to spare life, Human or Elementalist, instead only seeking power by force. They were equally as dangerous but failed to garner any support the way Dusk did. But when the Hero of Light emerged, the city was granted a blessing. He could outclass anyone using force to gain power, and he always used his strength for the benefit of others, never for himself. He managed to do what most thought was impossible. He united a country and repelled the scum back underground. The Hero of Light might have represented peace and unity toward those that he protected, but he also represented something entirely different to the underworld. He represented fear, and struggle, and oppression."

"You mean oppression from the freedom to do whatever they saw fit? Including stealing, assaulting, and killing those they think are the reason for their so-called oppression?" Coro almost spat the words in disgust. As far as he was concerned, all those beliefs sounded like sorry excuses for a group of people simply wanting to use their powers to do whatever they pleased, whenever they pleased. A group wishing to avoid any guilt for their actions. In his mind, it was a bunch of garbage.

"I never said it was right," Olivia replied. "But that doesn't change the facts. Anyone considered part of the underworld felt this way then, and they still feel this way now. But with their oppressor gone, they can smell freedom. That's why we as a collective force must stop them. Luminosa is the focus, but it doesn't stop there. We can't afford to return to those dark days."

"Agreed."

Every few minutes, Coro could see someone walk past the large window and stare into the shop. It was clear that their fixation was with Olivia, not him, but Coro sensed that it had more to do with her uniform and the allure of The 8 Project. He tried to ignore the prying eyes, though they did make him keenly aware of his surroundings at all times, even while sitting in a coffee shop.

"So that's why President Osiris planned all of this? Because he could see what direction the city was heading in, and he hoped to counter it?"

"Yes, although in one sense this plan was always in the works. I, and a number of others in the EC, had discussed this potential with President Osiris over the last five years, always anticipating the day we'd face such a conundrum. Admittedly, we weren't planning on having to enact such drastic plans on a dime the way we did, but outside of President Osiris, nobody knew that retirement for the Hero of Light was coming."

"So what was the original plan?" Coro asked.

"In most ways, it was the same—but we were expecting the Hero of Light to lead the charge. It was meant to be a more gradual integration into society to avoid causing a sudden panic. There's no doubt that some will view this change as cause for concern, losing faith in the EC while believing they're no longer safe. Unfortunately, the timing to avoid such concerns didn't work out, but even so, this is still the right move. Aside from that, those forming The 8 Project were also meant to be granted teams of their own, bringing in the younger generation to help act as mentors. Doing that would create a continual pipeline of young Elementalists ready to face the rigors of working in the EC."

Coro lingered on the last part. A pipeline of young Elementalists ready to face the rigors of working in the EC. "I thought that was the purpose of attending EA? To provide a place where Elementalists could train and learn the skills necessary to join the EC? But with the school now opening up to other fields, I guess that isn't as strong of a resource anymore."

"There's no doubt that EA is a well-constructed introduction to our world, but it's still a school environment all the same. And now with it becoming more education oriented rather than when I attended, we need to supplement that. Even when I was there, 95% of the students that graduated were ill-prepared to effectively join the EC."

"But clearly not everyone…some people can step right in and lead, can't they?"

"For a select few who really put in the work, they can step in, yes. Those who are the type to take it upon themselves and seek development or experience outside of class time come out far more prepared than most. Look no further than two of the other 8 Project members, Robin and Adelle. They're both by far the youngest of those selected, being only a year removed from graduating EA. But because of the work they put in, as well as their constant desire to improve and strengthen themselves in any way they can, they were far better than what most adult Elementalists could ever dream about."

"Actually, I did wonder about that. I know those two are in-credibly talented—I saw them at the Tournament of Elements. But if part of being in The 8 Project is about mentoring a young-er generation, then isn't it a bit counter-productive to have peo-ple so young themselves? Wouldn't it be wiser to pick people with a little more tenure?"

Coro had a fair point. Experience was the most important as-pect of their job, and no skill could make up for that. However, Olivia had a simple explanation.

"There's no doubt that most people would agree with that logic, and there was a decent amount of pushback when mak-ing these decisions. But in the end, they were the best choice. Though society may have been blind to the falling standards of the EC, others were not. Such was the downfall of relying on the Hero of Light."

"I don't understand."

"Despite all his accomplishments," Olivia explained, "the Hero often placed the burden of society on himself. He refused to allow others to be hurt, doing the dangerous lifting that otherwise would've been dealt with by groups. Unfortunately, that selflessness harbored unintended consequences. Because of him, many in society—not just students at EA, but even those in the EC—were able to take their foot off the gas pedal. They were allowed to become complacent in their training, instincts, and work ethic—all because they knew they always had the Hero of Light to pick up the slack. On top of that, many Elementalists who weren't in the EC often didn't feel the desire to use or improve upon their element. Some for lack of ambition, others in hopes that it would help ease tension with Humans and allow them to blend into society better. But with everyone becoming more relaxed, that left only one group continually working to become the strongest force they could."

"You mean those considered the underworld of society?"

Olivia nodded. "Those that truly seek to unravel the very fabric of this city continue to grow stronger—not only in power but also in numbers. And to place unprepared EC members in the way of those criminals without their own guidance would only be asking for senseless death. So the decision to choose those of a younger age was to help plant the seeds of a future generation. But, equally as important, we know they can be trusted to put in the work and seek help when needed, despite being so young."

"I guess I never thought about it like that. Since my father was always so hellbent on pushing me to be stronger by any means necessary, I never noticed the complacency of others setting in."

Coro thought back to his first full year at EA. There was little debate that he was near if not at the top of his class. And then there were others like Minisc who were always improving. But when he thought about the other students during his limited interactions with opposing classes, they were far behind. It was like they were in two different schools at times.

Olivia sighed. "The underworld is always looking to gather power, which makes me fear that with your father still on the side of Luminosa, they can now offer people a way to that power. We need to be prepared if that were to happen."

"But there's still one thing I don't understand. If those who are a part of the underworld are aiming for more power, be it in strength or in numbers, and Luminosa is in desperate need of support to achieve their goals, how have they not been able to unite the underworld under the promise of my father helping them become strong enough to live freely as they please?"

It was an interesting question, and one that Olivia had pondered herself. She shook her head. "That part I don't know. We've tried to figure it out, and there was certainly fear of that happening when Luminosa first returned, headed up by Brooklyn. But we've yet to really see anything materialize. There have been a few theories on it, though nothing more then rumours heard in passing from informants. The first is that unlike Dusk, Brooklyn has been far less charismatic in his moves. Perhaps he's failed to bring people on because of his age. Or his immaturity. It's hard to say."

"You said that a lot of these underworld types are really just looking for freedom and want to live more in a state of anarchy, right? Is it possible that most in the underworld don't want that either because Luminosa is looking to usurp and take over the power? It seems to me that the last thing they want is a new leader who's in control, so why would they have any care for some Elementalist's utopia if they're still under someone else's law?"

"We can only speculate on such theories, but if I were to put stock into anything, I dare say that you're not far off. However, if even a portion of the underworld were to join Luminosa, they could become dangerous very quick."

The waiter brought their bill over, and after paying, Olivia said, "Come on—it's about time we start patrolling for the afternoon."

The two started their walk down the busy streets, a number of people remaining fixated on their appearance. Not so much for Coro as he looked like nothing more than an ordinary kid, but with Olivia being the centre of The 8 Project announcement, not to mention the small speech she gave to the nation, many people were focused on her every move.

The clock struck one, which meant that soon their mission would begin—or at least that's what they'd been led to expect. Thanks to the tip they'd received a few days prior, they were bracing for anything. Supposedly an attack of some sort was to take place within that timeframe. Nobody could say for sure whether the information was credible, but that lingering question did cause some issues.

Logic dictated that if a dangerous attack involving Luminosa was on the horizon, and the EC were aware of it, that most if not all of The 8 Project should've been in the vicinity—but that also came with risks. A plan like that only worked if the threat was credible, and that in itself was dangerous to assume. If they were being fed false information, the rest of the city would be unprotected with not a single 8 Project member nearby.

Seeing no other option, they prepared everyone to be on high alert but left their daily routine intact.

Coro and Olivia sized up everyone in sight for any indication of a threat, but due to the masses moving back and forth, it proved difficult.

The breeze and snow picked up, and through the crowd they heard a woman growling, "Watch where you're going" as she stumbled forward, hitting another person. Olivia spun to her left, seeing a handful of people trying to hold each other up while a mysterious, hooded figure in a long black trench coat absorbed further into the far end of the crowd. He was hunched over as if he was hiding something, pushing and shoving anyone who blocked his path.

"Looks like we've got our first suspect," Olivia quietly said, just loud enough for Coro to hear. "Hurry, before we lose him in the crowd."

But, as she said those words and almost as if on cue, the character of interest disappeared from sight.

She glared at Coro and fired off her instructions. "Head to the Eaton Centre parking lot. And be ready — this guy is gonna take off the second he realizes we're onto him. I'll try to flush him out into the parking lot where you can trap him. It'll be harder for him to move with all the parked cars around, and there should be less people around to get in the way."

"Okay, I'll be ready."

When it came to handling business, Coro and Olivia were two peas in a pod. Most of their time was spent alone, and so trust didn't come very easily for them. For Coro in particular, being given orders was rarely an easy pill to swallow. But in the end, he understood that he and Olivia wanted the same thing. Also, Olivia had continued to show him respect and care for his well-being — even if she'd never admit it to his face — and because of that, as someone who often chose to lone-wolf all scenarios, he felt comfortable following her lead.

Just as Olivia had predicted when she began her pursuit, the hooded figure glanced back before taking off in a mad dash.

Coro headed to his left, making his way to the parking lot like he was ordered. With any luck, the culprit would run straight into their trap.

Olivia began hollering out for the man to stop running, but all that accomplished was drawing attention from the crowd around her. People began whispering, while others groaned and complained as they were shoved out of the figure's way.

She followed the clearing path and remained on his tail, but every few seconds, chunks of rock would spring up from the ground and sail back toward her — and also toward bystanders.

Those in danger dropped to the ground trying to avoid being hit, while others grabbed onto people near them and made for cover.

In a full sprint, Olivia cast her arms to her sides, and out came a series of shadowy hands. They smashed through the rocks with ease, keeping everyone around her safe. It might have slowed her pursuit, but her duty was to protect those around her above all else.

Past one street corner, around another, through an alleyway, over a fence…whoever the figure was, they definitely moved fast.

If Olivia could get in range, her shadows would be able to bind the person, but she wasn't having much luck.

While she continued her pursuit, she attempted to relay a signal though her comms. If other members of The 8 Project were around, now was the time to act.

As she continued her pursuit, something dawned on her—the figure was working his path away from the Eaton Centre. He was making no effort to blend into the crowd, or even use the civilians as bait.

No, they were never *supposed* to be bait. The cloaked figure was the bait. A seed of doubt was growing in Olivia's mind. *Am I being lured away?*

A number of scenarios played out in her mind, but Olivia wasn't one to remain indecisive—that's how the enemy would win. She came to a dead stop, watching as the figure disappeared farther into the distance.

Then she heard a massive bang, followed by a series of smaller but frightening sounds. She spun around and was met with an outpour of cries. People were now running toward her. And past her.

Then Olivia understood.

They played us.

CHAPTER 11
A SECRET WEAPON

SURROUNDING THE EATON CENTRE WERE PARKING lots as big as multiple sports stadiums. Normally, having that much room to operate would be welcomed, but there were thousands of cars jammed together due to the heavy traffic.

These obstacles brought up a number of issues for Coro to consider. The pathways between the traffic could barely fit two cars, which meant that the use of his element would be difficult. He'd have to be extremely cautious not to destroy much of people's property, which would only lead to more headaches for him and the EC, something that rarely paid dividends when dealing with Luminosa.

But second to that were the crowds, most of whom were paying little attention to him. He wasn't sure if making a scene, like telling people to get away, would be wise. If he did, it would open up his freedom to attack if need be, but it could also cause mass panic, and that brought about a dangerous unpredictability.

But all this was just speculation. It all depended on how Olivia's hunt went.

Coro positioned himself at the front doors of the Eaton Centre, his eyes darting back and forth and examining every path he could see.

There were seven sets of doors with people walking in and out, some taking a second to stare at the stoic boy while they did so. He tapped his foot repeatedly with his arms crossed as he waited for a signal.

One minute passed, and then another, but still no sign of danger. Confused, he pulled out his comms, but it remained silent. He questioned if Olivia had managed to apprehend the figure, but she would've told him if that were the case.

Did something happen to her? Should I be hurrying to back her up? No, he decided Olivia could handle herself better than almost anyone. He needed to stand firm and trust in the plan.

Finally his assumptions came to pass, as something sounding like a meteor hitting the ground sent shockwaves through the air and violent vibrations through the earth. Car alarms blared in the parking lot and ripples of commotion began circulating. Within seconds, Coro saw a frantic stampede of people rushing from their cars and heading for the mall doors.

At first it was mass hysteria, and Coro couldn't tell *what* was happening. He started looking around for Olivia or any sign of the cloaked figure, but he saw neither.

Unsure what to make of the situation, a man stopped in front of Coro, huffing and puffing. His face was pale, as though he'd seen a ghost, but still he attempted to warn Coro.

"Hey…hey, kid! You…you need to get away from here… there's…there's some sort of monster in the streets!" The man rushed past Coro and into the safety of the mall, leaving him perplexed.

A monster? But there was no time to question further, as the tremors below his feet returned. This time, they were short and periodic, like hard stomps. Then he heard the groans of crunching metal, leaving him even more confused. But if that wasn't enough, he heard a grotesque roar that sounded like a disgusting creature coming from his left to finish off the chaos. There was no mistaking it for human, but to call it some sort of animal wouldn't be accurate. It was far too menacing.

He glanced to his left, following the sound in question before seeing a strange object hurtling through the sky. Any signs of the sun were blocked out—it was large with a black, metal, rectangular bottom…as well as wheels.

That's when Coro realized that a car was soaring through the air, about to plummet in his direction.

Before his mind could fathom how the car found itself flying across the sky, his feet began to emit a frosty, pale-blue light. Pillars of ice sprung from the snow-covered concrete and punctured the metal frame of the car before sticking out the other side. The giant icicle wore the car like a hood ornament.

Coro took a deep breath as he realized that nobody had been in the car. Then he heard faint whispers growing behind him, and when he turned he saw a sizable group of people mesmerized by his heroics, but also horrified at what could've been.

Another strange roar, matched by a pair of thunderous footsteps, broke Coro and everyone else out of their trance. He looked at the crowd and yelled, "Everyone! You need to get as far away from here as possible! I'll handle this."

Nobody bothered to question Coro's orders after seeing his impressive display, so they hurried inside the building where they'd hopefully be safe.

Aside from those seeking shelter in the mall, a few cars were rushing into the streets recklessly. But those vehicles would soon find themselves panicked and stuck in traffic.

To Coro's left, there were a bushel of pine trees about ten feet tall that blocked any sight to the roadway. From over the trees flew a second car, this one a minivan, landing on other parked cars before tumbling over and catching fire.

Coro tried to picture what sort of creature could cause such destruction. What beast could be tossing cars like children's playthings?

But he wouldn't have to wait long — his culprit came plowing out of the trees, brushing them aside like toothpicks. That's when he saw what could only be described as a mutant.

"What the hell is that thing?!" The muscles in his body trembled as he stared down this abomination, wondering what sort of hell awaited him.

It was a creature, that much he was sure of, but it was also unlike anything he'd ever seen, or anyone else, for that matter. It was massive, with bulky shoulders and legs the size of tree trunks. Its skin was greyish black, but there were stitches all around its body holding the patches of skin in place. The creature looked like a giant deformed Human, but also prehistoric. It was an awesome sight — and not in a good way. Not even in his nightmares could Coro have pictured a more grotesque monstrosity. A creature of such ilk could only be made by one man.

His blood boiled at the thought. It was entirely speculation, but no part of him doubted his father's involvement in such a hair-raising spectacle.

But first he needed to stall the creature and let as many people escape as he could. If successful in that, then perhaps backup would arrive.

He took a glance around. Most people were able to flee, but there was no sign of Olivia — or any of the other 8 Project members.

In one way, the absence of those members brought Coro some small relief. In his mind, it meant that Olivia was still after the Luminosa member, and so he wouldn't have to worry about dealing with another threat.

This fight isn't about winning — I just need to keep people around here safe, which means using the powers Father forced upon me to keep him from doing harm to anyone else.

He placed his hands on the ground behind him, and a frost circled his body as the ground began to glow. Within seconds, a glacial wall rose in front of the doors to the Eaton Centre, blocking them off. Since everyone nearby had managed to scramble indoors, he'd be able to keep them safe as long as he prevented the monster from getting inside. Even if it meant sealing off his own exit strategy, he made sure that the ice was so thick that the monster would have to struggle long enough for help to arrive.

"All right, big guy—you don't seem to mind a little cold, so how about we turn up the heat instead?" Flickers of fire danced off Coro's fingers as he cast his hands in the air. "Inferno Flames!" he roared, as streams of fire exploded from his palms, wrapping themselves up and around the monster like a tornado.

Coro held firm, with the heat melting the snow around them. He needed to keep the monster from pushing too far into the parking lot so that he could keep damage to a minimum.

But the monster let out a violent growl that swallowed the spiraling tornado. Coro glared at the beast, noticing that his flames were failing to leave even a burn mark. All that resulted from the attack was a mildly agitated attitude.

"All right, if fire won't hurt you, then maybe I can freeze you in place!" Just like when dealing with the car, air swirled around his legs before paths of ice ripped along the ground toward the beast. It crawled up the creature's thick legs, working around his patchwork body until it reached his face.

"Got him!"

Coro put his hands on his knees, pausing to catch his breath. But before he could act again, another screech, this one even more high-pitched than before, pierced the air. The icy prison shattered like a glass house, crumbling into thousands of tiny shards.

"You've gotta be kidding me! I guess my father got sick

of experimenting on Elementalists and moved into monsters instead."

With no signs of victory in sight, Coro tried to think of his next steps. His hottest flames couldn't burn the threat, and his frostiest ice had failed to freeze it, so that ruled out any sort of fighting. But he also needed to maintain his distance. Based on the size of the creature, if it laid a finger on Coro he'd be snapped in half like a twig.

Unfortunately, the abomination appeared to be somewhat annoyed by Coro's heroic antics as it turned its blood-red eyes onto him.

For a moment, Coro swore that he could sense some sort of intelligence from the beast—the way it focused on him, the way it reacted to his attacks. If that were true, then he had a *real* issue on his hands.

The monstrous brute crouched down, snorting like a raging bull before taking off. Even the way it ran looked unnatural, using its hands and feet to move like some sort of demented gorilla. Each step left deep potholes behind while also shaking the cars, making them hop a few inches in different directions.

For a creature of such enormous size, it moved incredibly fast and closed the gap on Coro in seconds. He wanted to run, but he knew that at that speed he'd never escape. So he started making barriers of ice, one after another, hoping to halt the creature in its tracks.

But, just as before, the walls of ice shattered like glass and were nothing but a speed bump for the beast's arrival.

Within seconds, Coro felt the wind shoot out of his lungs as large sausage-like fingers wrapped around him, squeezing his bones tight. He tried to cry out in pain, but with no air to breathe, only silence passed over his lips. He could feel the bones in his body being turned to dust, hearing them cracking in his mind. If he didn't act quick, he'd be left in a pool of his own bone paste.

Damn it! I hate when I have to use my fire. Coro fought past the intense suffering shooting through his limbs, going back to the well of his flames once again. The heat in his body skyrocketed, causing him to sweat profusely, but he knew that basic strength wouldn't be enough—not when dealing with something straight out of his father's lab. He'd have to expend *all* his power.

His temperature continued to rise until the heat flooding his blood surpassed the crushing pain of his bones breaking. A sharp stabbing sensation prickled his skin in ways he'd never felt, and for a split second, he debated if what he was about to do was a good idea. He'd never pushed his fire so far, and there was a chance that he could internally damage himself permanently by attempting to generate the flames he needed.

The parking lot was rapidly heating up, and the tires of nearby cars were melting into the ground. Finally, Coro erupted in bright blue flames that exploded around his body.

The beast dropped Coro to the ground, shaking its hand from the scarring burn mark on its palm. A flesh wound wouldn't suffice, though—Coro wanted to send a message to both Luminosa *and* his father. He refused to let this grotesque creature bring about the destruction they sought.

The rage toward his father boiled over, and Coro's shimmering blue flames flashed to white. He glared at the abomination and roared with even more ferocity, "Inferno Flames, Extreme Heat!"

A volcanic eruption of fire burned off the sleeves of Coro's jacket, exploding toward the creature's chest. The flames began to engulf his enemy, but he refused to stop. Searing burns were rising up his arms, but he pushed any thoughts of self-preservation to the back of his mind. *Push it further. Dig deeper. I'll burn this thing to its core if I have to.*

Coro tried to make good on his words, keeping the heat coming and listening as the monster grovelled in agony. Still, as it did, so did Coro. His head was becoming fuzzy and the pain put him on the verge of passing out. He squeezed his eyes shut, locking in the tears so that his blurred vision wouldn't impede him.

Finally, the rush of heat to his head was too much. The flames evaporated as Coro dropped to his knees.

He fell forward onto his chest, his face and body shaking from the strain. He knew that it was over now. There was no chance of him getting up or protecting himself. His only hope was that his flames were enough to kill the beast.

But then he heard another roar, followed by the monster's thunderous stomps heading in his direction. Coro could only wait to see what would happen, his eyes still remaining shut. The steps became faster, louder, and before he knew what was happening, he felt like a truck had crashed into him. The wind shot out of him and he flew back, heading for the concrete walls of the mall's exterior.

Then he heard another pair of voices.

"Jules, break his momentum!"

"I'm on it!"

Swirls of wind wrapped Coro's body, like an opposing force to his increasing momentum. Thankfully, the force from behind managed to keep him from blowing right through the side of the building. Instead, he smashed into the ice wall and fell lifelessly to the ground.

CHAPTER 12
POWER BEYOND COMPARE

NOT FAR FROM ALL THIS DESTRUCTION AND MAYHEM, ignorance—at least for the moment—was most certainly bliss.

The ceiling of the Eaton Centre was generally a clear, glass semi-circle that stretched for miles, but for the time being, a thin layer of fluffy white snow continued to pile on top of it, blocking the sun from beaming through.

Just as one would expect in the days leading up to Christmas, the popular mall was packed with Humans and Elementalists alike as they pounded the slick white tiles. On each side of the long walkways were endless store fronts, stretching as far as the eye could see. Each had plenty of winter and holiday decor lining the entrances, with strands of tinsel and maybe a Christmas tree, while a few of the other stores were far more creative in their decorations.

A definite buzz danced throughout the mall —people were walking in and out of stores, carrying numerous boxes and colourful bags, all while wearing big smiles and regaling with friends and family. In the middle of the mall was a massive tree, decorated festively with a big throne at the base. In front of the chair was a lineup of children and parents, all waiting to have their picture taken with Santa Claus.

Of course, that wasn't to say that everyone in the mall was overjoyed. Some last-minute shoppers praying to find that special gift were less than thrilled to be in a crowded mall on the weekend before Christmas. Some would've preferred to be spending their time doing almost anything else.

"I hate Christmas shopping so much," Minisc griped as he and Jules stepped out of the brisk cold and into the Eaton Centre. "Why does everyone wait until the last minute to get everything done?"

Jules side-eyed his best friend, removing his mittens and stuffing them into his jacket pocket. "Really, you of all people are gonna say that? You dragged me to the busiest mall in the city on the Saturday before Christmas, and you want to complain about *other* people leaving things to the last minute?"

"Hey, now—it's not like I chose to wait this long. Training Celestial Light with Mr. Howland has been absolutely brutal. It's taking up all my time, and the fact that I even have today off is a miracle."

Minisc took a look around the endless crowd before sighing in defeat. "Trust me, if this wasn't important, I wouldn't be bothered."

Since coming to the agreement with his father and Mr. Howland about his training, Minisc had spent the previous few weeks—and what felt like every waking moment—working toward mastering Celestial Light. He knew that it wouldn't come easy and that the time involved would be extensive, but those were sacrifices he had to make.

Going to school all day and training until night, the only energy he could muster by the end was to collapse in his bed. The last thing he cared to think about was silly Christmas shopping.

And those were just the physical strains on his body; the

mental struggles were even tougher to deal with—in particular, the lack of time he'd spent with his friends recently. It made him sad, not getting to be a part of their lives as much as he wanted to be.

But lucky for him, Mr. Howland granted him a few days of rest before the holidays.

The rare freedom also meant that Minisc needed to finish off his shopping in what little time he had left.

"It certainly has been a little more boring lately without you around," Jules told him as they passed yet another bustling shop. "I can only have Lily complain about my math homework for so long, but just think about how strong you'll be when you do master Celestial Light. It's gonna be incredible. You can even take over being the light representative in the new 8 Project! We can be side by side, light and wind. It's gonna be sweet."

As taxing as Celestial Light was, Minisc could never ignore Jules' enthusiasm for his dreams. His friend's personality always seemed to carry a level of excitement that was infectious to those around him.

That being said, the last thing Minisc cared to worry about was joining The 8 Project, or even a future with the EC. The only thing he wanted to focus on was his next steps to improving control over Celestial light, until the day he could finally bring down Brooklyn and Luminosa. Without managing to accomplish that, nothing else in the world mattered.

Even so, for one day he wished to put all that aside. He had another task—one he viewed as equally important for many reasons. The only problem? He had no clue where to start.

Minisc and Jules continued sifting through the jam-packed mall, looking at different store fronts for anything eye-catching. Minisc rejected each idea his friend brought to the table, until Jules finally posed a question. "Just who is it we're shopping for?"

Minisc was silent, promoting Jules to react with, "Wait, it's not me, is it? You better not have waited until the last minute to get me a Christmas present!"

Minisc gawked at Jules with genuine confusion, trying to fathom how his brain worked. "Why on earth would I drag you to the mall with me if I was going shopping for you? Who does that?"

"I don't know — who waits until a few days before Christmas to go shopping at the Eaton Centre?"

Jules had a point, but even so, Minisc shook his head in defeat. "Either way, no — I'm not shopping for you. I got your present a month ago."

"So then who's it for? Your father? Robin?"

Minisc shook his head again, then he started sheepishly glancing at his feet. Jules began rattling off names of friends he could've left to the last minute, but it wasn't a long list; after all, it wasn't like Minisc had tons of people to buy for.

Then it hit Jules.

"No way! You haven't bought a present for Lily yet, have you!?" His jaw hit the ground as Minisc slowly nodded. "How could you have possibly forgotten to buy Lily a present?! She's gonna kill you if you don't get her something, you know that don't you? She's been bragging all week about how excited she is to see our reactions when we open our presents from her!"

"I know, I know," Minisc said, again shaking his head. "But I didn't forget about her — I've just been busy. And besides, I don't have the first clue about what to get her. It has to be something she's gonna like, but it can't be too over the top or she'll get mad at me for spending too much money."

Minisc groaned at the prospects. Celebrations were never his cup of tea — not holidays, nor birthdays, and certainly not Christmas. Not because he didn't want to celebrate, but the other kids in his school when he was growing up often looked at the holidays as a perfect time to display their love for the

Hero of Light in grand fashion. Every year, there was inescapable hype for the new Hero of Light action figure or Hero of Light signed posters, and all the kids at school cared about were things related to his father. It always left Minisc flustered and isolated because he had no interest in that sort of stuff.

But that was only a small part of the issue. His joy for celebrations in general had faded with the passing of his mother. Ever since her death, celebrating just never quite felt the same as it used to. The joy of waking up early on Christmas morning with wide-eyed excitement, running to the tree in hopes of finding that special present he'd waited so long for, only to find his mother and father already awake and waiting for him to arrive. Then being hugged tightly as he ripped off the wrapping paper with the biggest smile on his face. Those memories were so vivid—and also impossible to replace. Even years later with his father attempting to make the holiday season feel more special, both of them struggled to bring the same joy that his mother so effortlessly could.

Nevertheless, as was often the case, Lily wanted to help bring that joy back, and so this year she pitched the idea of celebrating together and exchanging gifts. She adored the winter season and the joyful memories she'd formed growing up in her family, so she wanted to help bring that joy to her friends like Minisc—but also Adelle, who was having her first true Christmas experience. But they'd also endured many difficulties over the last year, and she wanted to bring everyone together to relax and enjoy some time with the people she loved most.

Of course, much lobbying took place, but after Minisc's reluctant agreement they all decided to get together on Christmas Eve and host their own celebration at his place. Lily demanded that they all were to exchange gifts, and she wouldn't take no for an answer.

Not that it mattered; Minisc could never deny his best friend, but it did cause him a small headache.

Left with no choice, he put his frustration aside and focused on why he was at the mall. For Lily — to see her wonderful smile light up when he handed her the perfect gift. That is, if he could find it.

The two continued on their journey walking through another handful of stores, but each one provided Minisc with more angst than ideas. Feeling defeated, he and Jules took a seat on a nearby bench.

Minisc slumped deep into the bench and groaned, "This is ridiculous. Buying a single present for someone shouldn't be this difficult." He pushed himself up and placed his head in his hands, rattling off thoughts out loud. "The simple thing would be to buy her some clothes, but there's two problems with that: I don't know the first thing about girl's clothes, and plus, she'd rather make her own. She's not big on makeup, and obviously she doesn't want toys or anything like that. She owns all the books she could ever read, and I know she loves to cook, but heck if I know where to begin with that. And she absolutely refuses to give me any sort of hint, no matter how hard I try to pull one out of her. Sometimes I swear that she just likes seeing me squirm."

Minisc sighed, the wallowing of his conundrum washing over his face. Then he turned to Jules. "Hold on a second…what did *you* get her?"

Jules proudly smirked. "I bought her a new backpack. The one she's been carrying around since we got back to EA is a mess. And then, for good measure, I stuffed it full of school supplies as well. Practical and thoughtful. The perfect gift for our resident straight-A student."

Minisc laughed mockingly before saying, "Oh, please — you just want to make sure she's prepared for school so that *you* don't have to be."

Jules smirked, knowing that his friend might have a point.

"Hey, well if it makes her happy, and it happens to benefit me too, then I'd say it's a win-win. And isn't that really what Christmas is all about in the end? Besides, it's not like any of us are made of cash—I barely made any money from those apprenticeships and I didn't want to ask Yuri for even more money than I already do."

"That's true. Father said he would split the difference, but still, Lily would kill me if I spent too much money on a gift. But come on…we have to keep looking. We're not going home until I've got the perfect present."

Jules stood up, ready to follow his friend on their seemingly impossible quest, but as he got to his feet the ground beneath them began to shake, knocking Jules back onto the bench. Shrieks started to echo throughout the mall as people started running, while others attempted to grab onto something stable nearby. A few people even yelled, "Earthquake!"

But to call it an earthquake would be inaccurate—the shakes were sporadic and in short intervals, almost like heavy stomping.

From outside, they heard a violent crunching thud, like metal crashing into the ground. The abrupt noise made Minisc and Jules jump far more than the stomps had. They whipped their heads to the right to look at the entrance, and were stunned at what came next.

Waves of people came storming in like raging bulls in mass hysterics, yelling, "Everybody run! There's some sort of monster outside!"

Panic spread through the group like wildfire, and soon others began to follow the mob heading for the opposite side of the mall.

Another terrifying bang shook the mall, this one like a meteor crashing into the earth, causing tons of merchandise in the storefronts to come crashing down. More stampedes followed.

Minisc turned to Jules and said, "I don't like the sounds of that."

"Neither do I. We better hurry and make sure everyone outside is safe." The two took off, heading for the door.

They completely ignored the fact that they were on public property—not to mention that they weren't working with the EC in any way through the school or otherwise, and therefore weren't permitted to use their elements in public spaces. And as minors, no less.

But neither of them cared much for following the rules of the EC when it meant the difference between life and death. They'd just find a way to escape punishment later if need be.

Running opposite of everyone, the mall was a sudden ghost town once they popped out the other side of the crowd. They reached the same entrance doors they'd used only a short time ago, but now a gigantic wall of ice coated the glass in pale white.

Jules slammed his shoulder into the door, but he merely smacked off the ice, only cracking it open a few inches. He turned back to Minisc and said, "This had to be Luminosa's doing, right? Who else would do this?"

Minisc nodded. "If I had to guess, I'd say so. Step back—I'll see if I can blast through it using Celestial Light."

But for once, Jules was the one thinking. "Hold on. If you do manage to blast through, you could end up hurting people on the other side. We can't be sure who might've been trapped outside. Remember what Ms. Wright said about conducting a search and rescue mission?"

Minisc lowered his arms. "Right. We can't act rashly until we know that everyone in the area is safe. Looks like you were actually paying attention after all," he smirked. "But that means we need to get outside somehow."

The two began searching, hoping for a side entrance of some sort but saw nothing of note, which caused Jules to turn his attention to the ceiling.

"I'd say our best bet is going through the ceiling, but I don't think I can carry you that high."

Minisc joined him in staring upward, then took a quick glance at the area around him. "That shouldn't be a problem. If I use Celestial Light at 15%, I think I should be just fine."

"Really? That's pretty high up. Are you sure?"

"I know, but I'll be fine. Now we need to hurry, and I think I have a plan. First, I'll get up to the ceiling and blow out one of the glass panels to use as an escape. You use your wind to control the shards so that they don't scatter all over the place and cause unnecessary damage. Once that's taken care of, follow me up and we can head outside."

Jules could hear the determination in Minisc's voice—he was making decisions with logic and speed. Jules nodded without hesitation, putting full faith in his friend's plan.

After one last glance to see if anyone else was around, Minisc took a deep breath, the warm sensation of his power filling him from head to toe.

He pushed the power into his legs before crouching down, and after releasing his breath, he made sure that his heart remained steady from the sudden shock of the situation. Now was the time to remember the words of Mr. Howland, and to remain calm and confident in his actions.

In one swift motion, he jumped high off the ground, leaving waves of wind that nearly knocked Jules to the floor. Then Minisc ping-ponged off the lips of each floor in the mall, vaulting himself toward the glass rooftop. As he torpedoed at an insane speed, he forced his hand out and concentrated intently on the single pane of glass. *Keep calm, don't lose control, and just focus on the target. Let the power flow through you. You're in control.* A small ball of light burst from his palm that sailed through the sky, shattering his defined target in one fluid motion.

Thinking quickly, he formed a small barrier of light around

his body, shielding off the fragmented pieces of glass plummeting in his direction. In a matter of seconds, he landed on the steel beams that connected the entire ceiling.

Now that Minisc had reached his landmark, Jules braced himself to follow suit. But before he could do that, he needed to deal with the incoming razor storm of glass about to rain down upon him.

Like Minisc, he took a quick peek around, double checking that there was no one near by, and once they were in the clear, he raised his hands to the sky. Swirls of wind danced from his body like a massive funnel tube, capturing all the shards and tunneling them downward before directing them to the ground in a neat but broken pile.

"There we go—that should keep anyone from stepping on any glass until it's all cleaned up." Jules clapped his hands, proud of his work before looking up at his friend. Minisc was impatiently staring at him, signalling for Jules to stop admiring his achievement and join him on the rooftops.

Jules then turned his outward wind inward, allowing it to sink under his feet until it felt like he was walking on air. Then, with a burst of power, he began flying up to the sky.

Being able to fly is by far the coolest thing I've ever learned. Jules smirked as the wind flowed through his hair. That liberating feeling never grew old, especially not when impending danger awaited them.

Jules landed on the rails with far more grace than Minisc, but his friend was already busy staring in awe at the sight below.

"Uh, Jules? What is that thing?" Minisc stammered.

The view from such a height should've been stunning, but there was no time to admire the scenery. Hundreds of feet below them stood a monster, the likes of which they'd definitely never faced before. And it was most certainly not a member of Luminosa—or at least they hoped.

"It's like some sort of mutant! You don't think those bioweapons that Luminosa were using returned, do you?" Jules asked.

Minisc shook his head. "No, that thing is different, that's for sure."

"Well, whatever it is, it looks like trouble."

They looked at the parking lot and saw the remnants of a massive battle that had clearly taken place not long before. Layers of ice were strewn everywhere, although much of it appeared to have already melted, and there were cars flipped over in a messy, chaotic scene. Some vehicles even sat on top of each other like sandwiches.

And in the middle of all this mayhem was their new enemy.

The monster's back was to them. It was standing over something, but it was hard for Jules and Minisc to make out what it was.

"Come on, we need to get down there," Minisc said.

Jules nodded. "Right." He grabbed Minisc around the waist, just as he'd done with Lily in their training mission, and as carefully as he could descended from the roof.

While they continued down, they heard the monster roar menacingly. Then Minisc saw a boy begin sailing through the air toward the wall of ice.

"Look! That's Coro!" Minisc yelled in shock. "Jules, you need to break his momentum!"

Jules and Minisc hit the ground, tumbling from the awkward landing as Jules let go of Minisc and rolled to his knees. "On it!" Jules yelled, throwing his hands out in Coro's direction.

Gusts of wind crashed into Coro's back as he did all he could to brace his impact. Although not as effective as Jules would've liked, he did manage enough to ease the impact when Coro crashed into his self-made wall of ice.

Minisc rushed over to Coro, ignoring the beast. He wrapped his arm around him, helping to prop him up against the ice.

"Coro, are you okay? Are you hurt?" he asked, even though

the answer was obvious. Coro's face was beet-red and his brow was sweating profusely. Minisc could feel his muscles shaking vigorously.

"I've been better…" Coro groaned. He opened his eyes slightly to see a very blurry Minisc, and he could still see faint glimpses of the monster off in the distance as well.

"Jules and I will take things from here. Keep yourself safe!"

"Be careful…" Coro tried to sputter. "That thing…it's…it's not normal. Basic attacks…they won't hurt it."

"Right." Minisc turned his attention to the creature, glaring at it. "Do you have any clue what it is?"

"No, but if I had to guess, it's something my father created."

Those words forced Minisc to pause, making sure he heard Coro right. Once the words sank in, he said, "Okay…well, that brings up more questions than answers, but we'll talk about it later."

Meanwhile, in the fray of battle, Jules yelled, "Hey, Minisc—if you two are done catching up, I could use a little help right now!"

On the other side of the parking lot, Jules stood with his feet firmly planted in two broken potholes, staring down the prehistoric beast. Extreme winds flew from his body in an attempt to wrap up the beast, but it was doing little to hold the thing in place.

The monster growled, putting its hands in the ground to charge again. Jules did all he could to hold his position, attempting to push the beast back as it pursued him.

"I've got you, Jules!" Minisc yelled, exploding from his spot and stunning Coro with his speed.

Minisc sailed past Jules with trails of gold light following close behind. He absorbed into the wind, using it to give him even more speed as he cocked his fist. He hopped in the air just inches away from the beast, his fist shining in a coating of heavenly sparks.

"Solar Impact!" he yelled, slamming his fist into the creature's stitched sternum. Mesmerizing light gleamed in all directions as Minisc held his fist, continuing to push his punch further. The rush of strength through his arm was incredible as he tried to blow his fist right through the heart of the monster.

But even with his improved power of Celestial Light, he could feel the monster refusing to give an inch. Instead, the monster cried out in pain before taking its tree-trunk arms and smacking Minisc out of the way like a fly.

Minisc flew through the air toward the cars, but just like Jules did for Coro previously, he broke his friend's momentum, and this time with far more success. Minisc landed with a thud on the ground, skidding to a halt just inches away from one of the half-melted vehicles in his path.

Minisc groaned, pushing himself to his feet. He stared at the beast then glanced at his fist, which was still sending off sparks from his attack. "What *is* this thing? How can it hold up against my punch so easily? I was even using Celestial Light at 15%! That should've *at least* stunned him."

Minisc glanced back toward the beast. It was sitting idle, staring at him with an unnerving look in its menacing, glaringly red eyes.

But, at least for the moment, it gave Minisc a few seconds to assess his situation.

The first and most obvious thing he could gather was that they were facing a monster the likes of which he, Jules, and likely even his father had never encountered. Especially if this thing *was* a creation concocted by Dr. Normanday, as Coro had said, to act as a weapon for Luminosa. The only comparison he could draw came from the slime monsters released across the city a few months ago, which were also created by Coro's father. But those things were nothing compared to the monster before them now. A punch of that magnitude would've not only sent the bioweapons into oblivion but also shattered the elemental crystal that gave them life as well.

Were these supposed to be some sort of improved variant on those designs? They looked nothing alike, but if Coro's assumptions were true, then it wasn't out of the realm of possibility. And if the mad doctor had created monsters that could handle the likes of Jules, Coro, and even Minisc using Celestial Light… well, that was major cause for concern.

Minisc whipped his head around looking for help. He knew that it was only a matter of time until backup arrived; all the commotion going on couldn't be ignored. And besides, this was the reason for The 8 Project's creation, so that a bunch of teenage students didn't have to fight some horrific monster and get their brains beaten in.

Still, he saw no help along the horizon. He wondered for a split second if other similar creatures had been released upon the city in hopes of tying up The 8 Project, but there was no way to confirm such theories. Either way, for the time being, he'd have to fight to survive — and nothing else.

I know that Celestial Light at 15% doesn't seem to be effective, but if I go beyond that, I might leave myself useless. This isn't like fighting Dominos. Back then I had no choice. If I didn't let my power peak, we would've lost everyone. I was on my own then, but not this time. We still have a chance for help to arrive. I need to remain at 15%.

He watched the monster charge at Jules, who burst out of the way, forcing the monster to come to a skidding halt. There was something strange about the way the monster attacked. It was all physical. And though it showed an incredibly tough physicality, that didn't seem to fit a Dr. Normanday creation.

When he created the slime monster, they had different elements tied to their abilities which came through synthetic crystals. But so far, this thing had shown no signs of such power. There was no discernible crystal on its body, and to this point it had yet to display any form of element. But who said that the beast even needed an element to beat the boys — especially with the strength it already displayed?

Minisc thrust his hands out, a ball of light exploding into the skidding monster's chest. The force sent shocks through Minisc's body, but also managed to topple the monster onto its back. A trail of smoke rose to the sky from the blast, but nobody was prepared to celebrate — Minisc knew that he'd simply caught the beast off balance. A lucky shot, if anything.

Clearly enraged, the monster opened its mouth wide, bellowing an ear-splitting screech. The terrible sounds cracked through the ice wall and layers of ice on the road.

Based on previous fights, this enemy seemed to be less cognitive than the slime creatures as well. Those creatures were wired to hunt down Human prey and bring them to Luminosa, but this thing appeared capable of only destruction. Whether that was an advantage for them or not, Minisc still wasn't sure.

Once the creature got to its feet, it locked eyes with Minisc. Strange teeth flashed as the monster let out some sort of snarl. Like an angry gorilla, it began charging him, crushing the asphalt with each step. If Minisc didn't act quick, he'd meet a similar fate.

But his body was tired — not so much from the fight but from the last few weeks of training. He'd failed to give himself adequate rest, and now that was coming back to bite him.

He raised his hands, ready to fire, but then the burning pain returned. He'd felt it before, the same pain he'd endured in his training.

From the corner of his eye he saw Jules soaring passed him like a missile. His speed was far superior to the bulky beast, and the young wind Elementalist planned to make good use of his advantages. Jules flew over the beast's head, causing it to stop and take a swing at him. But the beast missed, and Jules landed right behind him.

"Take *this*, you freak!" Jules yelled. Wind pulses, one after another, struck the beast all over its body, causing small ripples through the thick hide until he finally got a clean hit in the monster's eye, which momentarily stunned it.

But, in the end, all Jules had managed to do was make the creature even more ferocious.

The monster reached for a nearby yellow taxi, picking it up like a brick and chucking it at Jules.

The young wind Elementalist flew to his left, narrowly dodging the flying hunk of metal and hearing the heavy, crunching impact behind him. It landed on another car—if not two or three other ones, as well.

"This is ridiculous—nothing I do even phases this thing!" Jules panted breathlessly. Spinning around, the monster swiped at Jules, hitting him square in the stomach. The air shot out of his lungs as he crashed into the wall of ice next to Coro.

"Jules!" Minisc yelled.

Jules landed slumped over on his back, moaning in pain as he tried to rub his tailbone. He glanced over at Coro, who was barely up to one knee by this point.

"Why does your father have to keep making these monsters?" Jules complained.

"Trust me, I hate them as much as you do." The two tried to return to battle, but their injuries were extensive. And even if they could get up, neither were in fighting condition.

Even though Minisc appreciated his best friend helping bear some of the load, he knew that this was his time—he needed to take things further if they were to stand a chance. Waiting for back-up was no longer an option. If they couldn't find a weakness in the beast, then the only option left was to increase his power.

He took a deep breath. He could feel his heart pounding, and the fear and worry of what could befall his friends was haunting him. But a growing sense of anger was also boiling his blood, the hatred for Luminosa and their threat on everything he held dear in life continued to hang over him. It was an overwhelming river of negative emotions that fought to seep into his mind, but Minisc refused to let them take over.

He knew that outputting his full power in such a state would be counterproductive. He just needed to keep his mind relaxed.

As he tried to draw out Celestial Light to its full potential, he steadied his breathing and eased his muscles. He began to challenge the negativity flowing through him until his mind calmed down. Then, once he felt ready, he channeled his power, letting it flow through him.

All right, I can do this. Celestial Light 100%!

Minisc burst forward in a cloud of smoke. "This time, you won't get back up!"

He took a direct line for the monster's back. He'd already learned of the monster's reflexes, and knew that even just the sound of him taking off would draw attention. But at 100% power, mixed with his knowledge of his opponent's speed, he held the upper hand.

Just as predicted, the beast spun around, swinging its meaty fist horizontally. To counter this, Minisc faked going to the left before springing up in the air, getting a clean look at the monster's ribcage. He thrust his hands out as they gleamed with a power only a select few had witnessed before—let alone felt—and a beam of light exploded with a thunderous bang.

The beast attempted to make a move to protect itself, but the attack was far to ferocious. It was swallowed in the beam of light, blinding Jules and Coro.

When Minisc landed, his shoulders bobbed up and down as he fought to suck back oxygen. He glanced up at the beast through his disheveled hair as Coro and Jules rested beside him.

"Did you get him?!" Jules asked.

"*Nothing* could survive that." Coro added.

But then they heard a vicious roar. All three of them were positively stunned to see the monster still standing.

Smoke continued to rise from its body, but unlike last time, there was now visible and incredible damage. Blotches of the monster's skin had been ripped apart to reveal strange, fleshy muscle underneath. Ugly, deep-purple blood dripped from the naked spots on its chest, pooling along the ground.

"Guess this brute bleeds just like anyone else. Well then, I think it's about time to end this!" Minisc clapped his hands together and then faced his palms outward. Another ray of light blew through the monster, striking it in one of the wounded spots on its arm. It let out an ear-splitting cry, and was suddenly frozen in place.

But it wasn't the only one wincing in pain. Minisc's outstretched arms shook furiously, and the golden lines on his body were beginning to dim from an awe-inspiring gold to a dark, blackish tone. He could feel his heart pounding out of his chest, and he suddenly couldn't breathe. His throat was beginning to close and his vision was blurry. He felt so exhausted, and his mind was flying out of control, allowing fear to seep in. But through all those emotions, his arms remained locked in place. It was strange; he simply couldn't move them at all. He was frozen. Then the temperature of his body sky-rocketed as though he was about to combust.

What's going on? Did I push myself too far? No, that can't be it. This didn't happen when I fought Dominos. What's happening to me?

After the symptoms of fear took over, there was no going back. He'd lost all control of his mind, and with it, his focus.

Suddenly, the heat boiling his blood turned to a chilling cold. It's like his body was numb or paralyzed. He couldn't feel the pain anymore. He felt nothing.

The moment lasted far too long, but once his senses returned, he wished they hadn't.

Rays of light started exploding from his body in all different angles—and not just rays of light but also potent attacks. From Minisc's lips came a screeching cry of agony that could be heard for miles as the light continued shooting from his body. It was like dancing spotlights but they sliced through trees, ice, and even the cars around him.

Ignoring his own pain, Jules rose to his feet and yelled, "Minisc, what's happening?"

A beam of light tore through the wall of ice like a hot knife through butter, and, thinking quickly, Jules grabbed Coro and flew out of the way before coming to a halt.

Minisc wanted to cry out for help, but the pain surging through him was unbearable, and he couldn't muster the strength to speak. He shut his eyes, fighting the tears as the repeated stabbing ripped through his body. Through gritted teeth, he managed, "I can't hold it back! It's too much!"

The radical power flowing through Minisc was beyond anything even close to imaginable. And he *knew* that it was dangerous—not only for him but also his friends and anyone else nearby.

With all his might, Minisc fought to keep the power inside, pledging to put a cork on Celestial Light and refusing to let it open.

With a grizzled scream from Minisc, the beams of light stopped escaping his body. But for how long could he hold it? The power refused to disappear, and now it was tearing his insides apart, just waiting to explode.

After a few seconds, he couldn't hold back anymore. No matter what he did, it was trying to find a way out, and it would end up overpowering him.

He cried out and a beam of light shot into the sky, like a pillar shining down from the heavens, absorbing Minisc. More rays of light shot out, slicing through parts of the Eaton Centre and the buildings across the street. He could only pray that nobody was getting hurt, but for the moment he was just focused on his friends.

He cried out in agony, "I can't stop this! Jules, Coro, run!"

The pillar of light grew even more intense before a dark energy started to swirl around it. Soon the pillar was mixed with light and dark, stringing Minisc up in the middle.

The monster was an afterthought now — even the beast itself looked terrified at the sight of the horrific events. The rays of light had managed to stab the beast, leaving it in even worse shape than before.

In a last-ditch effort, Minisc tried to focus the rays from sporadically shooting out around him. They felt more controlled but still shot along the ground like lasers. One ray sliced right through the monster's chest, causing it to cry out in grueling pain before collapsing.

"Jules, what the hell's happening to him?" Coro asked.

"I don't know, but if we get hit by those rays, we're gonna be diced to pieces."

The two were at a loss, not sure how to stop Minisc. But then after what felt like eons, backup began to arrive.

"Coro!" a voice yelled, causing both boys to spin around.

"Olivia! Finally! We need to stop Minisc — he's out of control!" Coro shouted.

Olivia had arrived onto the scene with Juno, who said, "What's he doing up there — trying to put on a light show for the entire city?"

"We don't know, but we need to stop it!" Jules cried.

They all fixated on the sky, seeing Minisc still growling in his attempt to fight the raging strength. More beams of light escaped his body, and the four jumped out of the way to miss them.

"If those rays hit you, you're gonna end up just like that monster over there," Jules warned.

The two 8 Project members quickly glanced at the remains of the mangled creature.

"Okay, what is *that* thing?!" Juno asked in disgust.

"We can talk about it later. First, we need to stop the kid," Olivia said.

But they had no idea how to stop him, and they were still confused as to what exactly was happening. What they did know was that the constant screams escaping Minisc's mouth were agonizing.

"Look out!" Juno yelled. With lightning speed, she and Olivia both cast shields—Juno's pillars of rock stretched high into the sky, while Olivia's shadows inhaled the rays of light. An explosion of smoke erupted and turned the pillars to ruble.

"How is one kid capable of such power? I've never seen anything like it," Juno gawked.

The commotion began to draw more brave people in. Robin emerged through the parking lot, though he wasn't in his new 8 Project uniform. Adelle was next to him, alongside Lily and Mr. Howland. They all came to a sudden stop before looking up at the blinding light.

Jules rushed over to Lily, with everyone joining behind him.

"Jules, what's going on? Who's causing that?" Lily asked.

"It's Minisc, we don't know what's happening to him. But we need to do something!"

Lily gasped as a sickening pain struck her chest. It was almost impossible to tell who was inside the beam of light from their distance, but when she stared up, she could see the agony on Minisc's face as plain as day. She could also feel it in her heart.

"Mr. Howland," she said to her best friend's mentor. "What's happening to him?"

But when they all fixed their gazes on the tenured EC alum, he gave them no sign of confidence. His face was becoming pale, the gears in his brain spinning rapidly.

"It's Celestial Light," he whispered. "His power is running out of control. This is bad. If we don't stop it quick, his body won't survive."

"Well then, how do we stop this?!" Lily cried out, "We have to do something! I won't let Minisc die."

"The only way Minisc can stop this now is to get his mind under control. If he doesn't calm himself down, then there's no way he'll be able to bring Celestial Light back under control."

"But there's no way he can even hear us from here to calm him down!" Juno said.

Before anyone could say another word, Jules launched himself high into the sky. "I won't let Minisc suffer alone up there. I'm going!"

Just hold on, Minisc. This time it's my turn to save you.

Jules refused to hesitate. He knew that if the roles were reversed, Minisc would do whatever was required to save him. It was time for him to return the favour.

More rays of light sprung from Minisc's body, but Jules stayed nimble, zipping between them until he could get in close. One beam managed to clip his arm, followed by an instant and unrelenting pain. The stinger shot up his elbow as blood spewed outward. He gritted his teeth and winced but refused to turn away. He wouldn't leave Minisc all alone up there, and he was the only one around capable of reaching him.

Once he got in close, he yelled, "Minisc? Can you hear me? It's Jules!"

"Jules…I can't control this…you need to run!" Minisc cried out. Jules could see the tears in his best friend's eyes, the black streaks of light along his body. Minisc barely looked like himself.

"I'm not leaving you, Minisc!" Jules shot to his left, narrowly missing another ray of light. "Listen, you need to calm down! Mr. Howland says that it's the only way to get Celestial Light under control!"

Minisc tried to take deep breaths but his throat still felt tight, and he could feel his body giving way to the pain. The muscles in his chest were ripping apart inch by inch. Try as he did, there was just no way of stopping it. He screamed, bottling up the power yet again.

Granted an opening, Jules saw his chance. Acting quickly, he dove into the beam of light, spearing his friend in the ribs. They both went crashing down toward the parking lot.

"I'm with you, Minisc! We all are! You can control this…I know you can!" Jules wrapped his friend up tight, knowing that if Minisc let the power slip he could die at any moment, but at that time self-preservation was irrelevant. Minisc would be willing do anything for him, including lay down his life. And if that's what it took to keep his best friend alive, then he'd pay that price, too.

He and Minisc torpedoed downward. Jules did all he could to brace their fall, but when they smacked into the ground, the two separated.

Jules groaned as he tried to lift his head up, then looked over at Minisc. Unfortunately, what he saw was not a boy who was gaining control of his power, but rather one who was writhing in pain, fighting the extreme burst of strength trying to break free.

Now on the ground, Minisc was still shaking. Fear gripped him tight, but he did all he could to seal up the power inside him. If he were to allow this power to hurt his friends, he'd never forgive himself.

"Minisc!" Lily cried out. She was about to start running toward him, but then she heard him cry out in response.

"No! Stay away! This power's too dangerous!"

Sparks began flying from Minisc's body, the gleam of light continuing to waver. With each second Minisc fought the power, he could feel it beginning to bottleneck. It was an erupting volcano, and nothing would keep it from coming out. He dug deeper and absorbed the pain.

But how long could he keep this up? Each nerve in his body was ganging up to cause agony unlike any other he'd felt in his life. Not when he first strained himself training, not when facing Dusk with his father…absolutely everything he'd been through paled in comparison to this.

"He can't calm down because now he's too scared of hurting his friends," Olivia quickly deduced.

"Well, what do we do? If we leave him, he's just gonna die!" Juno argued.

"I…I don't know!" Mr. Howland sputtered.

With everyone at a loss, Lily shook her head. "I'm *not* sitting back and just watching Minisc die." She took off, ignoring any of the others' warnings.

Jules did the same. Together they grabbed Minisc, engulfing him in a tight hug.

"We're here, Minisc," Lily whispered. "We're not letting go."

"You can control this. We know you can! It's all gonna be okay."

Minisc heard his friends' words, and suddenly he took his first deep breath. He squeezed his eyes shut, wanting to yell at them to escape, but no words formed. He'd soared past his pain threshold and couldn't find his voice.

Then, just as he felt his life fading and the cork on his power ready to burst again, his body went cold. He felt numb. His limbs, the pain, the pounding of his heart…all of it came to a sudden stop. More accurately, all of it froze. It was like everything running through his body had just paused.

Is that it? Am I dead? He tried to open his eyes, but he couldn't do that, either — nor could he turn his head to look for his friends.

Then he heard Lily's scared voice whispering to him, "Please be okay, Minisc."

Minisc tried to open his mouth, but even that was frozen. Then it dawned on him: This was no longer an effect of Celestial Light.

He was gasping for air, taking in the deepest breaths he could and feeling the chilled air filling his lungs. His muscles were still spasming and he lacked strength to push himself up, but the heat burning up his core had disappeared. His unrelenting power evaporated as he returned to his base form.

CHAPTER 13
A HEAVY BURDEN

THERE WAS MUCH TO DISCUSS AFTER THE INCIDENT at the Eaton Centre. First was the sudden appearance of that strange monster. The damage it caused could be dealt with by the city, but those witnessing its incredible power knew that its strength was the real threat. It was the cause of so much initial damage. Not only that, but it was impervious to almost every attack they could muster.

Unfortunately, after Minisc's explosive rampage, there was little left of the monster's remains, other than a pile of mangled limbs and pools of blood.

Even so, the creature's leftovers were handed over to the EC by Olivia and Juno. They had a number of questions about the monster, but most importantly, they wanted to know who was in control of the beast.

The group later learned that the cloaked figure Olivia had attempted to chase had managed to escape. Though apprehending the suspect would've been valuable, nobody could question her after understanding her reasons for abandoning the pursuit.

With more time to think about how events had played out, there was good reason to believe the hooded figure was simply a red herring to pull Olivia away while the monster wreaked havoc. At least that was the theory that Olivia chose to go with. Unfortunately, whoever was in charge hadn't planned on Minisc or Jules showing up.

Luckily, injuries were limited, as most bystanders had managed to take shelter in the Eaton Centre. Others succeeded in evacuating far enough away to avoid major catastrophe.

Everyone could take solace knowing that, but just because the injuries were limited didn't keep word from spreading about the incident. Gossip of an indescribable monster, strong enough to throw cars like bricks, ran rampant and struck fear into the city's hearts and minds.

Then there was Minisc. His display of power, or what most would call destruction, was making headlines. People could see the light show for miles, and there was no shortage of viral videos circulating around the internet.

He hated public attention on the best of days, but this time there was no avoiding it. People were connecting dots together and realizing who his father was, and they were ready to jump all over the story.

Of course, for those who'd witnessed the horrific event in person, they could care less about any of that. They were just relieved that Minisc survived.

Minisc sat up in his hospital bed leaning back against the pillow. He looked rather sick, heavy bags under his eyes and small black markings on his scars.

Enough time passed over the following few days that his mind finally managed to settle down, and he could breathe again without feeling like he would choke. The fog enveloping his thoughts took a little longer to dissipate, but it was beginning to gradually lift. Although his body still sporadically spasmed and his muscles were barely able to move, the pains were mostly few and far between.

He gingerly leaned his head back on the baseboard of the hospital bed, looking up at the stark lights. He was growing tired of staring at the same four white walls that surrounded him, but for the first time in his life, he was actually glad to be in a hospital.

There was no getting around the fears now planted in his mind. Comfort came from having medical personnel around, knowing that they could help him. Each day he managed to avoid those fear-inducing triggers was a win. Even so, he was scared. After all, how could he not be?

Everything felt like a bad dream, and if not for the lingering effects still manifesting, he might not have believed that such events were even capable of happening. Not that it mattered; even if he wanted to deny the truth, there was far too much evidence online.

With great caution, Minisc slowly reached for the table on his left, picked up his cell phone, and returned to his resting position.

His mind said not to, but his hands were working independently. His first instinct was to pull up one of the many viral videos of the extreme incident. He knew the feelings that would emerge with watching and thus reliving the nightmare, but he couldn't stop himself. The pit of nausea returned as he fixated on the beams of light ripping through the roads. Seeing Jules' terrified face as he dove into the pillar of light, the anxious tightness in his chest started to return but he tried to force his way through.

The videos served as an out of body experience, but there was one thing that continued to perplex him. Each video was no longer than a minute or two. Even the longest one he found, which showed the incident from start to finish, barely reached four minutes. But for him, floating in that spiraling pillar of death felt like an eternity.

The video ended when Jules smacked him out of the air and a flash of light blinded everyone.

He let out a sigh, falling back into his bed and weakly tossing the phone to his side. He didn't dare scroll thought the comment section of the video; the vitriol heading his way wouldn't be worth the time. And besides, Lily had already warned him that doing so would only make him angry, an expression he could see on her face.

Minisc understood why, though. They were scared of him. They were scared of someone who could display such destructive strength in a flash, and they had every right to be. After all, none of them were more scared than him.

He pulled the covers up to his neck and squirmed to find a comfortable position, but there was still so much running through his mind. Aside from the scare he'd caused his friends and family, the damage caused, and even the fear placed in the public, he'd failed to control Celestial Light.

All the work, all the time spent pushing himself past his limits, all the days of neglecting his friends...all in the hopes of bringing down Brooklyn and Luminosa. What was it all worth in the end? Was he just lying to himself when he demanded to learn Celestial Light, believing that he could follow in his father's footsteps, a task he never wanted to do in the first place?

Instead, all that came from his bravado was the near-death of his friends, not to mention himself, and the extensive damage to his city. He'd also caused more people to fear him rather than see him as a protector. There was nothing good coming out of his quest to master Celestial Light. Only destruction.

He understood that this was the path to defeating Luminosa, to stopping Brooklyn once and for all. If Brooklyn could find a way to master the same level of power as the EC feared, there'd be no stopping him. The endless bounds of destruction would wipe out the planet.

Minisc gripped the blankets tight and rolled over to his side, and through the window he could see heaps of snow. The skies were gloomy with far-reaching grey clouds, absolutely covering the city. He released his grip, taking a deep breath. If he'd learned anything, it was to not think himself into submission. It would lead him down the same path that caused so much damage in the first place.

He sighed and closed his eyes.

From down the hall, he heard faint pitter-pattering footsteps that made small squashing noises. Then he heard a knock on the door.

Minisc forced himself to sit up and then turned his attention to the door, undecided if he wanted to respond. But then he heard the handle twist and creak open.

Robin poked his head into the room, taking a glance around before saying, "Minisc, are you here?"

"Robin?" Minisc called out. He tried to sit up further, but a burn in his abdomen stopped him from getting very far. Still, he finally saw the friendly face of Robin—a welcomed sight for sure.

Robin popped his head fully into the room and the two boys locked eyes. "Is it okay if I come in?" His hand was shaking and his eyes were filled with worry, the total opposite of who Minisc knew him to be.

"Of course," Minisc responded, doing what he could to gesture to the nearby chair.

Robin slipped in through the door, partially closing it behind him. He took a seat in one of the visiting chairs beside Minisc.

"So...how're you doing? Those were some pretty intense moments while you were floating up in that pillar."

"I've seen better days, I suppose. But I'm getting better, I guess." Even Minisc's voice sounded defeated.

"Any clue what happened?"

Minisc paused, trying to think of how to explain it. He didn't really know himself, and he definitely lacked the energy to go into detail about Celestial Light…or whatever it was supposed to be.

He shook his head and said, "I wish I knew. All I remember is that Jules and I were fighting this monster, and then the next thing I knew, everything went black. I lost control of my element, and suddenly my power was just shooting out of me. I've never experienced anything like that in my life. And I really hope that I never experience it again."

"For real? That's crazy! But I'm glad you're all right. I've never seen anything like it, either. Mr. Howland and I were just walking down the street to meet with Lily and Adelle, but when we all met, the commotion started up. When that ray of light ripped into the sky, I've never seen Mr. Howland so scared."

The room fell silent for a moment, but then Robin caught Minisc by surprise. "This was related to Celestial Light, wasn't it?"

Minisc looked wide-eyed, not sure how to respond. Regaining his speech, he said, "Yeah, I think so. But how did you know that?"

"I overheard Mr. Howland say it while you were up there. But I had no idea that you were the one he chose to teach the technique to. When he mentioned it, I thought back to when you'd fought Dominos. That power you displayed…I'd never seen anything like it since the Hero of Light, and so I had a feeling that something was up."

"Sorry for not telling you." Minisc hung his head. "Mr. Howland mentioned that you'd struggled to learn it, and I didn't know if it was a sore spot for you or not, so I decided not to bring it up."

Robin laughed to lighten the mood, "No need to be sorry. Yeah, I didn't quite manage to get a grasp on the power, but that's all right. I'll just keep improving and eventually I'll surpass what Celestial Light could even do for me."

Minisc laughed faintly, refusing to rain on his friend's parade.

Robin continued, "Anyways, I actually just dropped by to see how you were doing, and to let you know that Mr. Howland wants to speak with you. Assuming you're up to it, at least."

"Oh, okay — yeah, I can manage that. And thanks for dropping by. I really appreciate it."

"Of course. That's what friends do."

Minisc waved goodbye to his friend, but once alone, he swallowed hard. He'd known that the conversation around the corner was inevitable. In one respect, he was surprised that Mr. Howland hadn't talked to him sooner. The same went for his father, too. Though both had been keeping careful watch over him — his father was around during most parts of the day — it seemed that they were granting him a few days to process everything that had happened. Good thing, because the extra time allowed Minisc to repeatedly run through the upcoming conversation in his head.

There were so many fears racing through his mind, about what happened and about the future. What did Mr. Howland think of the whole situation? Would he return to his belief that Minisc was too young and not mature enough to master Celestial Light? And, more importantly, would that even be in his best interest? He knew the consequences of abandoning ship, but what was the point if he died long before he used the power for its purpose?

Minisc continued staring at the door, anticipating Mr. Howland's arrival, but his mentor was sure taking his time. After a couple more agonizingly stressful minutes, he finally heard another knock at the door — the knock that would decide his fate.

Mr. Howland walked in. He was stoic on the best of days, but this time he had a somber frown, much like when Minisc had defeated Dominos.

Mr. Howland took off his jacket and sat down without saying a word. He locked eyes with Minisc, opened his mouth, and then shut it again. He glanced down, leaving Minisc feeling scared. A melancholy silence filled the room.

When Minisc looked at his mentor, his anxiety was replaced with shock. Mr. Howland looked worse than he did. The wrinkles in his cheeks were more pronounced, his eyes were red and bloodshot, and his usually well-trimmed beard was disheveled.

After the thick tension lingered a bit longer, Mr. Howland broke his silence.

"Minisc…does the name Chloe Hart ring any bells to you?"

Minisc furrowed his brow. "Chloe Hart…no, not that I know of? Should it?"

Mr. Howland shook his head. "No, I expected as much. It's not a name that's brought up lightly—certainly not by myself nor your father. But after what happened a few days ago, I think it might be beneficial for you to know."

The sinking pit in Minisc's stomach began to grow deeper.

"You see, before your father managed to master Celestial Light, there was another."

"Chloe?"

"Yes, she was part of my research team, and a talented Elementalist in her own right. In fact, at the time she was a bit of an idol to the Elementalists community, just like your father eventually turned into. She was also the first person to learn Celestial Light, or, as she liked to call it, Celestial Fire, because she was a fire Elementalist."

"Wait…but I thought that my father and Dusk were the only two who'd managed to learn Celestial Light?"

"That is not entirely accurate," Mr. Howland confessed. "Your father and Dusk were the only two able to master the power and make it their own. However, neither of them was the first to attempt the feat. As Dusk was only beginning his conquest, and I had yet to meet your father, Chloe was one of many who hoped to bring down Dusk. With her talent and skill, I believed that combining my technique with her powers would take her to new heights. She would be strong enough to defeat Dusk. It was a noble intention."

Minisc looked at his mentor, feeling his throat tighten. He softly asked, "What happened to her?"

"She was so determined to learn the power, but she was young and still growing. If I recall, she was only about a year older than you when she started, and although she was quite mature, she was also extremely stubborn. She refused to let anything stop her, including when she was feeling pain or overwhelmed. She always placed the burdens of the world on herself rather than let anyone else risk themselves in an effort to help."

Mr. Howland's voice became low as he continued.

"Unfortunately, at the time I was preoccupied with so much that I failed to notice just how hard she was pushing herself. One day, a small group of Luminosa sympathizers attempted an attack on our research facility. Chloe tried to stop them, but after she won, her power suddenly exploded. Flames were shooting out of her body in all directions, and she could no longer control her element. I remember watching in horror as such a magnificent power consumed her until there was nothing left. The power destroyed her body from the inside, and it ultimately killed her."

Mr. Howland hung his head, trying to keep his composure in check. It was evident why he'd never mentioned Chloe before.

"Once I saw what the destructive power my technique could cause within someone, I vowed to never teach it to anyone again. I never wanted anyone to die because of such an overwhelming state."

"Is that what happened to me?" Minisc asked.

"From what I could tell, it would appear so. When your power began to spiral out of control, do you remember how you felt? Or what was going through your head throughout the day?"

"Pretty clearly actually. Jules and I went to the Eaton Centre so that I could buy Lily a Christmas present, but we weren't having any luck. Then out of the blue, that giant monster showed up. We tried to hold our own, but Coro and Jules were injured, and when I used Celestial Light at 15%, I couldn't even put a dent into it. That's when I got scared. I was worried that we couldn't win and that that thing was going to kill us all."

Minisc dropped his head, recalling the vivid scene like he was watching it live. Perhaps the videos he'd just watched had helped jog his memory and fill in some blanks.

"I guess I panicked. I thought the only way to protect everyone was to use Celestial Light the same way I did against Dominos. But…when I fought Dominos, I had no fear. I didn't have time for fear—my body just reacted like it was possessed. This time, as soon as I used my element, I felt weird. Like I did back in my class training, but obviously this time it got way worse. I've never felt that sort of pain in my life."

Mr. Howland agreed. "I see. I believe that makes sense. Such a scenario is why I continued to preach the need for a calm and relaxed mind. When your brain became overwhelmed with negative fears, your body reacted in the only way it can. It was exactly what happened to Chloe. But, lucky for you, you have friends that refused to run even at the risk of their own lives. I don't quite know how they did it, but when they ran in to comfort you, it managed to quell your fears just long enough for you to gain control."

"Believe me, I know how lucky I am." It warmed Minisc to no end when he thought about his friend's actions, about the risks they took.

Silence filled the room once again. Mr. Howland took a deep

breath, composing himself before saying, "Minisc, allow me to ask you a question."

"Of course, Sir."

"After everything you have heard, and all that you have experienced…" he fell silent for a few more seconds, increasing the feeling of discomfort. "Do you still wish to learn Celestial Light?"

They could've heard a pin drop. It was a question Minisc had spent so long pondering himself, and yet he'd always failed to decide. Part of him wished that Mr. Howland would just make the decision for him — to say outright that they were to go no further, but instead he posed it as a choice for Minisc. After all, it was a choice that only he could make.

"I…I don't know," he said, barely above a whisper. "Honestly, I don't know what I should do anymore."

"I understand, perhaps it is still a bit premature to be asking such questions. I would advise you to take your time, talk with your father, and talk with your friends. I believe they know you best and will have your best interests in mind."

Minisc sighed with a nod. Those conversations could prove even tougher, but he knew that there was no avoiding the inevitable. "All right, I'll do that. Thank you, Sir."

***

With the afternoon sun winding down, Minisc once again passed out; most of his time in recovery had been spent sleeping. While Mr. Howland, far from resting, had one more person he wished to speak with.

He walked outside, his beard warming his face against the crisp air. He headed around to the back of the hospital, where his surroundings were silent. There he saw the Hero of Light, his former pupil. The bulky Hero sat on a bench hunched over, deep in thought. He wasn't wearing a jacket, but the cold had no ill effect on him.

Such a sight was yet another reminder of the times they were living in. There was no moment in recent memory in which the Hero of Light could sit on a bench in public without hordes of fans around. But now he was alone.

"Mind if I sit down?" Mr. Howland asked as he stood over Don. The former hero glanced up, and the sulking despair on his face was washed away in an instant. The demeanor of a man always showing his bravery returned like a reflex.

"Of course."

Mr. Howland did so, staring off into the parking lot of the hospital. Cars continued to pull in and out as people walked through the doors, some in distress, some rather casually.

"You know…you're not fooling me."

"Excuse me?" Don asked.

"That look of bravery. The same look you've worn every time you charged into battle, trying to bring hope to this city. I know you used it to place fear in your opponents, but I am no enemy."

Don's facade dropped as he slouched over again. "I guess you can see right through it, huh?"

"After what happened, no brave face could ever hide such fear. I felt it, too."

"It's just…" Don sounded broken as he spoke. "I knew that retirement would be difficult. Being the Hero of Light was so much of my life. But leaving Minisc to face such danger… knowing as he cried out for help that I was powerless to do anything for him…I've never felt so useless. That was my son, and not only did I place him in harm's way by introducing him to Celestial Light, but when it nearly killed him, I didn't even have the power to stop it." Don gripped his fists tightly, almost on the verge of tears. The vision of Minisc absorbed by that light was seared into his mind. He'd watched the videos on repeat more than anyone, wishing that he'd been there. "What use am I if I can't even protect my own son?"

"I understand. I felt much the same way. But don't allow yourself to be fooled. Such weakness doesn't mean that you are of no use to him. I don't need to tell you this, but you and Erika brought an incredible child into this world. Minisc has all of the tenacity and determination that allowed you to be the Hero of Light, but I can also see the love and compassion that Erika always displayed. Everything he has accomplished up to this point is a testament to your importance in his life. Even with retirement, that hasn't changed. And it never will."

Don raised his head and stared into the beyond. "I do know that. I've known it since the day he was born. He's everything I could've ever asked for in a son."

Don paused and took a deep breath, peeling back some emotions.

"And I know that I can't continue to protect him from the threats this world has to offer. That time was always going to come, and all I wanted was to prepare him so that he could face the world as best he could…but Luminosa and Celestial Light… putting all this on his shoulders…I never wanted that to be the case. He's still a child. No child deserves that burden."

"You're right—to have someone so young placed in such an unfair position, it's an unfortunate burden to carry. And Minisc knows that."

"I just don't know what to do. I can't risk losing my son, but I feel so powerless."

Mr. Howland held his hand out, a few sparks dancing off his fingertips. "These elements, this powerful phenomenon that has created the existence we know today, is both a blessing and a curse. No matter how hard we fight, there will always be those who seek to do harm. Such is an inevitable fate. But as long as we have something to fight for in this world, we can't give up."

Don's head rose as he locked eyes with his former teacher.

"A young irritating pupil of mine once told me those words after I refused to help him. I struggled to understand it at the time, but I think that after all these years, I finally get it now. Us, Minisc, everyone he cares about…I have no doubt they are still worth fighting for."

"I'm not sure I understand."

"Though you might feel that you have pushed Minisc down this path, I believe the truth not to be so simple. Remember what he talked about that day in my office? He has something to fight for, just the way you did. Just the way Chloe did. The difference is that neither Chloe nor you had the support that Minisc does. He has friends everywhere, and a father that loves him — things that many of us didn't grow up with. He made those choices because he wanted to protect everything he cherished in this world. Perhaps you can no longer protect him through pure strength, but he still needs you. He needs your encouragement, your love, and your support. Right now, he needs you to be his father more than ever."

Don exhaled, staring at his breath passing through the chilly air. He mulled the words of his mentor over, absorbing them into his mind. "I've always wondered…after the tragedy that happened to Chloe, you were adamant that Celestial Light was not something that anyone in this world should ever learn…so then why did you finally decide to teach me?"

Mr. Howland stroked his beard. "That is a question I have pondered myself on more than one occasion. But I'm afraid I don't have much of an answer. Perhaps it was a matter of desperation. Or maybe I could see the direction the world was heading, and knew that we could not continue down that path. But I guess, most of all, I came to believe that if there was one single person on this earth that could stay true to their convictions, it was you. And you did. I tried so hard to make you quit, not because I wanted you to fail but so you could avoid the same fate as Chloe. But then you did it anyways, and the world owes you a great debt for doing so."

"So what do I do? I can't ask Minisc to quit…but telling him to continue could be placing him back on a path that neither of us are ready for."

Mr. Howland stood up and turned to face his pupil. "You're right. In the end it must be his decision, but you are still his father. Talk to him. I'm sure that's what he wants as well."

CHAPTER 14
AT WHAT RISK

THE SHORT STAY IN THE HOSPITAL CAME TO AN END, and Minisc was finally released. And not a moment too soon—he could only take so many days away from his own bed and the comfort of his own home. Plus, he really didn't want to ruin Lily's Christmas plans by being forced to stay in the hospital.

Much like after his battle with Dusk, he'd still require routine check-ins to ensure that his body was healing properly, but there wasn't much they could do for him. Outside of lingering aggravation in his muscles, his heart rate was fine and his breathing had returned to a steady pace which was what they were most concerned about. But the scars on his body would likely never fade.

By the time he returned home with his father, the night was pitch black but the moon shone bright and the skies were calm.

Normally in such conditions, Minisc would linger on the front porch of his old home, letting his thoughts loose into the air as he watched the moon. However, with his new home lacking the same view from their porch, he was forced to make do elsewhere. Luckily, he had just the spot.

Minisc headed to his room and cracked the window open. A fresh frosty air hit his face, giving him a jolt, but it was just what he needed to stay awake. He dragged a blanket off his bed and draped it around him as he crawled onto the roof. He laid down its slant, overlooking the ever-growing forest in his backyard. He stared at the full moon, admiring the untouched snow on the ground and watching the beauty of the horizon. He hoped to let all his worries wash away.

When in doubt, he often turned to his late mother, visiting her grave and spilling his heart to her. Even long after the grave site had been destroyed, he still returned to his old coping tactics.

Jules, Lily, and his father were all in the living room, each one wanting to talk to him, but he needed a few minutes alone first.

He looked to the sky and said, "Mom, are you there? I really need to talk to you."

He wasn't expecting an answer, but that wasn't the point. He just needed to speak freely.

"I feel so lost, mom. I don't know what to do anymore. Ever since Father retired, I've been giving it my all to pick up where he left off. I've been working day and night to learn Celestial Light the way he did, all so that I can finally bring an end to Luminosa. So that I can help create the world you always envisioned."

Minisc sighed, sitting up and curling his knees to his chest.

"I know it's the only way forward. Even with everything the EC is doing, in the end none of it will stop Brooklyn if he can use such power the way I need to. But this strength...it scares me. The damage I could cause without even trying...it almost killed my friends and it almost killed me."

Minisc swallowed hard, burying his head. Though he was speaking alone and had nothing to be nervous about, the words were having a hard time coming out.

"I...I want to quit. I really do. I never wanted any of this. I never wanted to be like Father. I don't want to fight for my life all the time. I don't want to be the one tasked to learn Celestial Light. Why did it have to be *me*…the one they think can do this? Why does everyone always think *I'm* the one who can pull this stuff off? Just because of who Father is? And what if they're wrong? What if I was always meant to be just a normal kid?"

"Is that what you want?"

Minisc nearly jumped out of his skin, turning to stare back at his window. He saw his father standing with his arms crossed, staring not at Minisc but out at the view.

"How long have you been listening?"

"For pretty much all of it. I just came up to check on you, but I didn't want to interrupt. Mind if I join?"

Minisc nodded and scooted over as his father's large frame crawled out the window and took a seat beside him.

"So—you never answered my question. Is that what you want for your life? To just be a normal kid?"

The soft howls of the wind swirled through the air as Minisc slumped backward. "I didn't mean it like that. It's not that I don't appreciate my life or everything I've been blessed with. But sometimes it's hard. The last few months since you retired, I've spent every waking minute either in school or training to learn Celestial Light. I guess over time it's just worn me down. I never see Lily or Jules, and I'm always scared that I could wake up on any given day and learn that Luminosa has struck. That they're coming after me. I know that's why The 8 Project was created, and I'm sure that they believe in their abilities…but if what you and Mr. Howland fear most is true, then they'd never stand a chance against Brooklyn. The only way is Celestial Light. But the toll it's taking…I mean, I just never realized the destructive power that came with it. If I don't have full control of Celestial Light, I could end up destroying everything I want to protect. It all feels like too much for me to handle."

Minisc wrapped his legs into his chest tighter. A sad frown formed on his face, and he hung his head so he that could hide his tearful eyes.

Don reached for his son and wrapped his arm around him, pulling him close. He rubbed Minisc's back, just as he would when he was anxious as a child. "I get it, Minisc. I really do. You're right—it *is* scary. The uncertainty, the future, the danger—all of it's scary. When Mr. Howland told me what happened…when I saw the videos of you up in that pillar of light… knowing that there was nothing as your father that I could do to help…hearing you cry out in constant agony while I was powerless…I've never felt so useless in my life. It made me question every decision I made that led to that point. I wondered if asking you to learn Celestial Light was wrong of me, passing my failure to finish Luminosa onto your shoulders. Could it be that I was sending my only son to his death? I felt like a failure, both as a hero and as a parent."

Minisc finally raised his head, his hair disheveled and his eyes downtrodden with black bags. "Why did you do it, Father? Mr. Howland told me about Chloe Hart…about how she died from using Celestial Light, the way I almost did. Back in Mr. Howland's office when I demanded to keep learning Celestial Light, you said that you learned it because you had so much worth fighting for. But it has to be more than that, no? You knew at any moment that with one slip up you could die before you even made it to Dusk. How could you possibly not have that seep into your mind?"

Don rubbed his son's shoulder and looked out to the horizon, carefully considering his response. For him, recalling those times was not the easiest. Celestial Light had always just been an extension of his being. Rarely, if ever, did he worry about meeting the same fate as the woman before him.

"Perhaps I had one advantage over you. I was far too confident for my own good. At the time, I could never envision that what happened to Chloe could happen to me, because how could it? I was far too strong, and I believed that I was destined to defeat Dusk. There was no room for failure. Back then, I was so focused on where I saw the world heading. The streets were getting worse every day. People were dying, people I cared about. Sure, there were times when I was scared. I had that little voice in the back of my head trying to question my will the same as anyone would."

"And when that happened…what did you do? How did you get those thoughts out of your head?"

"Well, it wasn't done alone, I can tell you that. As was always the case, your mother kept finding ways to push me forward when I needed it most. She refused to let the world remain as it was, plunging into darkness. She wasn't physically strong, but she would never concede. We both knew the risks, and there were many times when she was terrified that I wouldn't come back alive, just the same way I worry about you every single day. But no matter how worried she was, she always said, "I believe in you. And no matter what happens today, I will always believe in you." She never lost her faith in me, or the people in this world. And in a way, that allowed me to keep the faith in myself."

Don took his arm off his son and met him eye to eye.

"I would be lying if I said I didn't have much of the same fears you carry now. After seeing what took place at the Eaton Centre, knowing the pain you endured, all for the sake of others…if it were up to me alone, I would no longer have you learn Celestial Light. I would rather do all I can to keep you safe from the dangers of this world. I think that most parents would feel the same way for their child. And perhaps I'm at fault for starting you down this path. It's been so long since I actually learned Celestial Light that I forgot the tolls it took, both mentally and physically. Losing your element is one thing; life might be different, but as Yuri has shown, you can still go on. But to almost *die* from it? As your father, I can't continue pushing you down a path that places you in such peril, fate of the world or not. That being said, also as your father, I know that you're growing up. The future of this world is yours to decide, not mine. So it's also not my place to stop you. All I will do is support you in the best way I can with whatever choices you decide in life."

Minisc sat intently, listing to his father's words and thinking in silence. His mind flooded with so many different emotions.

"I just don't know…what if we're wrong? What if this isn't something I'm capable of doing? I mean, I'm not you. I don't have that unwavering confidence. What if I only end up hurting myself or the people I love instead of what I need it to do? I almost killed Jules because of Celestial Light. All this was supposed to inspire hope in people, to bring peace of mind to Humans and Elementalists by defeating Luminosa. But none of that is what's happening. I've seen the comments on the news and on all the viral videos, and people are more scared of me than they are of Luminosa. They think *I'm* the monster." He sighed in defeat.

Through the silence, another voice spoke — but this one with much less gloom and doom.

"Come on, Minisc. Since when have you ever cared about what the public thinks about you?"

Minisc and Don both glanced at the window, where they saw Jules and Lily poking their heads out. Don moved over, knowing that he'd said what he needed to, and now it was time for the others who loved him to do the same.

They both wrapped him up in a big hug, filling him with their warmth and love.

"When have I ever cared about what people think of me? Uh, a lot, actually. My entire life, in fact," Minisc quipped sarcastically.

Lily sighed. "What I think Jules is trying to say is that it's not that big of a deal if people are scared of you — because they don't know the real you. They don't know all the great things you've done. One moment in time doesn't paint the full picture, and so they have no right to judge you."

Minisc turned back to face Jules. He fixated on the long white bandage that rolled up his friend's arm; there were still a few red blotches seeping through. He also had a number of small cuts on his face to go along with the injuries Minisc knew couldn't be seen on the surface.

"Even if it were that simple, think about how dangerous all this is. I could've killed you, Jules. I almost *did* kill you!"

"So?" Jules said without hesitation. "The point is that you *didn't* kill me. And I think that was because you knew, deep down, that even when you felt like you'd lost all control, you were still willing yourself to fight it. You refused to let it hurt me, or anyone else for that matter. That couldn't have just been luck."

"Jules…"

"And besides, how many times have you come to our rescue even when it could've cost you your own life? So it doesn't matter what happens, whether it be your power going out of control or Luminosa coming after us or whatever else the future throws our way. I'm still your best friend, and I'll never turn my back on you. No matter what happens."

Lily agreed. "Jules is right. We'll always have your back. And we know that if the situations were reversed, you'd give up everything to help us, because that's who you are. You're not some threat to society, and you're most certainly not a threat to us."

Lily squeezed Minisc tight until he stopped shaking.

"I know that learning Celestial Light is your burden, and I don't like it any more than you do. I've never been so scared of losing you in my life…but like we've always told you, this isn't on you alone. So when you're ready to break down and you want to quit, or you get scared and fear the worst happening, we'll always be here to pick you back up. We believe in you. I believe in you. And I always will."

"And together we'll show Luminosa that they picked a fight with the wrong people!" Jules chimed in.

Lily and Jules wrapped their arms around Minisc and squished him in the middle. Their words of encouragement were exactly what he needed at the time. His trepidations hadn't left his mind; it was still too soon after the incident for him to feel any kind of certainty. But hearing his friends and family refuse to give up on him brought a definite ray of hope.

***

A few hours later, Minisc was laying in his bed, groaning and rolling over while met with the glaring red lights of his clock. It was 1 a.m., but his insomnia remained strong. He sat up, staring into the black void of his room, his eyes struggling to adjust. He stretched his arm out and opened his palm. As he did, he could feel his heart thumping, but he took a deep breath and whispered, "It's just my element. I'm fine." Small flickers of light danced off his fingers like sparks in the night, and he sighed a breath of relief. He still had Celestial Light bottled up.

He shut his hand and tried to settle back into bed, but there was little chance of that happening. His mind continued to race, but this time it wasn't replaying the events from the Eaton Centre, or at least not entirely. Now he had much more to consider. The words of his father, his friends, and even Mr. Howland.

There'd been zero doubt in their words. When they said they believed in him and that they'd always have his back, they meant it. Even sitting now in the darkness alone, those sentiments brought him a great sense of comfort.

But that also made things more difficult. He was terrified by the thought of burdening them, hurting them, or losing them.

Out of habit, he grabbed his phone off the nightstand, clicking it on. The first thing he saw on his wallpaper was a picture of himself with Lily and Jules, the three of them, arms around each other and smiling. Such simpler times.

There were hundreds and hundreds of photos on his phone, but most of them were some kind of variation of the three of them together.

Minisc wasn't big on taking pictures himself, but Lily always had a camera ready and sent them all to him. At the time, he never paid much attention to it, choosing to focus more on the moment than commemorating them with pictures, but as he sat up in bed scrolling through the endless happy times and recalling all his most vivid memories of their days together, it made him happy. Days at theme parks, afternoons at the beach (even if Minisc hated the water), and so many times in school together having lunch, training, and studying. Those were the days he loved most. It took his worries away, just spending time with those who supported him best.

They all wanted to bring an end to Luminosa, there was no question about that. But no matter how hard he tried, the same thought continually popped into his head. Why did it have to fall on him to learn Celestial Light? Why could it not have been someone else gifted with the ability? Jules or Lily were far more mentally equipped to handle these things than him. Even Robin, the perfect embodiment of the Hero of Light himself. All of them were better choices.

But in that moment, his thinking changed. Seeing the joy of his friends, then remembering the fears of losing them, he wondered: What if the roles were indeed reversed?

He pictured Jules, Lily, or even Robin or Adelle being swallowed up by a beam of light. Their screams rang in his ears, sounding real enough to shake him. It made his heart pump in ways that Celestial Light never could.

When such a scenario played out in his mind, he felt different about his burden. Though he hated to admit it, he'd much rather be the one in that position than having to watch his friends suffer the way he did. Or even that sort of responsibility—he'd much rather have that put onto his shoulders than have his friends forced into it.

Each picture he swept through reminded him of what he wanted to protect, not just the memories but also the future.

Finally, he came to one last picture on his phone—of him and Lily when they went to visit the cherry blossoms over the past summer. A few hours after that picture was taken, he was ambushed by Ignis. He was sure that he was going to die that night as well, but Lily saved him, managing to get him the help he needed. Such a blissful day, marred in despair. But if he were to have more days like that with Lily, more memories with Jules, more opportunities to learn from Robin, he knew that the path forward would be tough. Still, it would be worth it. He had to believe that, because his friends did. Mr. Howland and Robin did. And his father did.

He held his hand out over his sheets and formed a small ball of light, acting like a night light. He stared at it while it shone brightly. Then, with a little more concentration, it grew a bit bigger and sparks started to circulate around it. Celestial Light at 1%. Even that sort of power was more potent than what most could ever hope to achieve.

Snapping his hand shut, he closed his eyes and slipped under the blankets again.

***

The next day, Minisc walked into Mr. Howland's office, closing the door behind him. No knocking, no announcement, and no warning to his mentor. His arms and face were still wrapped in bandages, his hair a disheveled mess.

Mr. Howland glanced up from his paperwork, noticing Minisc. It wasn't often that someone walked in on him without consent, but for Minisc he allowed it.

Without a word, Minisc took a seat on the couch where Mr. Howland often liked to talk. "I need to apologize," he said in a low whisper.

Mr. Howland dropped his pencil and examined Minisc's pained expression. "I take it you have made your decision then?"

"Yes I have, but that's not what I want to apologize about," Minisc said, hanging his head. "I lied to you. I told you I was fine with handling all the training we were doing every day. But I wasn't. I was exhausted, I was stressed, and most of all, I was missing my friends. And maybe, in a way, that was taking more of a toll on me than I realized."

Minisc glanced down at his hands, folding them up into his lap. He refused to look at his mentor as he spoke.

"It's just…I wanted to learn Celestial Light so badly. The sooner I was capable of that, the better my chances were of ending Luminosa once and for all, so that I could keep everyone I love safe. But in doing so, I was sacrificing myself. While I thought I was getting closer to my goal, I was actually causing myself to grow further away from it. Then even after you warned me not to go over my limits again, I ignored it. I ignored it because it worked against Dominos, and though I knew it could be dangerous, I thought it would work again. I just wanted to save my friends." Minisc took a long pause. "I want to learn Celestial Light, I really do. But I know that it starts with knowing my limits."

Mr. Howland left his desk and took a seat across from Minisc. "You know something, Minisc? I knew you were mature, but even now, you still continue to surprise me. It takes a lot to admit when you messed up, especially with all the pressure that's been placed upon your shoulders. That said, you alone are not to blame for your current state. I bear some responsibility in this as well."

Finally, Minisc took his eyes off his feet. "What do you mean?"

"You may have believed yourself to be deceiving me, but I was not oblivious to the toll that my training was taking on you. Yet I remained quiet and chose to see how you progressed, because that's what I did with your father. That was my mistake. The second I realized your well-being was degrading, I should have stepped in and slowed you down. I figured the way I dealt with your father would work the same for you, but that is simply not the case. He was such a natural, and his mind and body were always in peak condition. I never saw him grow tired. He loved to train; he could do it at all hours of the day. In some respects, after seeing what you did to save Robin and then your desire to keep learning Celestial Light when I suggested we stop, I attributed those same qualities to you."

"Yeah, that happens a lot, actually," Minisc sighed.

"But you are *not* him. You have shown that in many ways as well. And I do not mean that in a negative light. You have the heart of your mother, and that is a blessing in and of itself. But that means that you require different training. You are a young teen who requires breaks. You need to spend time with your friends, and be able to relax to be at your best. With that in mind, I shall ask you again: Do you wish to keep learning Celestial Light?"

The moment of truth was here. Minisc swallowed hard, knowing that this choice would dictate so much of his future.

"I've given it a lot of thought and even talked to my father, Lily, and Jules, and they still believe in me, even after putting their lives in danger along with my own. But I want to hear from you first. I've already made my decision, but I want to know what you think. And please, be honest. Are you scared?"

Mr. Howland's hardened face cracked slightly, and his voice became a little lower and softer. "Yes, Minisc. I admit that I have trepidations, and I always have. The same as you. I don't wish for you to get hurt, but that being said, the monster you fought I fear is only the beginning, and we saw the destructive capabilities something like that possesses. It is my belief that we are reaching a crucial point in history. I can see it upon the horizon. And I worry that it can go one of two ways, but at this moment I cannot be sure of the outcome. One thing I am sure of, and you know it as well, is that you Minisc — you will not be able to hide from Luminosa. Regardless of whether you learn Celestial Light, they will come for you. You said it yourself. So to answer your question more directly, yes — I'm just as scared as you are. But as much as I struggle with it, I do feel that this is the best path forward, both for you and for society."

Minisc nodded. "Thank you for that. I know this won't get easier, but I do want to continue learning Celestial Light. I want to follow this path and see where it leads me. I want to believe in myself the way everyone else does."

"I see. Well, then — if this is the path you have chosen, I shall continue to support it as best I can. That said, I believe that some ground rules must be established for your benefit this time around. Working on Celestial Light is paramount, yes — but not at the risk of your health. First and foremost, you are not to use Celestial Light at 100% until we are both fully confident that you are safe to do so. None of this will matter if you lose control the way you did at the Eaton Centre."

"I understand. I promise, I won't do that again, no matter the situation," Minisc agreed.

"Good. The second rule is that you must tell me when you need a break or are fatigued. No more hiding the tolls of training. It is clear that training every day while in school is just too much for someone your age. So we shall scale it back. Yes, it means that you will be learning Celestial Light slower, but that is still better than not at all. If we are to do this, we are to do it right."

"All right, I can accept that. Anything else?"

"Yes, I have one last thing I want you to keep in mind, and this is the most important part. Remember—this is not all on you. No matter how it feels at times. The 8 Project is more than adequate to defend the city from any sort of attacks, and until we see proof that Brooklyn has emerged as the threat we believe him to be, there is no reason to push you. The time to fight will come when it comes, and I'm sure when it does that you will be ready. You and your friends."

Minisc smiled. It was all he needed to hear. "Thank you, Sir."

CHAPTER 15
A BREWING POWER

IT WAS CHRISTMAS EVE, WHICH MEANT THAT NEARLY all of Toronto was closed. The bright lights of the city still lit up the sky, but on this night the normally hyperactive city was quiet. Juno stood atop one of the many buildings damaged from Minisc's impromptu explosion of power, her hair fluttering in the wind as her jacket rasped back and forth. She wasn't wearing her 8 Project uniform but rather inconspicuous winter clothing.

From her perch, she watched a few stragglers walking down the streets. They too were mesmerized by the damage.

Juno shook her head. *It's unbelievable. How could one kid cause so much destruction? A power like that…it's unnatural. No wonder Luminosa is scared of this kid. If he manages to control such power, all their plans would go up in smoke. Of course, if Brooklyn manages to master the same power, it's more than just Humans that are going to be in danger…*

There was much to consider for the state of the future, but she still had her role to play as well.

She took a seat on the lip of the roof, letting her feet hang over the edge. She relaxed her shoulders and leaned back looking across to the Eaton Centre, checking her watch and wondering if the guest of honour would arrive or not. She couldn't blame him if he didn't; every chance Luminosa took meeting with her was a risk, but she could say the same for herself. Being on the inside had more than a fair share of risks.

While waiting, she went back to examining the damage. Yes, Minisc had caused much of it, but that wasn't to overlook the other source, which was the reason Minisc was using such power in the first place.

What the hell was that thing, anyway? It wasn't an animal, and it wasn't an Elementalist…but the brute strength it had could be impossible to stop. How could they've made such a monster…and can they make more? I need to find that out as well.

Time continued to tick, and Juno was starting to have her doubts. But before she bailed, she pulled out a small pocket watch, clicking it open and looking at the picture inside. "I can't be wrong. I *know* I'm not wrong." She closed the watch and whispered, "I will find you, Lucas. I swear it."

A slithery tone caught her attention. "I figured you'd be too busy cleaning up the aftermath of that little mess to show up here again."

Juno casually got to her feet, keeping the composure she'd displayed in their first meeting. She turned, staring down Bronx.

"I told you I would, didn't I? And here I am."

But there was something more threatening in Bronx's eye this time. He wore not only a glare but also a menacing snarl.

"And you think I believe a word that comes out of your mouth?"

Juno could feel the tension growing. "Have I given you any reason not to?"

"Don't try that crap with me. I've done my research on you."

Juno's heart skipped a beat, but she sustained her farce. "Excuse me?"

Bronx pulled out a thin brown folder and tossed it into the snow just a few feet away from Juno.

"Juno Barns, one of the inaugural graduating students of Elemental Academy. You were a top student for all four years. Smart, skilled, popular…nobody had a bad thing to say about you. But when it came time to work for the EC, you backed out. Everything you'd worked for, and at the last second you got cold feet and moved to another country."

Juno eyed Bronx, mulling over the information as fast as she could. Nothing he was saying was of any real substance. She shrugged, "And your point?"

"That's not all I found out," Bronx continued. "You had two best friends in school. Olivia Middleton, who's now not only a high ranking official in the EC but also the newly appointed shadow representative in The 8 Project. She was voted most likely to succeed and was widely considered a protégé among the EC. However, your other friend, Lucas — he was a bit harder to find information on. Quite talented, but not exactly the student you or Olivia were. Unlike most, over his four years he appeared to become disillusioned with joining the EC, to the point that he even thought about quitting school altogether. That is, until you two tried to talk him out of it, and then a few weeks before your graduation, he mysteriously disappeared. Nobody has found a trace of him ever since. Don't you think that's interesting?"

Now Juno was becoming distressed, and her face showed it.

"Struck a nerve, did I?" Bronx laughed.

Though hearing him mock the situation irked her, she shook off her anger and spoke cautiously.

"All right, so you did your homework. You know who my friends were in school. I fail to see what this has to do with me being part of Luminosa."

"So why did you come back?"

"Huh?"

"Why did you come back to work for the EC? What made you uproot your entire life and return here? You wouldn't do that *just* to join Luminosa."

Juno could tell that she was losing Bronx. He was already a hard egg to crack, but it appeared that giving him time to dig deeper only increased his suspicions.

"I told you already. I didn't come back to join Luminosa. I came back because I could see the writing on the wall. You think this city is any different than the rest of the world? Elementalists and Humans are not unique to our country. There are conflicts everywhere you look. As you already said, Olivia, who always kept in contact with me after I moved, requested that I come back. She told me that the EC had a position for me. At the time, I believed that the EC would have things under control, but it didn't take long for me to see how delusional that thought was. They're desperate, clinging to what little hope they have against the rising masses. Like I said, I'm just trying to be on the winning team here. Otherwise, what's the point?"

She shrugged, delivering her best acting job to get the conversation back on the rails.

"Now I think it's only fair that I get to ask you a question of my own."

Bronx remained silent.

"If you're so suspicious of my intentions, then why trust me to lead the doctor's boy into such danger?" She ran her hand through her hair. "I did exactly what you instructed. I gave you the best shot to take him out with that freak monster of yours."

"And yet here we stand. The kid's still alive and Brooklyn's precious pet has been diced into mincemeat. Oh, not to mention that you were there ready to fight alongside them as well. So what did you really help us accomplish?"

"Well now, that's a bit harsh, don't you think? How was I

supposed to know that some kid would just show up out of the blue and create a light show like that? He damn near killed us all!"

Bronx brushed past Juno and stared out at the destructive remains in front of them. "I'll admit, that kid *did* do a number on this place, and certainly without any help from us. Minisc Premier, the Hero of Light's kid…to have that sort of power sealed away…I think I'm beginning to understand why Dusk had such a fascination with him. I always believed it to be about revenge. The best way to gut the Hero of Light was to take something he could never regain. The life of his son."

Juno could sense his guard dropping—or maybe was he baiting her. She remained vigilant as she spoke.

"I think that, if anything, Dusk knew what sort of power that boy had, and he feared that if such power became controlled by the EC, there'd be no stopping him. Luminosa would never stand a chance against someone capable of such destruction. Also, for the record, that area was my post. You can't just let loose a horrific monster and expect a member of The 8 Project to sit back and do nothing. I still have a public reputation to keep up around here. Without it, I wouldn't be of much use to you, now would I?"

"Yeah, well you're not much use to us now."

Juno let out an exasperated sigh. "Fine. Don't trust me. What do I care? But a deal's a deal nonetheless. That night on Scotia Coliseum, you said that you'd let me in on the secret of that beast if I met your demands. I held up my end of the bargain, and so now you'd better hold up yours."

It was obvious that there was little hope of gaining Bronx's trust, which meant that any attempts to extract information were limited. Now was her chance to gain the insight she was owed, and she refused to pass it up.

"It's called a Manoah," Bronx said in a hushed tone, refusing to look at Juno as he spoke.

"A Manoah?" She side-eyed the Luminosa member and said, "That some kind of slang for 'deformed monstrosity,' or what?"

"Beats me what it stands for! I didn't come up with the name. All I know is that lunatic doctor has been working on his prototype day and night for months. Needless to say, he was pretty pissed to know that his precious pet's remains are now in the hands of the EC. But that's fine—he can make more. Being able to see his pet get a workout was worth it in the end."

"And you're not worried at all that the EC could find a way to dissect it and create their own versions of a Manoah? You know they'll try to do that, don't you?"

Bronx scoffed at the notion. "Create their own monstrous brutes? I doubt it. They don't have the stomach to go down that route. If they did, it wouldn't even be a contest."

Juno remained silent, and Bronx turned around and glared at her.

"Besides, the EC can't afford that sort of public reputation. People have been losing faith in them for years, and of course that will only get worse now. Everyone has seen that boy's power explode, and it'll put fear in the hearts of them all. The son of their greatest hero will soon be viewed as a monster. It's only a matter of time."

CHAPTER 16
THE PERFECT PRESENT

BRIGHT, COLOURFUL CHRISTMAS LIGHTS WERE DRAPED along the roof of the Premier household. On the door hung a large green wreath with a fancy red bow tied neatly in the middle, and the snow on the ground lit up the black sky in stunning fashion. Never had their house looked more festive. It surpassed even when Minisc was a child.

Of course, none of this festive adornment came from Minisc or his father. The credit went to Lily who took it upon herself to create such merriment in the decorations. Seeing as this was Adelle's first Christmas, she was determined to make it the most memorable possible. And for her, that meant making sure that the entire house was beautifully decorated from top to bottom.

She knew that Minisc wasn't particularly interested in the holidays, and after talking with Don, he admitted that without his wife, they just weren't the same. That said, neither of them objected to her take-over of their home and using it to celebrate.

But it wasn't solely for Adelle that Lily was going the extra mile. *Everyone* was in need of some holiday spirit especially after the scare they'd all just endured.

The work on the outside of the house paled in comparison to the masterpiece on the inside. With the generosity of Don, who'd spared no expense in his wish to help Lily, the two managed to make the house glimmer like a Christmas extravaganza.

In the living room stood a tree that nearly scraped the ceiling with a bright golden star on top. Lines of silver and gold tinsel fell along the branches, with even more red and white lights wrapped around each layer. Underneath were also dozens of different presents, all wrapped with snowman and snowflake wrapping paper. It was exactly what Lily had envisioned, her smile growing wider with each task completed.

But it wasn't quite done yet, and she still had a few rooms and the front hall that needed a makeover. In other words, she needed the boys to decorate.

Of course, Minisc or Jules didn't mind in the least. Though they didn't exude the same level of excitement as their festive taskmaster, they both wanted to make sure that this Christmas was the most spectacular in memory.

An electric energy filled the home as Minisc and Jules ran back and forth, hanging strings of lights and taking orders from Lily. Since she and Don were working on much of the cooking, that left the two boys to handle the finishing touches of the house.

"Man, if Lily ever decides on a new career, she could totally decorate homes. This place looks amazing," Jules said as he handed Minisc a line of tinsel. Minisc stood on a ladder, as he stuck the tinsel along the wall and fiddled with it until everything was exactly how Lily envisioned things.

"She really spared no expense. I just hope Father didn't use my inheritance to pay for it all," Minisc quipped. He stepped down from the ladder before taking a whiff of the scent wafting from the kitchen — the smell of a freshly cooked turkey, seasoned to perfection, filled the house.

With all the tasks done and the house in a standard that Lily was willing to accept, everyone changed into more festive attire. The remaining time was used to catch a breather before the guests arrived.

Under normal circumstances Minisc would be dreading even just the thought of a house party, let alone agreeing for Lily to host one at his own home.

He could recall far too many times when his mother and father hosted celebrations during the holidays. He hated each and every second of those experiences. The stuffy clothes, the never-ending swarm of people trying to ask him questions, and his inability to hide from the spotlight.

But this year was different, and even *he* felt an excitement bouncing in his stomach. From the beaming enthusiasm of Lily to the fun times decorating with Jules, even doing odd tasks were a joy as long as he was back with his friends again. No fears of Celestial Light and no concerns with Luminosa. Today was all about relaxing with those he loved, which he'd sorely been lacking of late.

Though it was late in the afternoon, the sky was already black and gleaming with stars. One after another, guests stared to trickle in, embracing the festive spirit as they arrived with their gifts in hand.

Thankfully for Minisc, the house wouldn't be as crowded as when his father hosted celebrations, but there was still a decent sized guest list. But unlike as a child, at least he knew all the guests this time around, which made the situation far more tolerable.

Yuri was the first to arrive, then Dwayne and even Bailey and her sister Maya. Coro also showed up, much to the surprise of everyone.

That made Minisc feel more comfortable since he wouldn't be the only one who felt out of place. If he ever got sick of the social interaction, he could always fall back and have a simple chat with Coro. He said few words on the best of days, but he was working to improve that, and he and Minisc seemed to share a mutual connection.

Even Mr. Howland came, who remained dressed in his usual formal clothing. There was nothing festive about him, but just having him be there was important enough.

Beside him was Robin, dressed in a red and white sweater with reindeers and carrying all the gifts himself.

Finally, after a few minutes of talking, admiring all of Lily's decorating, and eating from the table full of baked snacks, Minisc and Lily heard a knock at the door.

The room fell silent. Everyone had been informed that this was Adelle's first Christmas, and so they wanted to surprise her.

Lily made her way to the door, breaking out into a cheerful grin as she did. There stood Adelle, and though not dressed quite as festive as Lily, she did wear a Santa hat and a shirt with little snowmen on it.

"Whoa," Adelle said, seeing Lily and the shrine to Christmas through the entrance foyer.

Everyone popped out and merrily shouted, "Merry First Christmas, Adelle!"

She stood in shock, almost dropping her presents. The love, the care, the kindness—all of it was stunning.

"Guys, I…I don't know what to say!"

Lily grabbed Adelle's hand and dragged her inside. "You say 'Merry Christmas,' of course!"

Adelle grinned the biggest she'd ever grinned, cooing, "Merry Christmas everyone!"

With everyone finally in attendance, it was time to let the celebrations begin. The night would be one of the best experiences of everyone's lives.

In an effort to make sure that Adelle got the full Christmas experience, they even made Don dress up as Santa Claus, having him put on the hat and fake beard before coming in through the backdoor with a bag of gifts.

At any other point in time, it would've been a hokey gimmick, and one even the Hero of Light would never partake in, but when they all gathered around, there was just no denying the infectious joy.

Everyone took their turns sitting on Santa's lap and receiving a present, with plenty of pictures taken throughout. Remembering their time at the Christmas market, Lily grabbed Adelle and said, "Come on! We're finally gonna get that picture with Santa!" before hopping on Don's knee. He handed the two girls a present each and boomed with a laugh and a ho, ho, ho.

Even a reluctant Coro participated in the festivities, although he was certainly less lively than the rest of the group.

Everyone had a blast, and, most importantly, they were all laughing and enjoying each other's company—just the way the holidays were meant to be spent. For just one night, there was no need to worry about Celestial Light, Luminosa, or about what the future might hold. Everyone could focus on living in the here and now, which is exactly what they did.

Once the evening grew long and the huge amount of food began to settle into everyone's bellies, the festivities started to die down. People were getting ready to leave for the night, and even Adelle—who'd adored every moment of her first Christmas—had been worn empty. She was fighting back yawns as she left the house, but there was no removing her smile. She hugged Minisc and then Lily before saying, "Thank you. I can't tell you how much this means to me. I couldn't have asked for a better night." The smile on her face was immovable.

After most of the guests had departed, the night finally started to sink in for Minisc. Everything had been perfect. The joys of opening their presents, the smell of the wonderful food, and the warmth of being around so many happy and loving people gave Minisc exactly what he'd been lacking. These were memories that they'd all carry with them for the rest of their lives, proudly.

But with the night drawing to a close, there was still one last thing to be taken care of.

Once Minisc was able to find some free time from his hosting duties, he slipped away and into his room. From under his bed, he grabbed a small box. It was the perfect size to fit in his palm, and wrapped to perfection, though it had taken far more tries than he cared to admit.

While holding the gift in his hand, he could feel nervous butterflies fluttering in his stomach. He'd hoped that by waiting for most of the group to leave he could avoid such feelings, but they seemed to be inevitable.

In the aftermath of Minisc's incident, it was hard to remember what had spurred the whole event on in the first place. But Minisc never forgot. He and Jules were at the Eaton Centre because he was in desperate need to find Lily a Christmas present.

He never *did* find a gift that day, but while recovering in bed with his mind racing all over the place, it finally came to him — something he was sure that she'd value more than anything.

Of course, at the time there was a minor problem, as he was in no shape to go back to the mall when he first came up with the idea. That meant that Jules had to return to the scene of the crime on a solo mission, but this time he was more than gracious to help.

When the commotion had all but petered out and Lily was alone in the kitchen stacking plates, Minisc grabbed her by the arm. "Shh, come with me."

Minisc guided her down the hall and away from any potential prying eyes, taking Lily by surprise. Her heart skipped a beat as they walked, but she could put two and two together.

Throughout the evening, even when exchanging presents

with others, she'd been eying her best friend. She'd said nothing about her lack of a gift because there was no reason to worry. She knew that Minisc had come up with something wonderful. Not that it mattered, it was the thought she cared about, but still—she knew that he was holding out until the end of the evening to give her something special.

Minisc led her to the patio door, handing Lily her earmuffs and jacket, which just added to the confusion.

"Minisc, what on earth are you doing? Where are you taking me?"

Minisc zipped up his coat and then stopped to look at Lily with a sheepish smile. He realized that it would probably be best to add a little bit of clarity before surprising her.

"I'm ready to give you your present now, but I don't want to do it here. There's too many people."

Lily let out a soft giggle. "Aww, you're embarrassed—that's too cute. This must be the greatest gift a girl could ever ask for if you're this shy about it."

Minisc blushed, but Lily was already ahead of him, her cheeks rosy with anticipation. She slid open the door and grabbed his hand. "Well, come on then—it's rude to keep a girl waiting for her present, you know."

Minisc's cheeks grew even warmer as he slid on his boots and followed. Behind them, he shut the door quietly, making sure not to draw any undue attention.

The backyard was a mosaic of snow, untouched by the world and shining with the moonlight's soft, blue glow.

Minisc took a few steps into the snow as Lily followed. His mind was focused on the moment and completely immune to the cold, but Lily wasn't nearly as comfortable. She released his arm and clasped her hands, rubbing them together feverishly to stay warm. "Come on, come on! You've kept me waiting all night—I want to know what you got me!" She was hopping up and down on her tiptoes in anticipation.

In truth, by the end of the night, the present itself didn't matter. The effort of the whole day was better than anything she could've expected. She knew everything she'd asked of Minisc, and even his father, wasn't ideal for them, and considering the timing of events, things were even harder. But they did it with smiles because they loved her, and that was more than enough to warm her heart.

But aside from that, the presents they all exchanged with each other were supposed to be more practical and affordable. She'd even knitted Jules and Minisc scarfs for the winter, and she got Adelle a small ornament in the shape of a snowflake to represent her achievement of making The 8 Project. So she was at a bit of a loss regarding what Minisc could've bought that would be so embarrassing.

"Okay, okay…close your eyes and hold out your hands."

"Okay, now you're just being cruel," Lily joked, but she did as instructed.

Minisc reached into his pocket, failing to realize that he was holding his breath. He pulled out the miniature wrapped box and gently placed it in her hands.

Her eyes opened up and she stared at the box. "Did you wrap this yourself?" It was perfect, and so she knew that it couldn't have been him. Since she'd wrapped almost all of Minisc's other presents, she knew that he wasn't exactly skilled in that department.

Minisc rolled his eyes. "Yeah, yeah—I can't wrap. We get it… just open it already."

Done with her teasing, Lily started to gently tear away the paper until she caught the corner of the box. It was sea blue and had the texture of felt.

She continued unwrapping until she held a small jewelry box in her hands. Lily popped open the lid and her eyes lit up as she saw a small blue and silver pendant in the shape of a teardrop tied together with a silver chain.

"Minisc, you—"

Before she could say another word, Minisc said, "Open it up first."

Lily's eyes grew wider as she ran her finger along the edge of the pendant, feeling a small clip on the left side. With a click, the front popped open, and she looked up with a glimmer in her eye before pressing the locket against her chest. She sniffled from the cold, before grabbing Minisc and wrapping him up tight.

"This is the sweetest gift I could have ever asked for. I love it, Minisc. Thank you."

PREVIEW
ELEMENTS IN THE SHADOWS

THE TEMPERATURE WAS QUITE WARM CONSIDERING the snow that was still falling to the ground. After a long night, the sun was beginning to peek over the horizon. The forest remained quiet, but critters were starting to rustle around freely in search of their breakfast.

However, all that failed to register with Brooklyn as he stepped over broken branches and fallen logs. The path he continued to follow was loosely marked by what was once a dirt road but now was barely visible through the snow. His mind should've been focused on the meeting that had taken place a few hours ago, but that didn't mean much to him, either.

He'd given Bronx and Bex the orders to dig up dirt on Paradise, but then he went his separate way for the time being.

His fingers and toes were numb from how long he'd been walking through the night. It felt like miles. Normally, his destination would've been a short trip by car, but even then, his memories recalled that those times had felt like hours.

But the notion of pain was far from an issue, and he continued taking one step forward at a time until he reached his destination.

The closer he got, the stronger he could sense his dread rising. He came to a stop in front of an obscure tree at the end of the path. The roots grew in and out of the ground like tangled speedbumps, and nailed into the bark was a small, engraved sign that read WALKER COTTAGE.

Beautiful flower carvings adorned the edges, and despite the white layer of snow caked on like thick, frozen icing, there was a warm and inviting feeling from the sign. He grabbed the brittle edges of the wood and ripped it down before stomping on it.

AFTERWORD

The ending of this book was written with the intention of bringing a little bit of levity and happiness to you in the Christmas and holiday season. I know it can be tough for a lot of people, myself included, and so I hope that I was successful.

One of my goals when writing this series was to have it essentially grow up with its audience, sort of in the same way the Harry Potter series went from a children's book to a much darker, more serious series as its audience aged. I don't intend to go as dark as that series did, but I do hope you can sense that things are becoming more serious as the full plot moves along and the characters develop. As for what will happen with Minisc, Lily, Jules, and the rest of the Elements gang, you'll just have to keep reading to find out.

Thank you to StalkingP for her continued commitment to this series, especially as her art continues to blossom.

Thanks also to Rob Peace for his care and dedicated focus with the editing process.

Thank you to my family and friends for not being the kind of people to tell me to "just give up" and that "nobody reads these books." I appreciate your support immensely — and hopefully the next book won't take nearly as long to come out!

Thanks one and all for your continued support, and I'll see you in the next book.

William Richards

CHECK OUT MORE BOOKS!

IN THE VAST AND MYSTICAL LANDS OF ALTERRA, ANGELS—RARE SUPERNATURAL BEINGS BORN THROUGH A PROFOUND BOND CALLED UNITY WITH HUMANS—ARE WHISPERED OF IN LEGENDS. FOR 17-YEAR-OLD NOAH, UNITY WITH AN ANGEL WAS THE LAST THING ON HIS MIND. CONTENT AS A SMALL-TIME MERCENARY IN THE QUIET VILLAGE OF BERRIOS, HIS LIFE IS UPENDED WHEN THE MIGHTY NATION OF ENGVALL, A DOMINANT FORCE IN ALTERRA, DEMANDS HIS SERVICE IN THEIR ARMY.

BUT THE CALL TO ARMS HIDES DARK SECRETS, AND NOAH IS THRUST INTO A WORLD FAR MORE PERILOUS THAN HE EVER IMAGINED. AS BETRAYAL AND CRUELTY UNRAVEL AROUND HIM, NOAH MUST EMBARK ON AN EPIC JOURNEY ACROSS ALTERRA, FORGING UNEXPECTED ALLIANCES, UNCOVERING HIDDEN TRUTHS, AND CONFRONTING A LOOMING THREAT THAT COULD OBLITERATE BOTH HIS WORLD AND THE ANGELS'.

ADVENTURE, MYSTERY, AND THE BOND BETWEEN HUMAN AND ANGEL COLLIDE IN A TALE OF COURAGE, UNITY, AND THE FIGHT TO PROTECT A FRAGILE PEACE. WILL NOAH RISE TO MEET HIS DESTINY, OR WILL THE SHADOW OF DESTRUCTION PREVAIL?

RIMOR DYNEX IS HAILED AS THE GREATEST MERCENARY IN THE HISTORY OF THE GALAXY. BETWEEN HIM, AND HIS ONE-OF-A-KIND DYNEX SUIT, THERE IS NO MISSION HE CAN'T HANDLE. HOWEVER, THAT DOESN'T MEAN LIFE IS EASY. WHEN RIMOR IS TASKED WITH SEARCHING FOR CALAX CRYSTALS, ONE OF THE RAREST, NOT TO MENTION, ILLEGAL MATERIALS IN THE WORLD, HE SOON FINDS OUT HE'S GETTING MORE THAN HE BARGAINED FOR.

FINDING HIMSELF STRANDED ON THE DESOLATE PLANET OF RG-87, HE IS NOW BEING HUNTED BY A RACE OF ANGRY SPACE MONSTERS KNOWN AS THE UUZIKS. AND TO MAKE MATTERS WORSE, HE ONLY HAS 24 HOURS OF OXYGEN TO SURVIVE. BUT ALONG THE WAY, HE DISCOVERS A NEW PLAN BY THE UUZIKS LYING UNDER THE SURFACE. CAN RIMOR DODGE THE UUZIKS LONG ENOUGH TO FIND A WAY OFF RG-87? OR WILL HIS TIME RUN SHORT, BEFORE HE CAN FIND HIS ESCAPE?

AUTHORWILLIAMRICHARDS.COM

www.ingramcontent.com/pod-product-compliance
Lightning Source LLC
Chambersburg PA
CBHW060540190726
48283CB00003B/807